I0617815

Up North

A Novel

Jim Trainor

UpNorth
Press

Also by Jim Trainor

Grasp: Making Sense of Science and Spirituality (2010)

Waverly's Universe (2012)

The Sand People (2013)

UP NORTH

Unless otherwise noted, Scripture quotations are from the New Revised Standard Version Bible, copyright © 1989 National Council of the Churches of Christ in the United States of America. Used by permission. All rights reserved.
Quotations from the Book of Common Prayer, including the Psalms, are taken from the 1979 version.

Jacket photos by Jim Trainor

ISBN: 0692307346

For Mary and all those who love
the beauty of northern Wisconsin

Because of our almost forgotten past there is a restlessness within us, an impatience with things as they are, which modern life with its comforts and distractions does not seem to satisfy.

—Sigurd Olson, *The Singing Wilderness*

To those devoid of imagination a blank place on the map is a useless waste; to others, the most valuable part.

—Aldo Leopold, *A Sand County Almanac*

Who is ever really alone? I have my conversations with the red squirrel. I share the industry of the carpenter ant. I celebrate the miracle of this day with the leaping trout. The white pine stands with me against the wind. I am not alone. I've been more alone in the big city than in these quiet woods.

— Sven Norstaad, from his recovered diaries

Prologue

October 2004
Angeles National Forest, California

The hot coals glowed and crackled, then hissed as water was poured over them. More water sloshed over the coals, and they dimmed into blackness, poofing a burst of steam like a dying breath. They lay there dark and dead for minutes, cooling in the crisp mountain air.

Then a swirling puff of wind stirred them, arousing a new glow from the dark ash. One coal crackled, and a spark leapt beyond the fire ring and wafted on the gentle breeze before landing in dry pine needles. One of the needles glowed orange, then ignited. The glow quickly spread to other needles. Within minutes a small fire had begun—nothing threatening, a tiny patch burning slowly, probably unnoticeable to any passersby, if there had been any.

Another soft gust blew across the needles like the whoosh from a bellows, causing new flames to dance through them. The flames engulfed a bush, but still the fire was small.

Consuming dry undergrowth, the fire meandered slowly up the hillside, smoke now swirling up into the treetops.

At the mountain's ridgeline, a stiff wind blew energy into the fire. It spread out along the crest, now leaping skyward and touching off the dry ponderosa branches. Craving air and fuel, the fire surged across the crest and down into the tree-clogged canyon on the other side. Roaring. Hungry. Unstoppable.

A young father paced in his kitchen in the early morning, bobbing and rocking his crying week-old son. His wife slept in the bedroom nearby, after nursing and caring for their child most of the night. He heard the fire before he saw it, a crackling sound that began almost as a whisper, barely audible above his baby's cry. Then it grew louder. He moved to the patio door and looked up toward the mountains. He gasped when he saw it: a raging wall of flames roaring down the canyon toward his home.

Chapter 1

Ten years later
September 2014
Northern Wisconsin

I hope the bus is empty, like this town. I need to just sink back into a deep seat and watch the night fly by, all the way over to Escanaba, where I'll transfer at midnight to the 1490 that'll get me into Milwaukee by four. The last thing I need right now is some noisy family, or some chattering local who wants to talk my arm off.

It's Sunday night, and the main drag of White Pine, Wisconsin, is dead. The street light on my corner has just flickered on, a dim yellow. Both sides of the street are lined with old brick storefronts, all dark. Only the CITGO station, several blocks down, looks open, its bright red and white sign broadcasting the prices of regular and diesel to the lifeless night.

My name's Wil Weathers, and that's all I know about White Pine, since I just got here myself. Ron dropped me off five minutes ago; then his 4Runner slipped quietly down the empty street and turned right at the traffic light onto Highway 2, westbound, which will get him home to the Twin Cities in three hours. I'm here by the bus-stop sign in front of Danny's

Northwoods Café, closed, at the corner of Main and Eighth Avenue, where the Indian Trails bus stops every night at 8:15.

I almost said no when Ron called last week and suggested we get the old backpacks out and head up north into the Nicolet National Forest, up near the U.P., for a few days. Said he was in Milwaukee for a conference and could pick me up, but I'd have to find my own ride home. I hadn't talked with Ron for several years, since graduate school back at UCLA, when we'd head for the mountains almost every weekend. I haven't stayed connected with any of my old friends for that matter, not even on Facebook. I'm sure that's where Ron learned that I'd lost my job at the University and broken up with Megan. Not that I'd ever post anything like that, but Megan's a Facebook junkie, and I know she wouldn't have been able to resist spilling the beans. That was enough for me to cancel my account.

So when I got this call from Ron, I was pretty sure it was an act of charity to a poor down-and-outer. Well, maybe that's what I am, but I don't need anyone feeling sorry for me, so that's why I almost said no. But I'm glad I didn't, because the trip was just what I needed, and Ron, to his credit, never said a word about my personal life until I brought it up on our second night out.

I ease the backpack off my shoulders, then pull out the Nalgene bottle and swig down the last of my water. So yeah, I got laid off at UWM, that's the University of Wisconsin at Milwaukee. That was last April, five months ago today, in fact, on Good Friday. I remember such things because I'm a numbers guy. And I know it was Good Friday, not because of any religious thing, but because Del Behrens, who, like me, teaches the Physics 101 sections, had been lurking outside the department office. When I told him what had happened, he shook his head, then cracked, "Well, I guess it's a good day to get crucified."

It was a funding shortfall that led to my termination, or so they said, but let's be real. It was obvious they were looking for an excuse to trim some dead wood out of the system. Not that I see myself as dead wood. Let's just say that when I got called into Grace's office, I was pretty well braced for what she said.

Dr. Grace Michaels, the chair of the physics department, probably isn't any older than me. Usually informal and collegial, Grace sat behind her desk that morning and made minimal eye contact, while she calmly informed me that my contract would not be renewed at the end of the semester. Then she said, with compassion I couldn't be sure was authentic, "Wil, this is the part of my job I hate most." I remember thinking that the part of my job I hated most was losing it.

Okay, I don't need to relive that for the millionth time. The Indiglo dial on my Timex shows 8:17. No sign of the bus. I pull the bus schedule out of my hip pocket and angle it toward the street lamp to check the time again. It's 8:15, yep. But wait a sec. The times in bold face are p.m., and the ones in regular type are a.m. Why hadn't I noticed this before? My bus leaves at 8:15 a.m. This is definitely not the kind of dumbass move a detail guy like me should be making.

I do a slow three-sixty, as if some answer might be discovered in these sleepy surroundings, like maybe an unscheduled bus coming down the road. I feel the sudden need for more oxygen, and I'm aware that my breathing has become faster, almost gasping. I have to fight this off, my tendency to hyperventilate when stressful things happen.

Breathe into a paper bag. That's the advice a woman gave me when my car broke down in an intersection. But I don't have a bag.

The water bottle might work. After a few breaths into the bottle, I feel better. I sit down next to my pack and wonder what to do next. There are no motel signs down the main drag, but you'd think, being so close to a national forest, there'd be lots of motels around. Guess most overnighters either camp or head to a larger town, like Iron River. But I can't spare fifty bucks right now anyway.

This isn't complicated. I have all my camping gear with me. I'll just head down a side street, find a vacant lot out of sight of any bored small-town cops who'd love nothing better than to roust some vagrant. Eighth Avenue looks perfect, a narrow, wooded residential street disappearing into the darkness. I'm beginning to enjoy the idea of my impromptu extra night camping out. After all, what do I have to be back in Milwaukee for anyway?

So what am I going to do when I get home? If you can call the depressing Bali Hai Apartments home. I've filled out at least a dozen job applications, had three interviews, and mailed off another hundred copies of my résumé. Nothing. My unemployment benefits run out in two more months, and if I still don't have a teaching job, I'll be making pizza deliveries for Domino's. Or worse, crawling back to L.A. and moving in with Mom and Dad at age thirty-three. Now *that's* depressing.

My eyes struggle to adjust as I make my way into the darkness along Eighth Avenue, where only a few shafts of light streak down from the corner street lamp. There is no sidewalk, so I have to watch my footing along a narrow strip of dirt between the road and the thick vegetation that fronts a few modest houses, widely spaced along the block and set back from the street. No lights on. Either everybody's already in bed or they're all in the back room watching the tube. The stillness is eerie, not like the natural quiet of the wilderness where I camped last night.

At the first intersection with another unlighted street, a pickup appears from nowhere and accelerates toward Main Street. I back out of the road, against a dense hedge, to let it pass, certain the driver hasn't seen me. As the truck turns and vanishes around the corner, I continue on. But my foot seems caught on something in the bushes, a root or a vine. I try to kick it loose, but it holds fast.

I look down, and even in the darkness what I see is unmistakable. My ankle is encircled by a human hand.

Chapter 2

In an adrenalin burst, I rip free of the hand, toppling awkwardly atop my backpack like a flipped tortoise. I roll quickly onto my side and then up on all fours.

Moments pass, my panic subsides, and there is no motion from the hedge. Now on my feet, I edge forward to where the hand grabbed me. I've pulled out my iPhone to use the flashlight app, but the battery is dead. At the edge of the hedgerow, the hand still extends toward the street, but now I can see it's still.

"Hello?" I call out tentatively.

No response.

I lean in cautiously for a better look. I'm thinking maybe this is just some drunk collapsed in the bushes on his way home from the bar. But another part of me is jumpy with a primitive fear.

I see a body, face down, dead still. The person wears a heavy plaid shirt. It seems to be a man. *Is he alive?* I try 911. Forgot, battery is dead.

Part of me wants to leave. But this person may need help. *Shouldn't I check for a pulse?* I take a deep breath, then slide my hand to the person's neck, where I might find an artery. There's something wet and sticky. I jerk my fingers back. Even in the near-darkness, the bright red blood is almost blinding.

I swipe my hand over dirt to rid myself of the blood, then I leap to my feet, spin, and make a fast scan for dangers that may lurk nearby. For just a moment, so brief that I could have imagined it, I think I catch the reflection of two eyes, far back in the bushes, looking my way.

Gasping, I bolt, looking for a place where I can call for help. There's only one light, across the street, coming from a window in a door up several steps from street level. Through wavy old glass, I make out a person moving. I rap hard on the glass, and the person stops, then heads in my direction.

I'm greeted by a woman with a mop in her hand.

"There's a body across the street. I think someone may be dead. We need to call for help." My words gush out in breathless bits.

The woman wears loose jeans, a baggy sweatshirt with the letters MTU in bold yellow and a scarf around her hair. She stares at me for a second, then turns and races into a small room. I follow her. She makes a call, then reaches into a desk, pulling out two flashlights. "They'll be here in a minute. In the meantime, let's go have a look," she says, her calm voice helping to head off my hyperventilation. She's already moving toward the door.

I lead her to the hedges across the street, then stop abruptly, sweeping my flashlight beam back and forth along the hedge row.

The body is gone.

Chapter 3

"It was right here," I blurt out.

"You sure?"

"Of course I'm sure. Something strange is going on. Maybe—"

"Maybe your dead guy made a miraculous recovery and just went home. Sure it wasn't just a drunk who—"

"No, there was blood all over his neck. Or her neck. I'm not sure if it was a man or a—"

"Seems like there's a lot you're not sure about."

I'm starting to dislike this woman. "I swear there was a body here just a few minutes ago. He had on a plaid shirt. He …" I feel my face flush.

I sweep my flashlight again along the dense shoulder-high foliage lining the road. I peer back into the shrubs, but can see nothing.

"What's this?" The woman kneels and picks up a scrap of paper, illuminating it with her flashlight while tipping it toward me so that I can see. It looks like it was ripped from the corner of a larger page. On the scrap, hand-printed in pencil, are the words "HOME Skill."

Just then a police car with flashing red and white lights turns onto Eighth from Main and accelerates toward us. It comes to a stop next to the hedges, and a policeman emerges, leaving the lights flashing. He approaches us, then says to the woman, "So what's up, Sally?" He doesn't look at me.

"Darby, this guy thinks he saw a dead body in the bushes here, but now it's gone."

The cop turns toward me, and I feel his suspicious eyes checking me out in the strobe lighting from the car. But he says nothing.

"I'm Wil Weathers," I offer. "I just got back from a backpacking trip in the Nicolet National—"

"Where in the Nicolet?" There's an edge of doubt in his voice.

"Around Porcupine Lake. Look, the body was right here. There was blood."

The cop walks around the area, takes some photos with a small camera, then turns to me again.

"Don't see any blood."

I extend my hand to show him the blood, but the wipe across the ground apparently removed it all.

The cop glances at my hand, then back at me. "So what are you doing here?"

"I thought the bus left at 8:15 tonight, but I misread the schedule, and—"

"So you thought you'd just wander down this peaceful residential street and look for dead bodies? You got some identification?" Officer Darby's probably in his mid-twenties, but in the low light he could pass for a teenager. He's got a chubby boyish face, and I can make out a wisp of peach fuzz that he's trying to grow into a mustache. There's a macho swagger about him that makes me uneasy, and he's dressed like Barney Fife, with a neatly pressed gray uniform that his mother probably irons for him, boots that squeak as he walks, and a thick leather belt supporting a large holstered handgun on his right hip. He wears a shiny brass badge that reads "White Pine County Sheriff's Office."

I fish my wallet from my backpack and show him my driver's license. He takes it back to the car, where he studies it for a long time. When he returns he says, "So if you've got a driver's license, why are you taking the bus?"

I launch into an explanation, but the woman cuts me off. "Darby, I don't think this man is a criminal. Why don't you just focus on why we called you, on whether there was someone in these hedges?"

Officer Darby seems flustered by this. He pulls out a small notebook. "Okay, William, so tell me what you saw."

I recount my experience. I wish there was still some blood on my hand to show him.

"So you saw a pickup before you supposedly saw the body? What make and model?"

"I couldn't tell. It was dark. Only saw the shape."

"Almost everyone in White Pine has a pickup." He shoots me a skeptical look, like I'm withholding information. "Anything else?"

"Well, there was one thing. I think I saw a set of eyes back in these bushes, looking at me."

"Eyes, huh?" Darby scratches his jaw. "If there was a body, and I'm not sayin' there was, then it could have been wolves. They're active in this part of the state, you know." He looks at the woman. "You remember a couple weeks back when some wolves killed that dog out on old Spafford's farm?" He looks back at me. "Yep," he says, "coulda been wolves. But by tomorrow we'll know for sure if your story holds any water."

"How's that?" I ask.

"It's a small town, city boy. If nobody's reported missing, then there was no body." He chuckles, apparently pleased with his pun.

"One more thing," interjects the woman. "We found this." She hands Darby the scrap of paper.

"'HOME Skill'? What the hell does that mean?" He stuffs the scrap into a baggie, pronouncing in an official-sounding way, "I'd better hold onto this." Then he looks at me again. "And you. When are you leaving?"

"The 8:15 bus tomorrow."

"And where are you staying tonight?"

"I'm not sure, uh, I thought I'd …" but then I stop. Not going to tell Officer Darby my plan to camp in a vacant lot.

"Maybe you'd like to come over to the jail with me. Make you real comfortable, keep you out of trouble." He laughs, resting his right hand on his gun, and I feel the hyperventilation surge back to life. I'm not used to dealing with cops. He continues, "I can't allow strangers wandering into our little town to just loiter around, 'specially ones bothering the police with wild stories. I have a duty to protect our—"

"He'll stay here," the woman says.

Officer Darby's macho bluster is now tinged with a bit of a whine. "But Sally, you don't know anything about this guy. He could be Jack the—"

"Darby, this is a church, after all. We're supposed to welcome the stranger."

"Sally, I can't let you—"

"Of course you can. Didn't you learn anything in Sunday school? Now you've got your information. Why don't you just run along and protect the community."

Darby blows out a loud breath, then looks at me, narrowing his eyes again, but says nothing.

"Run along, Darby," says the woman.

Again Darby seems flustered. He places the little notebook back in his hip pocket, mumbles something about checking for more wolf sightings, then gets into the car and leaves.

Back in the building, the woman undoes the scarf from her head and shakes out long dark hair. "I'm Sally Ladke," she says, extending a hand. I realize that she is young, probably in her late twenties. Her face is fair and smooth, which helps accentuate her intense brown, almost black, eyes. She's tall, I'd say five-eight.

"Look," I say, "it's nice of you to offer me a place to sleep, but I don't want to get you into trouble with your boss."

"My boss?" She laughs—a soft childish laugh, almost a giggle—rolling her eyes skyward. "I'm pretty sure my boss approves." Then turning and pointing to various places in the room, she rattles off a string of directions. "You can bed down on that couch over there. There's a bathroom down that hall. Sorry, no shower. And there's a kitchen right here. There should be something in the fridge if you get hungry."

"You said this is a church?" The room is large and plain and evidently very old. Its hardwood floors are worn and creaky. A few posters and colorful hand-made signs adorn the plain white walls, with old wainscoting that looks like it's been painted over many times. Folding tables and chairs are stacked against a wall. In one corner is a row of several unmatched bookcases filled with books. Next to them is the couch, sagging and worn.

"That's right. St. Paul's. Actually, you're in the parish hall. The sanctuary is a little farther down that hall, past the bathrooms."

"And you're the janitor?"

"Heavens no." She runs a hand through her thick hair. "I'm just a volunteer. Trying to help out. These floors get pretty dirty after a Sunday. And anyway, we couldn't afford to pay a janitor. I've got a little more mopping to do. Then I'll be leaving, so you can make yourself comfortable."

"Look, I know what I saw. This is not right. And for what it's worth, I don't have that much confidence that Officer Darby is going to—"

"Darby's okay. I've known him all my life. He's always had a little crush on me, so he tends to start pulling his macho law-enforcer act when other guys are around."

Okay, I get it. I'm now in the middle of some small-town soap opera. The best I can do is hit the sack and get to 8:15a.m. as soon as I can. If the citizens of White Pine aren't going to worry about this, then why should I? I nod and give Sally a weak smile, then begin unrolling my sleeping bag onto the couch.

Sally turns out the lights as she leaves. I plug my dead phone into its charger, set the alarm on my Timex for 6:45, then stretch out fully-dressed atop my mummy bag on the couch. I study the old hammered metal ceiling of the parish hall, faintly illuminated by a night light near the door. The room smells of soap, from Sally's mopping, and musty, like an old library. It stirs childhood memories of mornings at my grandmother's house in San Bernardino, where she'd bake me blueberry muffins.

My parents lived closer to L.A., near Pasadena, where my dad worked as a draftsman at a defense-related company and my mom stayed home, so I got to visit Grandma only every other weekend or so. As I close my eyes, I see her kitchen, the big old O'Keefe & Merritt gas range surrounded by worn counters crowded with spice containers, cookbooks, piles of recipes clipped from magazines, and dishes that had not been put away into the cupboards. There was a tall wooden stool in the corner, where I would sit and watch Grandma cook, singing as she worked and telling me tall tales about her childhood. The other thing I remember about her house was that high bed with the extra-soft mattress and the fluffy down comforter I could get lost under …. My thoughts blur and slowly segue into dreams.

I'm back in the forest with Ron, on the far side of Porcupine Lake, setting up our tent. I'm inside the tent laying out the foam sleeping pads and bags. I hear a scratching on the side of the tent. "Is that you, Ron?" I ask. No answer. The scratching sound becomes a ripping sound as something cuts into the tent. I bolt upright from my dream, look around and try to orient myself. It takes a moment to figure out where I am. Then I hear the ripping sound again and realize it's in the room with me.

Chapter 4

My heart almost stops. In the dim glow of the nightlight I make out the silhouette of someone climbing in through one of the windows of the parish hall. The hair on the back of my neck stands up, and I can't catch my breath. I roll off my mummy bag, hit the floor and crawl behind the couch. In the shadows it appears the figure is a man, but I can't be sure, and he's carrying something, maybe a gun.

I stay frozen behind the couch as the figure pauses then moves toward the light switch. I could try to drive off the intruder by confronting him or making a loud noise, but given my experiences of the evening, he may be looking for me. I've got to get out of here fast, like in the one or two seconds before the intruder hits the lights. In my socks I make it safely into the darkness of the hallway just as the parish-hall lights come on behind me.

I move quickly toward the sanctuary, hoping there's another exit there. I don't have much time. If the intruder's looking for me, he'll be coming right behind me.

The heavy door at the end of the hallway creaks as I pull it open, and I hope the intruder doesn't hear it. I step into the dark sanctuary, holding the door so it closes quietly. A lighted candle over a high altar provides a flickering glow in the large room. I fumble my way toward the rear of the church, where an exit door must be located, but when I'm about halfway through the pews, I hear the door creak again. I dive between pews and crouch down. When I peek over the top of the pew in front of me, I can make out a figure near the door, apparently feeling for a light switch.

I hope the switches are hidden away in some back room. Then a flashlight comes on, and a narrow beam sweeps across the walls like a searchlight seeking out an escaped prisoner in an old jailbreak movie. I go flat and squeeze my body under the bench of a pew. I work hard to regulate my panicked breathing to maintain absolute quiet. I hear the intruder pacing the sanctuary, and I see an occasional splash of light from the flashlight. I'm being hunted.

A minute passes, but it seems like hours. I hear the door creak again, and the flashlight beam disappears. I wait another minute, then shift out from under the pew, rise onto my knees and peek over a pew back. I see no sign of the intruder. I begin to rise, then stop. This could be a trick to lure me out. I do not know that he is not hidden somewhere nearby in this room, waiting for me to move. I drop back into my hiding place and stay there. The luminous dial on my watch says 2:10.

At 2:30 I'm still quaking. The intruder may still be here. I slip out from under the pew and peek over the seat back again. There's no movement, only the soft glow from the candle over the altar. I weigh my options. I could leave through the rear door of the church, where the intruder could be waiting, or I could venture back into the parish hall—but how can I be sure he has left? Better to remain here, where I've been safe so far.

I come awake with a start, as the alarm on my watch goes off, and bolt up so quickly that I thump my head against the pew bottom. It's 6:45. Somehow I'd fallen into a dreamless sleep. I stand in the aisle, rubbing my head, as shafts of color flood from a huge stained glass window above the altar, bathing heavy fabrics and polished woods in streaks of warmth. Emboldened by the daylight, I make my way back toward the parish hall, pausing near the sanctuary door to dip my fingers, still trembling, into a small basin of cool water mounted there, then touch them to my sweaty, sore forehead.

To my relief, the parish hall looks the way I left it. My sleeping bag is still spread out on the couch, with my boots nearby. But then I realize with a jolt that my backpack is gone. And so is my phone. My hand instinctively goes to my hip pocket, and I'm relieved that my wallet is there, along with my bus ticket. But with the ID tag on my pack and whatever information might be found on my phone, the intruder now knows far too much about me.

Chapter 5

Highway 2 cuts a line through dense second-growth forest east of White Pine. On the Indian Trails bus to Escanaba, I stretch in my comfortable seat and watch the pines fly by. Fifteen minutes out of White Pine and I'm already feeling better. The morning was uneventful, after my harrowing night. Maybe I should have called the police, but after my experience with Darby last night, I figured it was best just to get out of there. Back home I can worry about finding my phone. I know it has a tracking app, but I need to log into a computer to use it, and there was little prospect of that before my bus left.

I found a sweet roll and a Diet Coke in the fridge, and I washed up in the bathroom. I left my sleeping bag at the church, since the intruder also took the stuff sack for my bag, and I also left Sally a note explaining about the intruder, so she can follow up with the cops and won't think I was responsible for the ripped window screen and who knows what else. And I said I'd be in touch about how to return my sleeping bag. I didn't want to leave any of my contact information in a note that might be seen by God knows who. Then I headed for the bus stop, where I could wait out in the open. Still, I was antsy until that big bus rolled up, and its doors whished open.

It's unsettling that the intruder knows where I live, but the Bali Hai has a security entrance, so it won't be that easy for some small-town criminal to get to me. And I'm pretty certain that whatever I'd become involved in was a local thing, not anything that would follow me to Milwaukee. And if it did, at least I would be on my home turf, where there are real policemen, not backwoods bullies like Officer Darby.

The Bali Hai Apartments. Who'd think I'd actually be looking forward to seeing that place again? Like I said, it's depressing. The Bali Hai is a sprawling complex built in the seventies and showing its wear. The ads draw people in with the claim that it's near the action, and, truth is, it's not that far from Brady Street, with its trendy bars, Italian restaurants, and funky clothing stores. I moved there after Megan split, needing a change of scenery. I also needed lower rent, as our previous place near the lakefront hardly fit in with an income exclusively of unemployment checks.

Despite the ads, life at the Bali Hai turned out to be about anything but action—not that action was what I was seeking. There's no pool at the Bali Hai, just a small patio with some cheap web chairs and chaises and a few plastic flamingos that give the place a fake tropical look. Oh yes, I noticed those shapely girls lounging around the patio area during the summer with skimpy bikinis and beckoning smiles. And there are scheduled community cookouts and happy hours designed to help busy people meet. But it's not as good as it sounds. The place reeks of desperation, and I recall overhearing one person down in the laundry room refer to the Bali Hai as the divorcee's cathedral. At least that's the way the place has struck me, maybe because I'm not a pick-up-sexy-girls-on-the-patio kind of guy or maybe because the real desperation resides in me. Yes, I've considered that possibility.

Anyway, I'll move out of the Bali Hai as soon as I get my employment situation sorted out, and that had better be pretty soon. Meanwhile, my life is anything but nonstop parties and casual sexcapades. Most days I've taken to showing up early at Starbucks, just down the block and one of the few really good things about the Bali Hai. It gets me out of my dreary apartment, with its blank white walls and popcorn ceiling. It also keeps me from becoming one of those poor souls who's still in his bathrobe at two in the afternoon, which I fear I could become.

When I first started hitting the Starbucks, I would keep insanely busy researching potential employers, filling out online job applications and tweaking my résumé. Now I like to claim a comfortable seat in the rear, plug in my laptop, then order a small house coffee—my four-dollar venti latte days vanished with my last paycheck from UWM. Then I settle in for the morning. I keep my earbuds on, and folks probably assume I'm jamming with some current hot band, though in fact I can't even name any current hot bands. Actually, I'm not listening to anything, because it's the background noises I want to hear.

Busily engaged with my laptop, I look like I might be drafting a critical report for an urgent corporate deadline or maybe writing a novel. At least, if some comely Marquette coed wanders by, that's what I'd like her to think. In fact I'm usually just surfing the web, giving a superficial once-over to the news sites, then lingering a while longer at ESPN to savor the latest baseball rumors, surveying the next week's weather predictions for an assortment of cities and frequently checking back on my email just in case an important message—maybe a job lead or, who knows, a desperate plea from Megan—might be coming in. Usually, though, there is nothing, other than the occasional spam informing me of a million-dollar inheritance or offering insider discounts on Viagra. But more than I enjoy the surfing, I find it soothing to be there with the calming background noise: the laughter, the shuffling of newspaper pages, the cheerful voices of the baristas.

The driver announces that we'll soon be stopping in Florence for ten minutes, if anyone wants to get off. I'm quite happy just to sit here in my plush lounger seat. The bus is nearly empty. Up front, an elderly couple share the morning newspaper. Across from me, a teenager in a Brewers T-shirt is popping gum and moving in rhythm to some beat coming through his headphones. I glance over my shoulder to the rear of the bus. No more than a half-dozen other people. A matronly woman reads a magazine. A man with a shaved head and frameless glasses gazes out the window. A young couple cuddle. My gaze switches back to the guy with the shaved head, just as he looks at me. For an instant, as the light reflects from his glasses, I'm seeing the eyes in the bushes from last night.

Chapter 6

I turn forward and try to calm myself, but now I'm spooked by the guy with the shaved head. I risk another glance in his direction, and he's looking directly at me. Quickly, he looks away.

The bus pulls into Florence, another small northwoods town that looks larger than White Pine. The driver reminds us that we have ten minutes. I decide to get off to see if the man with the shaved head gets off too. If he doesn't, at least I can ride the rest of the way to Escanaba without panic attacks.

I step off the bus at a street corner on Highway 2, in front of an antiques store. Across the street is a gas station and convenience store; kitty-corner is the Black Bear Inn, which looks like a local hangout. The other corner is a vacant lot. Not the kind of place where I can easily disappear into a crowd. I cross the street to the convenience store, and my worst fears are confirmed. The man with the shaved head has gotten off too and is coming my way. Though my heart is in my throat, I try to walk with a leisurely stride, not letting on that I know he's following me. Of course, maybe he just wants to use the john at the gas station.

I go to the rear of the store and select a soft drink, then grab a plastic-wrapped muffin near the check-out counter. The man has entered behind me and looks at the newspapers. I flop down my ATM card to pay for my food, while keeping the man in my peripheral vision. Then I exit back toward the bus. He follows. As far as I can tell, he has purchased nothing in the store.

Back on the bus, I take the front seat, next to the door, across from the elderly couple. The man boards and passes me without looking my way. As the doors close with a whishing sound, I leap forward and thrust my arm into the opening, counting on a safety switch that will open the doors again. Indeed, the doors reopen. As the driver protests, I jump out and race toward the small downtown section of Florence. I don't even pause to look over my shoulder to see if the man is behind me.

After running a block, I'm out of breath. I turn to look back. The bus is gone, and I see no sign of the man. I'm standing in front of Barb's Café, a cozy looking diner, trying to figure out what to do next. Although the man is nowhere in sight, I can't be sure he didn't get off.

I go into Barb's Café and take a seat at a long counter at the rear of the restaurant, beyond booths still bustling with the morning breakfast business. I order a coffee, while casting frequent glances over my shoulder toward the door. When the waitress, a perky redhead, brings me my coffee, I ask, "Is there a pay phone around here?"

"It's a ways down the street," she says, "right after the stop-and-go light. Where do you need to call to, hon?"

I consider calling the police, but what do I have to report? That some guy got off the bus at the same time I did? "White Pine," I say.

"You can use our phone for that." I follow her down a hallway to a phone on the wall. I call information and ask for the number of Sally Ladke. The operator says there is no listing for Sally Ladke, but there is a Joan Ladke. Would I like that number? I say yes.

Sally picks up. "Sally, I wasn't sure I had the right number. This is Wil—"

"You dialed my mother's number. You didn't miss your bus, did you?"

"I'm in a bit of a mess. I think someone followed me on the bus this morning, so I got off in Florence. He may have gotten off too, I'm not sure. Anyway, I'm stranded here now. I was wondering if you could pick me up. Look I know this is a big imposition on—"

"It's no imposition at all. Where are you?"

"Barb's Café. Do you—"

"I know where it is. Get the Swedish pancakes, they're famous."

"'Fraid I don't have much of an appetite right now. Look, if you're willing to pick me up, can you suggest a place I can walk to from here, where I can be sure I'm not being followed?"

She's quiet for a moment, then says, "Why don't you go about four blocks north, until you come to—I think it's Olive Street. Make a right and that should take you to the library. By then you ought to be able to see if you're being followed. Wait inside the front door and be on the lookout. I'm in a green Subaru Outback. Should be about a half-hour. If the coast is clear, come on out. If it's not, stay put and call me on my cell. Here's the number."

"Sally, I appreciate what you're—"

"No problem. I'm still not sure you're not some weirdo, but I'm gonna take a chance for now." She laughs—that little girl's laugh, bubbly and enthusiastic. And for the first time in a while, I feel like laughing too.

Chapter 7

I don't want anyone to have the impression that I'm heartbroken over the Megan experience, that she left me a pathetic emotional wreck. Though she left suddenly, informing me through email no less—and that part does hurt, I'll admit it—I had seen the breakup coming for a long time. At least, looking back now, I should have seen it coming for a long time.

I'm not so heartbroken as embarrassed by the whole experience. I should have known better, my buddy Del Behrens told me, when we met for a beer one night after she left. "She never was your type to begin with," he pronounced, as if he were some dating expert. Del's a confirmed bachelor, and his relationships never seem to go beyond the first date. "I can size up the possibilities pretty quick," he once boasted, "and I don't need six months of stress to get the lay of the land." Right.

"But we did have some good times," I said to Del.

Del leaned forward in the booth, with his head so low I could see his bald spot, and looked up at me through his horn-rims like he was sharing a sensitive confidence. "Maybe, but you know as well as I do that a professor dating a student is a recipe for disaster."

"Oh, come on, Del," I said so loudly that he looked around like I was making some big commotion and we'd probably get asked to leave. I'm hardly a guy who ever makes a big commotion. "First of all, I never was a professor—just an instructor like you. And second, Megan was anything but some innocent-eyed coed just in from high school. She's as old as I am."

But there was some truth in what he said. Megan and I met one afternoon in my Physics 101 class, where ninety non-physics majors were trying to stay awake for my lecture on the physics of falling bodies. After class she asked me about the acceleration due to gravity, and I realized that the falling body that afternoon was mine and that gravity had nothing to do with it.

But I have other things to worry about right now.

I find the library right where Sally said it was, on Olive Street, and I only have to wait a half-hour—which is mostly spent peering through the lobby doors in case the man with the shaved head should appear—before a dirty Outback slips in under some trees across the street. After one last scan of my surroundings, I dart out to the car, a small, dark-green station wagon with a widespread collection of dents that looks like the result of many fender benders. A half-dozen bumper stickers share an environmental-advocacy theme. One that catches my eye reads, "I don't just hug trees, I kiss them too."

Sally looks over at me with raised eyebrows. "So, Mr. Bourne, I guess you haven't seen the assassin again?" There's a teasing twinkle in her dark eyes that I find annoying. She wears blue jeans, quite a bit tighter than the baggy ones she had on last night, and a white T-shirt that says "Isle Royale National

Park" above the outline of a moose. Her dark brown hair is tied in a ponytail.

I just say, "No, but thanks for coming to get me."

"So, where to, Wil?" Her right hand rests on the shifter, ready to go.

Good question. I can't ask her to drive me down to Milwaukee. That'd take all day, and her old jalopy might not make it anyway. And I'd rather not hang around Florence for the next twenty-four hours, waiting for the next bus. "Well, I'm not sure yet."

"Okay. Then let's just head back to White Pine. You can hang there until you figure things out." As we pull away, she adds, "Too bad about you getting your backpack and phone stolen. If that happened to me, I'd be really pissed. But I called Darby and he's working on it."

Oh great. "You could just drop me at a motel, and I can wait there until the bus tomorrow." I'm doing a quick mental inventory of my finances. I'll have to use my ATM card. I've got less than forty bucks cash, and I haven't made a payment on my Visa card in months, so that probably won't be accepted.

"You don't have to do that. There's plenty of room for you at the house."

"Your mother's house?"

"Actually, it's my grandmother's house. Big place. Nobody will bother you, and by the way, Wil, just how many days has it been since you've had a shower?"

"Oh, God, I'm sorry if I'm grossing you out. It has been a few days." I lower the window.

"It doesn't bother me." She gives me a reassuring smile. "I'm an outdoors girl."

Yeah, kissing trees. The inside of Sally's car is a mess. At my feet are a daypack, a pile of maps and several bottles of water, all of which I had to rearrange just to climb in. The back seat is piled with books, a pair of dirty hiking boots, and a tangle of sweatshirts, parkas and other stuff I can't identify. The cargo area behind the back seat is similarly filled.

She notices me looking around. "Sorry my car's so cluttered. It's my base camp."

"Base camp?"

But she's moved on to other things. "So, when I talked with Darby this morning, he said that no one's been reported missing."

"Well, that doesn't mean anything. What if the guy lived alone, so that nobody was missing him? What if he wasn't from around here? Look, let's work through this logically. Assume that the guy was dead and—"

"But we have no proof that—"

"Please, just go along with me for a bit. Assume the guy was dead. And assume the body wasn't dragged away by wolves. Then someone removed it. Quickly. To me that indicates foul play, maybe murder."

"I still think the drunk theory is the most likely—"

"Maybe, but let's say I did see eyes in the bushes. That means someone knows I found the body. And if that body was murdered, whoever was watching me probably wasn't too happy about it. Plus, they may not be sure how much I know. After all, the person was still alive when I found him. They don't know if he told me something, like who killed him."

Sally appears to be thinking this over. "And that could explain the break-in, to find out who you are or … yeah, maybe to take you out. So that's pretty creepy."

"And the guy on the bus. He could have been there to do the job."

"Or, Wil." She turns to look directly at me. Her eyes are sparkling. "Or all of this is really nothing. Maybe in fact there was no dead body. Yeah, I know you said there was blood, but maybe the drunk cut himself when he fell."

"But we still have the break-in to explain."

"Okay, I agree that's fishy and too coincidental if it doesn't involve you. But maybe someone just wanted a new iPhone and some nice backpacking gear. And the guy on the bus, maybe you just imagined that he was after you. If you hadn't panicked, maybe you'd be heading home now to your life in Milwaukee."

I shrug. Maybe I'm just letting my emotions control me. I'm normally an analytical guy who looks at data and makes a decision based on that. I know you also have to consider intuition, the so-called gut-feeling, but I've learned to trust data over feelings. I need to trust the data here. And the data do not support the theory of the commission of a crime, much less some killer determined to get me.

I look straight ahead at the narrow strip of blacktop cutting through the woods. So why does my gut still scream that something here is terribly wrong?

Chapter 8

There's not much to distinguish the main street of
White Pine, which is becoming a familiar sight, from
that of any other small town up north. A red-brick post office
on the corner of Main and Highway 2 is the most impressive
structure along the four blocks of downtown. Down the block
is the only other building of any stature, a two-story structure
with a faded stone façade, Corinthian columns at the corners
and the words "Northwoods State Bank" chiseled in the stone
crossbeam supported by the columns. In another era this no
doubt conveyed stability and permanence. Today the space is
occupied, according to the paper sign below the crossbeam, by
Irene's Hair and Nails.

Most of the cars along Main are clustered around the
Ace Hardware, with a line of snowblowers and wheelbarrows
displayed curbside. Several gift shops and bars dot the
boulevard, and I wonder if the man from the hedges tied one
on in one of these watering holes before I found him.

Sally turns onto Sixth Avenue, just two blocks past my
bus stop, and we are immediately in the shade of an arching
canopy of maples. They're just now turning yellow in the
cooler days of mid-September and causing the midmorning
sunlight to streak down golden on the narrow street. Along
both sides of Sixth sit orderly rows of old frame houses—a

few stately Victorians, but mostly simpler homes that I'm guessing are at least a century old. There are no sidewalks along Sixth, and there are no fences between the houses. A peaceful rural scene it is, and I half expect to see Huck Finn heading toward the local fishing hole, with his cane pole over his shoulder.

Sally pulls into a narrow gravel drive next to a white clapboard frame home with a high peaked roof, three stories if you count the dormer window looking out from an attic space. Simple, not ornate. A long front porch that runs the length of the home looks like a good place to watch the unfolding fall colors from a rocker. "Home sweet home," she says.

"This is your grandmother's house? Won't she mind having—"

"It's only me who lives here now. My grandparents bought this place back in the twenties; then my mom and dad lived here. I was born here. But now it's only me. So there's plenty of room."

We enter a door on the side of the house, and I notice that it was unlocked. *Even after a body was found just a couple of blocks away, she's leaving her doors unlocked?* We step into a large kitchen, which appears to have been upgraded back in the fifties. The old appliances are clean and the counters are tidy, unlike the interior of Sally's car. A round oak table commands the center of the room.

"So where are your grandmother and your parents?"

"They're dead," she says matter-of-factly, as she reaches into a cabinet, then hands me a bath towel. "There's a room at the top of the stairs and a bathroom next to it. Sorry again about your backpack. Maybe I can find you some clothes. There'll be some lunch down here when you're settled in."

Spending the night at Sally's. I can't help but wonder where this might lead. Yes, she is attractive, in a woodsy, park-ranger kind of way. And my imagination is fully able to create a romantic fantasy about the lonely local janitor-girl who kisses trees.

My room on the third floor is small, with a peaked ceiling. The dormer window, framed by wispy white curtains, looks out into the yellow foliage of a huge tree. There's a twin bed and a small dresser and not much room for anything else. An oval toss rug is centered on the well-worn hardwood floor. A tiny bathroom is across the hall, spotlessly clean, with antique fixtures that look recently polished.

Sure, I could fall into some casual fling here, but do I want that? That's sort of the way it got started with Megan. After that first afternoon when she approached me after class, Megan would come up after almost every lecture, always with some pertinent question about physics. It was hard not to notice her petite body in those tight jeans and that curvy black turtleneck. Her red pageboy set off her cute features—yes, I'd say cute instead of beautiful. A kind of pixie look. But it was her eyes that got me. I remember how she'd look up at me with near reverence as I explained inertia or momentum. She told me she was just getting back to school after a dead-end job and a bad relationship that had caused her to drop out of college years ago. It was a fresh start she was looking for, and she told me that one afternoon with such an earnest look that I knew, or maybe hoped, that her fresh start included me.

It wasn't long before we were having coffee together after class. Two wild months later, when my momentum was sky high and my inertia was all but gone, she suggested we move in together.

I head into the shower, but stop to check myself in the mirror, surprised by what I see. I haven't gone three days without shaving for a long time. Normally I'm not a guy who studies himself in the mirror, but I've been looking in the mirror a lot more the past few months. Maybe because I'm not sure who that person in the mirror is anymore. He looks like a stranger. The wide-set light green eyes don't show emotion, don't give a clue about the stuff that's going on inside. The boy-like features have a carefree look, giving no evidence of those down times. The brown tousled hair, shaggy and curly, is the only thing about this person that looks a little reckless, a little wild. It's not a bad-looking face, but not an exceptional face either. Quite average. But I'm not sure I can see him objectively, not sure I can draw any conclusions at all about him. And maybe that's why I keep staring.

Enough of that. "What a dork," I say out loud, shaking my head, suddenly self-conscious, even though I'm alone.

The shower is great, and it seems like the hot water washes away more than just some trail dirt. My edginess about the body and the man with the shaved head seems to dissolve too. Even though I have to put on the dirty clothes again, I'm feeling better about everything. I make my way down the stairs toward the kitchen and my luncheon rendezvous with Sally. But she's not there. A note on the table, written in a hasty scrawl, says, "Gone to the church. Plenty of stuff to eat in the fridge. See you later."

In fact there's not much in the fridge. Some healthy-looking salad stuff, which I pass on, a six-pack of yogurt cups, several unlabeled Ball jars that contain something unrecognizable, a gallon of skim milk. In the back of the fridge I find some sliced meat in a plastic tub. I'm going to assume that it's roast beef, but from what I'm learning about Sally, it could be squirrel. There's also a loaf of what looks like homemade bread in a plastic bag, with which I'm able to make a sandwich that tastes quite good. I wash it down with iced tea from a large jar, while I lean back and stretch in an old wooden chair and stroke the smooth surface of the pedestal oak table, which I imagine going back to Sally's grandmother's day.

Afterward, I wander out into the living room, which looks like a museum. Stately old furniture pieces, the kind your great aunt wouldn't let you sit on, look rarely used. A large grandfather clock, taller than me, dominates one wall. An intricately patterned rug that gives the room a warm look covers most of the hardwood floor. The only thing that doesn't fit this scene from yesteryear is a folding plastic table, piled with books and papers, against one wall. I'm not a snoopy guy, but I can't resist a peek. Books on ecology and biology. Photocopies of scientific papers. Several topographical maps spread open. And a laptop.

I go to the front door and look out into the early autumn afternoon. Two old rockers on the long front porch look inviting. As soon as I sit down, I lock eyes with an elderly woman raking leaves in the next yard over, even though very few leaves have fallen yet. She's clearly checking me out, but when I wave at her, she looks away.

I see Sally coming down the street, toting a large plastic bag in one hand and a small box in the other. She stops to speak with the old woman. Then they both look my way, and Sally waves at me to come over.

Sally introduces Mrs. Verlander to me, and I extend my hand, but the woman keeps her hands on the rake and gives me a suspicious look. She obviously thinks I'm some slime bucket moving in on Sally.

As Sally and I head into the house, Mrs. Verlander calls out, "Oh, Sally, I meant to ask if that man ever found you."

We both turn to face Mrs. Verlander. "Which man?" Sally asks.

"I didn't catch his name. Nice fellow ..." She pauses and gives me a disapproving look, then continues. "I said you were over at the church. Seems like that's where you spend most of your—"

"When was this, Mrs. Verlander?"

"A couple of nights ago. No, wait, maybe it was last night. Oh my, I'm really not sure now. But he said he needed to talk to you."

"What did he look like?" Sally's obviously thinking what I'm thinking.

"Hmm, it's hard to say. He wasn't a spring chicken, that's for sure. Wearing a plaid wool shirt, I think." I glance at Sally, but she's focused on Mrs. Verlander.

"So where'd he go then?"

"Well, he left his car here and walked over to the church. Must have found you, huh? When I looked out a little while later, the car was gone."

"What kind of car was it, Mrs. Verlander?" Sally's voice remains steady.

"Oh my, I'm not sure I remember. Now isn't that terrible? You'd think I'd remember a thing like that."

Sally smiles at Mrs. Verlander. "If you remember, you'll let me know?"

"I sure will, Sally. You take care, you hear?" Mrs. Verlander shoots me one last disapproving glower before resuming her leaf-raking.

Inside the door, Sally stops and hands me the plastic bag. "I found you some clothes."

"You didn't need—"

"I think they'll fit you fine. You're about six-one?"

"Right on, actually, but where did you find—"

"We collect clothes for the needy at the church. Actually pretty nice stuff, should get you by. Unless of course, you want to keep wearing—"

My impatience is building. "Thanks, Sally, but there are more urgent things to talk about, don't you think?"

Sally gives me a blank look, but doesn't say anything.

"So tell me, did that guy ever find you?"

"No," whispers Sally. "Look, I don't like where this is going."

"Well, I don't either, but it sounds like the man who stopped here might be the guy I saw in the bushes."

"Maybe, maybe not."

"So where'd the guy looking for you go, if that wasn't him?"

"Look, I don't know. Maybe he couldn't find me, so he drove away. That guy in the bushes could've been anybody."

"But the guy in the bushes had a shirt like Mrs. Verlander mentioned."

"Lots of guys wear shirts like that around here."

"So who was the man who stopped by here, then?"

Even in the low light of the living room, and even given Sally's fair complexion, I see that some of the color has drained from her face. "I don't know," she says.

I switch gears. "I see you have a laptop. Maybe I can at least try to track my phone."

Sally leads me to the plastic table and logs on. "All yours," she says. I bring up my phone account, and click on the Find-My-Phone program. "Offline," the screen says. I click for some help and learn that the app won't work if there's no signal for the phone. I groan.

Sally says, "Reception's spotty around here. Sorry." Then she holds up the small black box she's been carrying. "I for one have work to do. Need to take communion over to Mrs. Grabowski. Why don't you come with me?"

"Look, Sally, this is not the time to—"

"It'll only take a half-hour, and it'll get your mind off all these other things you're so wound up about. Why don't you go change, and we'll leave when you're ready?" She flashes a smile that seems forced.

I sigh and move toward the stairs with my bag of new clothes. Sally can't seem to face it, but she must be thinking it. The man in the bushes was probably murdered while he was headed to the church to see her.

Chapter 9

While I'm changing into my new duds, a Carhartt work shirt and well-worn Levi's 501s—which fit perfectly, it turns out—all the recent events churn in my head. Okay, I admit I have a bit of a reputation for working myself up into a tizzy over things that never really amount to much. Sometimes I can become paralyzed by too much mental fervor. "Analysis paralysis," a co-worker once called it. I didn't appreciate that remark. What I really need to do is get myself a new ticket and be on that bus tomorrow morning, making sure the guy with the shaved head isn't hanging around. Before heading back downstairs, I sit on the bed and put my head down between my knees. This always makes me feel better when I get stressed out.

In the car, Sally acts like everything is just fine. "Thanks for coming along," she says with a light air, "Hazel always loves to have company, and she'll enjoy meeting you."

"Where is it we're actually going now?" If Sally told me before, I missed it.

"To see Hazel Grabowski. She's homebound and in hospice."

What I don't need right now is to be around some depressing dying person. Maybe I can just wait in the car while Sally runs in. "Oh," I finally say.

We drive to the other side of town, which takes all of two minutes, then pull in under a towering maple, in front of a modest one-story frame house. "Think I'll just wait here while—"

"You'll do no such thing." Sally is full of bubbly enthusiasm. "This'll make Hazel's day. And it won't take long." She's already climbing out of the car. "C'mon."

I'm learning that arguing with Sally is not a profitable enterprise. If she's worrying about the mystery of the last twenty-four hours, she's certainly not showing it. I tag along behind, up a weathered brick walk in mid-day sun filtered golden through the turning maples, admiring Sally's curvy sway in the tight jeans.

At this moment, it's hard to consider that all is not right with the world. I silently chastise myself for jumping to conclusions. Not everything that happens indicates gloom and danger. Could it be that my thinking has been tinged by my misfortunes? Probably. "Get a grip," I say to myself out loud, loud enough that Sally turns and looks at me. I audibly clear my throat, as if what she heard was just a cough.

Sally knocks, and a voice says, "It's not locked." In a small, square living room, furnished simply, a woman sits in a recliner under a large, colorful quilt. She's small, with distinguished silver hair drawn tight around her head and pinned in back. I'm guessing she's in her mid-sixties.

"Hazel, you're looking great today. Oh, and this is my friend Wil."

Hazel smiles at me with blue eyes magnified through thick bifocals. Hospice? Doesn't that mean a person is dying? This woman doesn't look all that sick to me. "Wil, thank you for coming. I don't get too many visits from good-looking young men these days."

I give what I think is a friendly smile.

Sally kneels down next to Hazel and asks, "So how are you feeling today, Hazel?"

"I'm having a good day, dear." She reaches out and lays a hand atop Sally's hand.

On the small table next to her chair are a book of brain teasers and a Sunday *New York Times* crossword puzzle. The crossword is completed. Impressive. Apparently whatever is wrong with Hazel hasn't affected her mind. I say, "I notice you're good at puzzles." Sally gives me a reassuring smile, obviously pleased that I'm joining in the conversation.

Sally says, "So what's the visiting nurse's schedule now?"

"She's coming twice a week. She says at some point I'll need more care." Hazel grimaces, then casts her head down. "She says I might not be able to stay here much longer."

I look around the living room. A small fireplace, its brickwork blackened from years of use, takes up most of one wall. The furnishings look inexpensive and old.

"I brought you communion," Sally says.

"That'll help my spirits, that's for sure," beams Hazel, suddenly more cheerful.

Sally raises the hinged lid of the small black box. "I'll set up our altar here as usual," she says, nodding toward the side table. She carefully shifts Hazel's books, then spreads out a white cloth, upon which she places a tiny silvery chalice and a small plate. From the box she produces three small wafers and arranges them on the plate, then pours what looks like red wine into the chalice.

Sally looks up at me and says, "Wil, I assume you'll join us for communion."

I've never had communion before. I've seen it on TV, but never paid much attention. It's great that Sally's doing this for Hazel, though I don't understand what either one of them is getting out of it. I guess I've studied too much science to buy into this religious stuff. "Think I'll pass."

Sally nods, apparently unconcerned with my refusal, then turns toward Hazel. While the communion takes place, I look around the room. On the mantle above the fireplace sits an arrangement of artificial flowers and a white porcelain urn bearing an ornate scrolled pattern. Above the mantle, a large painted portrait, the centerpiece of the room, is obviously of Hazel and her husband, no doubt done many years back. It's a formal studio painting, the kind people dress up for. The man is seated, while Hazel stands at his side with her hand on his shoulder. They look healthy and confident. The painting is sad, as I'm guessing her husband is dead.

Now Sally stands. The service is apparently over. Hazel looks up at me and asks, "So, Wil, what do you do?"

I guess she means my work. I haven't even mentioned this to Sally yet. "I'm a physics instructor at the university down in Milwaukee. I'm just up here for a camping trip." Okay, so I said *am* a physics instructor instead of *was*. My unemployment woes aren't a topic that needs to be aired right now.

I must have hesitated a second too long, because Hazel gives me an odd look, her big eyes full of questions and that *New-York-Times*-crosswords brain clearly mulling things over. This makes me squirm, but she doesn't comment on it.

Instead, she says, "I sure would like to see you again some time, Wil."

"That would be nice, but I'm leaving tomorrow. Maybe next time I'm up this way," I say, knowing that I won't be this way again. And more grimly, Hazel probably isn't going to be around much longer.

Outside, I say to Sally, "She doesn't seem that sick. What's wrong with her?"

"Cancer. She's pretty good most days, but I guess the doc thinks it won't be long now. Hazel's ready to go, not scared at all." Then she adds, "What makes me sad, though, is that she might have to move. She's been here forever. That'd probably kill her in a week."

An image of the Bali Hai Apartments, my home, pops into my mind. It sure wouldn't kill me to leave that place. And then a sadder thought surfaces, which I work hard to dispel. *Maybe I've never really had a home at all.*

Chapter 10

In the car, Sally says she needs to stop by the church to drop off the communion kit. She explains that she is a lay eucharistic minister, a lay person who takes communion to homebound members of the church. Another volunteer activity of hers. But I'm thinking about my bus trip tomorrow morning. When I get to Sally's house, I'll call Indian Trails and purchase a new ticket, which will set me back fifty-seven bucks. My ATM card should work, but I'll try to use my Visa card first—to conserve my cash until my next unemployment check comes in—although I'm sure it will be rejected.

Yeah, I should have kept up my payments on the card, but the past few months I've let some things slide. I just couldn't stand to look at all those Visa charges Megan and I racked up, while we were living the good life. I made the minimum monthly payment for a while, but stopped. What kind of dent would ten bucks a month have made on the thousands I owe anyway?

It's hard to believe that a numbers guy like me would be in such a financial mess, but since losing my job, anything regarding money gets me down pretty quick.

The church is a stately gray-stone building with a square bell tower. The only thing colorful is the bright red front door. A carved sign in front reads "St. Paul's Episcopal Church."

Sally leads me through the sanctuary, where I spent most of last night. The high-arched ceiling is all wood, layered in struts and planks like the inside of a wooden canoe. The wooden pews, with which I am quite familiar, look simple and well-worn. There is no light except for what streams in from two large stained-glass windows at either end of the church. The one over the altar depicts Jesus, I presume, ascending into clouds with arms outstretched, while people kneel and look up in amazement or fear. The window at the rear of the church shows four robed men—some guys from the Bible, I guess.

We enter a small back room, where an elderly man, polishing candle holders, barely looks up as Sally enters. "How'd it go with Hazel?" he asks.

"She's doing pretty well today, Hans." Sally starts washing the vessels from the kit. "Hans, I want you to meet Wil Weathers."

The old man stops and turns toward me. I can see that he was once a large muscular man, but now his body is bent with age. He has a broad seasoned face, pale and tired looking, and his hair is thin and white. The man gives me a faint smile as he extends his hand.

Sally says, "Hans has been leading our altar guild work here at St. Paul's for … how long Hans? Before my time, that's for sure. Not sure what the church would do without him."

"Thirty years. Too long, if you ask me. And the church would do just fine without me." There's a devilish twinkle in Hans's eyes as he lets out a low grumble of a laugh. "So, you new here in White Pine, Wil?"

I explain that I'll be leaving tomorrow.

"Well, that's too bad, son. There's a lot of beautiful stuff to see around here, if you ask me." Then he lowers his voice and leans toward me, "Not the least of which is standing right here." He gives me a sly smile, as he rolls his eyes toward Sally.

"Oh, Hans, you silly man." Sally quickly shifts the conversation away from herself. "Wil's a physics professor down in Milwaukee. Thought you'd be interested." She then turns to me and says, "Hans's son Joe is our high school principal."

"Science professor, huh? That's a good profession, Wil. Lots of demand for smart people like you these days." *Oh yeah? I could tell you something about that.* I just nod as Sally leads me toward the door.

Late afternoon sunlight pours in through the tall stained-glass window in the rear of the church. The four men in long robes look disapproving, and I could easily be convinced that they're looking at me. Sally stops beside me and says, "Those are the gospel writers. They're quite imposing, don't you think?"

"I think they look grim."

"I guess they were taking their jobs seriously."

I nod. *Or maybe they've seen my Visa bills.*

Outside the church, I look across the street to where I saw the man last night. The scene looks much less menacing on this brilliant afternoon. Dense, head-high hedges parallel the street. Behind them are more shrubs, extending toward the rear of a house on the next block over. A perfect place to seek refuge from an attacker or to drag a person you've just killed. "Let's check out those hedges again," I say. "Maybe we missed something in the dark."

But fifteen minutes later we've discovered no sign of anything out of the ordinary. As we're heading back to the car, Officer Darby's cruiser pulls up.

Darby saunters slowly toward us, as if the weight of keeping the peace is a heavy burden upon his strong shoulders. He grins at Sally, then shoots me a hard look. "I thought you were leaving this morning."

"Well, I was, but then—"

"Wil's staying an extra day," Sally says. "He's been helping me make my rounds." She glances at me, then back at Darby, and doesn't allow us to dwell on this subject. "So what have you learned about the break-in at the church?"

Darby shoots me another disapproving look, then says to Sally, "Not much. Gotta say that some transient getting his junk stolen is hardly a federal case." In other words, he doesn't plan to do anything about it. Then he adds, "But I do have news that might interest you, Sally." He pauses to let the suspense build, then says, "We had another wolf sighting this morning, just a mile from here, back behind Ed's place."

Sally grimaces. "That doesn't mean—"

"Look, I still think what our city boy saw was some drunk last night. Still nobody missing. But if there is, looks like my wolf theory—"

"Darby, your wolf theory is a bunch of hooey," interrupts Sally, her eyes smoldering. "And I hope you know it. Sure, the wolf population is increasing up here, but there's no indication that they're a danger to—"

"All I'm sayin', Sally, is that if it is wolves, then I've got some of my huntin' buddies alerted about this, and they'll take care of it." Sally's fuming, and Darby's clearly enjoying it. He finishes his statement with an air of authority that essentially says "case closed."

Chapter 11

I've been a big-city guy all my life. I was born in L.A. and lived there straight through graduate school, after which I moved to Milwaukee. Twenty-four hours is about as long as I've ever been in a town as small as White Pine. Sure, I've spent a lot of days backpacking and camping in the boonies—well, at least, I used to, back before .... Anyway, I really love it there. Those have been some of the best days of my life. It's natural that an introvert like me would blossom in the solitude of the wilderness. But I've never had to live in a tiny town like this one, away from twenty-four-hour supermarkets, malls, Starbucks everywhere and a dozen movies showing within a few miles of my house.

There's more to it than that. Cities are where civilization has flourished, where museums display the best of our culture, where great minds have wrestled with the big questions, where decisions are made that affect everyone.

I'll concede that's a glorified view of the city, a view that neglects the darker aspects. And perhaps a guy who loves the wilderness should be turned off by the nerve-rattling noise, the stench of pollution, the millions of anonymous and seemingly uncaring others sharing the same crowded space with me. But for me, there is a comfort being surrounded by these nameless millions, who help stem the tide of loneliness. Maybe that's why I love the city.

Back at Sally's, I use her phone to call Indian Trails, and it's no surprise that they reject my Visa card. I'll have to use the ATM card, even though this will drain my already critically-low checking account. But I don't see my ATM card in its usual sleeve inside my wallet. It takes only moments to search the other compartments of my wallet and conclude that the card is gone. I stand and go through my pockets, but it's not there either. Could it have been in my backpack?

No, wait. I used it this morning at the convenience store in Florence. I blurt out an obscenity so loud that Sally comes out of the kitchen. "What's wrong?" she asks.

I let out a huge sigh. "I think I left my ATM card at a convenience store in Florence."

Sally seems nonplused about my crisis. "Well, let's call them. Do you know what store it was?"

"I don't know the name. It's across from the bus stop."

"I know the one." She goes back into the kitchen, then returns with a thin phone book. "Here it is," she says, handing the book to me, then returns to the kitchen.

I call the convenience store and speak to the manager, while pacing Sally's living room. She tells me that they have no card that's been left or turned in. She takes my name and Sally's number and says she'll call if it turns up. "If it was me," she says, "I'd call the company and get that thing cancelled right away."

Which I do. From the kitchen, Sally calls out, "Did they have your card?"

"No," I snap, frustrated at my stupidity in letting the man with the shaved head distract me enough to walk off without my ATM card. I've had enough trouble for one day.

"Oh Wil, I'm sorry. Maybe you left it somewhere else?"

"No, that's where I left it. I just cancelled the card."

"Do you have another credit card?"

"Uh, I've got it under control." She's trying to be helpful, but I'm in no mood for a review of my sketchy financial resources.

My other option for getting my ticket is to get my bank to transfer cash. I check my watch. 5:15, the bank's closed. Maybe I can do it online. I call out to Sally, "May I use your computer? Still trying to get my ticket for tomorrow."

"Sure," she calls back. "The password is *mitosis*." Mitosis? Some kind of biology word, isn't it? I find I can get money transferred to a bank just down the street from where Irene does hair and nails in the old bank building. But the White Pine bank doesn't open until 10:00, and the bus leaves at 8:15, which means I'd be stuck here for another day. I decide I'll ask Sally to float me a loan. Some time tonight when the time is right. No shame in doing this. So, how come I feel like a deadbeat?

In the kitchen, Sally's stirring something on the stove. Over her shoulder, she asks, "Did you get your bus ticket?"

"Not yet," I say with nonchalance. This isn't the time to bring up my cash problem. "What are you cooking?" I ask, feigning interest.

"Just spaghetti. Something quick. Don't want my guest to starve." This statement is concluded with that soft laugh of hers. Then, more somber, she asks, "Aren't you missing work today?"

"I don't have any classes today." Technically not a lie. Still, I feel lousy saying this.

It's a simple dinner around the oak table. The spaghetti is whole wheat, of course, with a carbonara sauce, served with more of that homemade bread and a half-full bottle of red wine Sally's pulled from the back of the fridge. "So tell me about yourself, Wil."

"What would you like to know?" I'm filling my mouth with a twisted fork-full of pasta. The sauce on the spaghetti is quite good. "I'm a pretty ordinary guy."

"Where do you teach?"

"UWM." Then I add, "That's the University of Wisconsin, Milwaukee."

"Yes, I know." She takes a sip of wine, then says, "So you're a professor?"

I respond with a nod that's more a duck of the head than confirmation, then say, "So what about you?"

She shrugs. "I'm in between things right now."

"How so?"

"Last year I was working on my master's up at MTU—"

"That's Michigan Tech?" I'm pretty sure I sent them one of my résumés.

"Yeah, up in Houghton. Environmental biology. That's my passion. I was looking to do research with some environmental group or work for the DNR—"

"Department of …?"

"Natural Resources. You really are a city boy, Wil." There's that little-girl laugh again—like the cheery giggle from a child with rosy cheeks—and I'm starting to like it. Then she turns serious. "Anyway, my mom got sick about a year ago, and I had to come home and take care of her. She died six months ago, and I'm just now starting to get my life back together."

"I'm sorry." This all seems consistent with the nurturing acts of Sally kneeling beside Mrs. Grabowski, and how she so readily offered me a place to stay. "So where is your dad?"

"He's been gone a long time. Died in an accident when I was in high school."

I nod with compassion.

"He worked for the DNR as a hydrology tech, assisting the scientists who studied the lakes and rivers." She sits back in her chair and looks at me with those penetrating dark eyes. "So you have a Ph.D., Wil? Most professors have Ph.D.s, don't they?"

"I've got a master's," I say, trying not to sound apologetic. Okay, so there's a big story there, about why I don't have a Ph.D. And not one I hope to get into tonight. I've done a lot of rationalizing about it over the years, tried to make it look rosier than it is. But the plain fact is that I had to leave grad school. Not because I was a troublemaker or anything like that, but because ... I usually try not to think about that, that dark time in my life. Let's just say I couldn't cut it academically. I mean, I really am good at physics, but ... when the written qualifiers came along, I got killed. So I got this letter from the academic dean saying ... you get the idea. I clear my throat and say, "The spaghetti's really good."

"Thank you." There are questions in her eyes. The kind of eyes that it's hard to lie to. "So, what do you think of White Pine so far?"

I try to sound positive. "It's really a nice little town." *Nice if you don't include dead bodies, thieves in the night, or men with shaved heads chasing you—and throw in a bully cop for good measure.*

She seems pleased with my answer, obviously proud of her home town. "If you had more time, I'd show you the white pines."

"Oh, I saw plenty of white pines on my camping trip."

"Those are all second-growth white pines. You've probably never seen one of the old trees, because there's less than one percent of them left."

"What happened to the rest of them?"

"They were all cut down. At one time the northern half of the state was covered with white pines. Then men came from the east and saw their fortunes in these woods. The whites were great trees. Up to two hundred feet high, and they grow so straight and true their trunks were prized for making masts for sailing ships. It must have been beautiful, but now they're all gone. All except a few."

"You mean nothing was done to manage the forests or to replant or keep some of the trees?"

Sally's eyes flash with determination and something that looks like a mixture of love and anger. This stuff clearly touches her deeply. "Don't get me started. Not everybody agrees with me, but I say it was just greed, plain and simple. The lumber barons made fortunes for themselves, and the state was clear-cut."

"That's so sad. But you say there are a few of the old trees left?"

"Yes, a few. In secret places that most people don't know about. I call them the sentinels."

"I would love to see them," I say, really meaning it.

The fire in her eyes softens to kindness. "If you had another day, I'd take you out and show you. But you've got a bus to catch."

A plan may be hatching. If I stay another day, I could get my cash wired to the local bank and be all set to take the bus the next morning. I could see the white pines. And I wouldn't have to ask Sally for money. But this is probably a bad idea. I say, "So, I'm guessing you were working on your environmental biology degree so you could protect those white pines?"

"Unfortunately it's too late for them. What's done is done, and it'll be centuries before there are new sentinels in these forests. But there are other parts of our environment where it's not too late to—"

"Like where?"

"Like the Great Lakes, that's where. I want to see that no one ever does to these beautiful lakes what the lumbermen did to the white pines."

"I didn't know there were any threats to the Great Lakes."

Sally sits up straight. "You've got to be kidding, Wil," she snaps with such energy that for a moment I think she might take a swing at me. "The lakes are under all kinds of threats. Pollution. Invasive species. People trying to steal the water and pipe it to other parts of the country." Then she sags. "I get sad just thinking about it."

Now we are quiet while we finish our meal. This is certainly not the right time to ask Sally for money. Finally, I say, "You know what? I probably could stay an extra day, if your offer to see those white pines still stands."

She looks me over for a moment, probably wondering how a busy physics professor like me can afford another weekday off in the woods, then says, "Got yourself a deal, Wil.

I think you'll be amazed." She has an easy smile that enhances the sparkle in her eyes.

Maybe it's the red wine we just finished off, but I'm already becoming amazed, and not about the white pines. I lean forward, then pause while I craft some romantic line.

But before I can say anything, Sally jumps up. "So it's set. Now, since I cooked the supper, you get the dishes. Sorry there's no dishwasher. I've got some work to do. See you bright and early." With that, she strides into the other room, leaving me there with my empty wine glass and the dirty dishes.

Chapter 12

I lie on my back, eyes closed, trying to will my way into sleep, but my mind's churning like crazy. The dormer window is open because it's warm up here on the third floor, and the slight breeze that produces a comforting swishing sound in the maples outside, shaking loose more leaves for Mrs. Verlander to rake tomorrow, also keeps the air moving in my room. Maybe a change of weather is coming.

So I'm staying in White Pine for another day. Now I'm having second thoughts about what seemed like a good idea while I was bantering with Sally over dinner. I guess I'm still a sucker for girls. And that hasn't always worked out for me, has it? Sure, for a year there was that romantic apartment by the lake with my pixie who seemed madly in love with me. Life with Megan wasn't bad—the full time student and her professorial stud. At least that was the image I was awash in for a while, and it felt good. Then I got laid off, and a month later she was gone. Just moved out one afternoon, taking her clothes and the Keurig, while I was giving my lecture on friction. There was only that email informing me that the relationship wasn't going anywhere, that she needed another fresh start, and that I shouldn't try to contact her, which I didn't. That's how it ended. Okay, so the email did say a little more than that. Some stuff about not wanting to hang with a guy who felt sorry for himself all the time, who was struggling with self-esteem issues when she had enough self-esteem issues of her own. I admit I was going through a down period, and yes, it wasn't the first....

I don't want to get into that again tonight. I roll onto my side and double up the pillow under my head. My mind returns to the disappearing body in the hedges, Darby's loony wolf theory, the intruder in the church, the man with the shaved head, and the man Mrs. Verlander says was looking for Sally. How do these pieces fit together? Or do they? Taken as individual incidents, each has an innocuous explanation. Taken together, though, do they add up to something more?

But on this peaceful autumn night, the bursts of terror I've experienced in the past twenty-four hours now seem distant, and my thoughts return again to this evening and the passion in Sally's face. I drift into sleep, and I'm back at UCLA, on the day of my written qualifiers in classical mechanics. I feel the fire in my gut, the anticipation, as the test is handed out. Classical mechanics is my best subject. I need to ace this baby.

The professor passes through the classroom, handing each of us a copy of the test. When he says we can start, I take a deep breath and look at the test. My sheet is only a torn scrap, blank, except for the two words written across the top. In pencil, the first word in all caps: *HOME Skill.*

I come awake with a start, breathing hard. Just a crazy dream, but it was, after all, that exam in classical mechanics that did me in. Every student dreads the written qualifiers, a week-long series of exams given after two years of graduate coursework and covering the gamut of physics subjects. But I had a special reason to dread them. Not because I didn't understand the physics—but quite the contrary: I loved the physics too much. Maybe that doesn't make sense. But I never could solve physics problems against the clock. You give me a problem to solve, and I immediately get engrossed in it. I want to ponder it, savor it, try all the different ways it might be solved. I just can't help myself. So, if I'm facing a test with, say, four problems to solve, I have a hard time getting past the first problem before the time is up. That's what happened, and I wound up getting a big fat 40 percent, finishing at the bottom of the heap.

There are two outcomes for the written qualifiers. You can pass at the Ph.D. level and continue to the next phase of the graduate program. This, of course, was what I was hoping for. If you fall short of that, you may still pass at the master's level. That is, you are awarded your master's degree, kind of a consolation prize, and you leave. My scores weren't even good enough to warrant a master's, but someone must have put in some good words for me, enough to keep the dean from just throwing me out.

There is more to it than that, but I won't allow myself to rehash it again tonight. These things have already caused more than enough sleepless nights. I shouldn't be ashamed, but when I'm talking to a person like Sally, I guess I am.

I need to get some sleep, but I need to calm down first. I sit on the side of the bed and stare out the dormer window into the pitch black of the night. It's cooler now, and the evening breeze has turned into a moderate wind. Rain may be on the way. I pull the window closed, leaving just a crack at the bottom, and try to settle back into sleep.

But as I begin to doze, I'm aware of a rattling sound outside my window, and I'm suddenly wide-awake again. A loud thud against my window jolts me up and off the bed. Then everything's quiet except my pounding heart. Memories of last night in the parish hall still fresh, I quietly move toward the edge of the window to peer out. There on the roof, resting against the window, is a large branch, snapped off by the wind. But now I'm too agitated to go back to sleep. I lie back on the bed and stare into the darkness, my mind racing over a hundred things and wondering when the morning light will come.

Chapter 13

Danny's Northwoods Café, at the corner of Main and Eighth, is hopping by the time we walk in. Seems like half the town is gathered around the closely packed tables, huddled in the tall pine booths that line the walls or perusing the morning paper at the U-shaped counter that fronts a large pass-through into the kitchen. There's a lively din of laughter, clanking silverware and rattling coffee cups that guarantees to raise sleepy spirits.

If you're looking for up-north, woodsy ambiance, Danny's would be your place. A high ceiling of knotty-pine tongue-and-groove arches over the tables. Numerous mounted fish, the heads of trophy deer, and a black bear adorn the walls. Rough-cut pine shelves display various antique pieces of farm equipment, old galvanized buckets, a washtub, part of a plow, old brown bottles and a railman's lantern. It's a homey place that feels good. Behind the pass-through two young men move briskly to fill the orders, working beside an older man, who I suspect is Danny.

Sally and I have come for some serious carb loading before our trek into the woods to see the sentinels. She wears a bright pink Patagonia fleece vest over a "Life Is Good" T-shirt and khaki hiking shorts that show off shapely legs. Her hiking boots look well-worn. They probably came from the back seat of her car, her base camp. Her hair is tucked up under a white ball cap that says "Live Green," and her pony tail pokes out through the opening in the rear of the cap. Though her ears are pierced, she wears no jewelry.

Sally introduces me to Marge, the waitress, who's pouring our coffee, which prompts me to say, "Sally, do you know everybody in this town?"

"It's not hard when there are only twelve hundred people."

"It looks like it was once much larger than that."

"It was at one time, back when the lumber industry was thriving. But that's pretty much gone, except for the young trees they still cut for the paper mills." She pauses to stir some skim milk into her coffee from a small metal pitcher, then continues. "There also used to be iron ore mining around here, but that's petered out. You've probably heard about the taconite mines, and how that process poisons people just like asbestos does. But they're out west of here."

I nod knowingly, although I don't know anything about taconite mines. I don't even know what taconite is, but I'll figure that out later. I want her to go on, which she does. "Today, White Pine exists pretty much by being the county seat, although there are only eight thousand folks in the whole county. The businesses make money just being on US 2, with all those cars passing through from Duluth to Escanaba. Then there's a little farming and some tourism catering to fishermen, snowmobilers and hunters. That's about it. It's enough to keep the place going. Barely."

She takes her first sip of coffee and looks up at me with eyes full of morning energy. Sally's in a good mood, and so am I, considering I didn't get any sleep last night. After breakfast, we'll stop by the bank to pick up my cash, then head off into the woods to see Sally's sentinels. I ask her about the kielbasa and eggs, which seems to be a special on the menu. I've never heard of kielbasa, but Sally informs me that it's a kind of sausage from Poland. "It'll spike your cholesterol," she cautions with a giggle, "but it's worth every bite."

I order the kielbasa and eggs and get the German potato pancakes too—another specialty, she tells me—instead of toast. I've got enough cash to cover breakfast, and once I hit the bank I'll be fine.

A guy heading for the door spots Sally and comes over. After introductions, the man says, "You must be the physics professor." He sees the surprised look in my eyes, then says, "My dad, Hans Gerlach, met you yesterday and told me about you."

Joe Gerlach is a big rangy guy like his dad must have been at one time, with wavy blond hair thinning in the front, a rough red Nordic face and a warm genuine smile. There's a gentleness in his pale blue eyes, like you want to see in a person who's a school principal. He extends a large hand, which I shake.

"Do you teach and do research?"

"I mainly teach."

"Physics is a pretty hard subject," he says with inquiring eyes, expecting me to elaborate.

Marge comes by with more coffee, and Joe steps aside to let her fill our cups. Then I say, "It can be a hard subject, but I think it's a lot easier than some make it out to be."

"How so?"

"Most textbooks bury students from the get-go with a lot of memory work and stuff that's boring. Memorize how to convert units from one system to another, memorize equations and so on. It's no wonder the students' eyes start to glaze over on day one."

"And what do you do about that?"

He's just lobbed me a slow pitch over the middle of the plate. I set my fork down, then say, "I start out by telling my students that they already know a lot more physics than they think they do. You see, I want to reduce the intimidation factor, which has hit many of them already."

Joe leans forward, pressing his palms onto the table, his eyes locked on me. "Say more."

"Well, I might say, 'Have you ever thrown a tennis ball against a wall?' They all nod, 'Sure.' 'So what happens when you do?' I ask them. They look around like it's a trick question, then some bold student will say, 'It comes back to you.' 'Of course,' I say. 'And what happens when you throw the ball harder?' Now more confident, several students will say, 'It comes back faster.' 'Exactly,' I say. 'See, you already understand an important law of physics called conservation of momentum.'" I realize I'm really getting into this, and I notice Sally looking at me with some surprise.

"That's great," Joe says with what appears to be real appreciation.

"I think if you can create excitement and give students confidence, then learning's going to be a lot easier. I couldn't care less if my students learn how to convert ergs to joules or whatever. I want them to leave with a sense of curiosity about the world around them and a few tools to understand it a little better." I stop and take a sip of coffee, look at Sally, then back at Joe. "I'm sorry. I get carried away with this stuff. Don't mean to talk your arm off." There's something inviting about this guy that makes me ramble on more than I normally do.

"No problem, Wil. I can see you love this stuff."

"Yes, I guess I do love physics." I struggle to keep last night's dream about the written qualifiers at bay. Loving something isn't always enough, as I learned at UCLA, as I learned at UWM.

After Joe leaves, Sally says, "Wow, that was an impressive lecture you just gave there, Professor Weathers."

Impressive. Sure. The recently fired marginal member of the physics department, holding court in a coffee shop at some wide spot in the road in the middle of nowhere. I give out a little forced laugh. "Thanks, Sally."

Chapter 14

We stop at the bank right at ten, then Sally takes us west on US 2 through a dense mixed forest of maple, oak and birch, interspersed with low second-growth pine, spruce and fir. The woods are interrupted only by an occasional cabin, a rustic tavern where I imagine Darby's wolf-huntin' buddies hang out, and a few forest service roads shooting off into the trees. The rain hinted at by last night's wind has not yet materialized, but there is an abundance of billowy cumulus clouds moving fast across an otherwise brilliant blue sky, causing us to be in bright sun one moment, then plunged into shadow the next. I've been in Wisconsin long enough to know that when it comes to weather, anything can still happen today.

The stop at the bank was uneventful. The wire I finally sent last night had gone through, and the teller had four crisp twenties waiting for me, enough for my ticket tomorrow and a snack when I change to the Milwaukee bus in Escanaba. Two minor things left me a bit unsettled though. I learned that I have just seventy bucks left in my account after the wire, much less than I assumed. My next unemployment check isn't due for another ten days, so I'll have to worry about that when I get home.

The other thing was rather odd, though I probably wouldn't have given it a second thought if I hadn't gone through the events of the past two days. As I was receiving my money, I couldn't help but notice a man at a desk behind the counter checking me out. When I looked at him, he looked away, but as soon as I returned my eyes to the teller, I could see in my peripheral vision that he was looking at me again. Finally, as I was about to leave, the man, a distinguished pillar-of-the-community type, silver headed and wearing a well-tailored business suit, approached me. "Mr. Weathers, isn't it?" He wore a broad, pasted-on smile, as he extended his hand.

"Uh, yes," I said, trying not to let my apprehension show, wondering how this man might know me. Of course Joe at the café had known who I was, so maybe this was just a small town thing.

"Mr. Weathers, I'm Dennis Yardley, the bank president. We hope you're enjoying your stay in White Pine. Planning to stay long?"

Planning to stay long? Why would he want to know about that? Maybe he's been talking to my pal Darby? "Actually," I said, then paused. I almost told him I'd be on the bus tomorrow morning, but then thought better of it. "I will be leaving soon." I'm hoping to slip out of town unnoticed and not repeat my experience with the man with the shaved head. Mr. Yardley nodded and gave me another big banker smile, then returned to his desk. Yet I could feel his eyes on my back as I left. It was probably nothing, but it kind of spooked me. I didn't mention it to Sally. She already thinks I'm paranoid enough.

Now Sally slows and makes a right onto a dirt road, marked by an easy-to-miss wooden sign that says Forest 1277.

We head more or less north through forest that becomes more dense the farther in we go. We encounter no other cars. We pass several lakes, and I remember my camping buddy, Ron, telling me that this area has the highest density of lakes in North America. "Sure, they call Minnesota the land of ten thousand lakes," he laughed while we sat around our campfire at Porcupine Lake, "but Wisconsin actually has over fifteen thousand."

Sally drives faster than I would on these forest roads full of loose gravel and blind curves. I recall the multitude of dents in her Outback, and I hold on tighter. But she seems to know where she's going. Several miles in on the dirt road, we enter a range of low rolling hills, not high by out-west standards, but a change from the perfectly flat geography we've been traversing. A few more miles, then Sally slows and pulls off into the pines. There is no parking area or even an indication that other vehicles have stopped here. She kills the engine and looks at me. "This is it," she announces. "We walk from here."

"Is there a trail?" I ask.

She gives me a condescending look. "No trail." She rummages around in the cluttered back seat for awhile, then hands me a daypack and a water bottle. "There's a poncho in the pack. It may be a bit small for you, but it looks like it might rain later."

These woods are dense, a tangle of all kinds of trees, shrubs, and vines. I'm concerned. It's the kind of place where you could get lost fifty feet from the road. "How do we know where to go?" I ask.

"I have been here a few times, Wil. Many times, actually." She laughs, then adds, "Plus, I have this." She holds up a small plastic object. I look closer and see that it's a GPS.

"So are you into geocaching then?" I realize immediately that this is a stupid question.

Sally rolls her eyes. "Geocaching is a game, Wil. This is a tool. I use it as a tool." Okay, so she takes this stuff seriously. She enters some information—coordinates I assume—into the GPS, then says, "This way."

I follow Sally off into the thick of the woods. On my backpacking trip with Ron, we'd stuck to maintained trails that were well-marked and identified on our topographical maps. But this is bushwhacking. The branches of the pines and spruces are well above head-high, but we have to contend with a thick understory, which Sally points out is mainly ferns and alder, sumac, and hemlock saplings. The footing is precarious, uneven stepping through the ground vegetation and pine needles laced with fallen branches and small rocky outcroppings. I'm struggling to keep up. After what seems to me like several miles, we emerge into an open area and find ourselves on the shore of a small lake. Sally drops her pack and pulls out her water bottle.

Before us is a pristine wilderness lake surrounded by conifers and low shoreline vegetation. A slight breeze stirs the water and reflects the sunlight as a million sparkles. Near where we sit, a layer of lily pads, their white flowers in full bloom, reaches out into the lake. "What's the name of this lake?" I ask.

"It has no official name, but I call it Lake Warren. After my dad, Warren Ladke."

"Did he bring you here?"

She gazes out across the lake as she speaks. "Yes. He's the one who showed me where the biggest sentinels are. He walked these woods all his life, and for years with the DNR."

"So your mom and dad were both born around here?"

Now she looks at me. "Sure were," she beams with pride. "My dad's family came here from Poland back in the late 1800s. Ladkes helped start White Pine. My grandmother was an English girl. Her parents moved here to be school teachers back in the twenties. They built our house and got my mom and dad and then me going to that Episcopal church."

I nod, pondering how different Sally's upbringing was from mine, as we watch a stately great blue heron stalking its prey in the shallows across the lake.

"Better get going," she says, jumping to her feet. "It's a ways farther. Maybe we can get back before it rains."

We follow the shore of the lake around to its far side, where Sally turns to face me. "Ever been in a Wisconsin bog?" she asks.

"No."

"Well, we'll be crossing a bog at the headwaters of the lake, so follow me closely. One wrong step and you could be up to your neck in muck." Of course I know what a bog is, and I bristle a bit at the idea that an experienced backpacker like me needs coaching about how to walk through the woods.

We stop at one point and admire a pair of loons patrolling the waters of Warren Lake. "I love them," sings Sally, imitating their haunting call. "They'll be heading south pretty soon." So will I.

While we watch the loons dive for fish, Sally asks, "So where are your parents, Wil?" She looks at me with those dark eyes full of interest.

"In the L.A. area. That's where I was raised. Actually, they now live in Orange County, in a condo, since my dad retired."

"So they're both in good health?" A reasonable question, considering both of her parents are gone, and she just lost her mom recently.

"Yes, quite good actually. I'm fortunate." But if I'm so fortunate, how come I haven't seen my folks in almost two years? Sally would probably not consider my monthly phone call as staying connected. In truth, I have thought about asking them for a loan, but I just can't bring myself to do it. They don't have much—my dad being a draftsman, after all—but I know they'd readily send me some cash. Maybe in another month I'll have to make that call, but I do still have a few shreds of pride left.

"You are fortunate, Wil, and blessed. Not a day goes by that I don't miss my parents. I still cry about my mom, Geez, it's all still so fresh. And when I'm out here in these woods, it's like my dad's right here with me." Sally looks like she's about to cry, but then she glances up at the gathering clouds. "Yep," she announces, pulling herself back together, "I think we're in for some rain." Then she laughs, "Ready to get wet, Wil?"

At the far end of the lake, we make our way through an alder thicket, then cross a small creek. "This is a good spot for brookies," she notes. I jump when a bird suddenly flies up from the underbrush before us. Sally tells me that it's a woodcock. I've never even heard of a woodcock.

This place is stunning—much more eye-popping than Porcupine Lake, where the effects of generations of campers are quite evident. I follow behind Sally, my head turning to take in as much of the beauty as I can. Then I'm in some ankle-deep mud. I side-step to avoid it, but I only go in deeper. I look around for a better route around the mud. Sally, up ahead, has somehow made it through this spot. Over to the left—that looks like my best bet. But two steps later, I'm sinking deeper. Suddenly I find myself thigh-deep in the mud, and I can't move.

Sally turns, and I expect her to laugh. I brace for the calls of "I told you so" that will soon be heading my way. But she doesn't laugh. Instead she hurries back to where I am, stopping just beyond the deep mud. "Don't try to move, Wil. That'll only make it worse. I'll get you out." Sally forages around at the edge of the trees for a few minutes, then returns with a fallen tree limb, so large she can barely carry it. She flops it across the muddy stretch that separates the two of us. "Okay, Wil, grab ahold, and let's see if we can get you out of there."

As Sally pulls hard, I begin to budge. It takes a while, but I make it out. "Oh, Wil, I'm so sorry, I should have stayed with you." She lays a hand on my arm, then pulls it back like she's inadvertently crossed some boundary.

I laugh. "So, now I guess I know about Wisconsin bogs." But I'm really thinking about her hand on my arm.

Beyond the bog, we climb up a steep ridge and soon find ourselves traversing the rocky ledges of a high cliff. The view of the forest, dotted with lakes, is stunning. "It's because of these cliffs, I think," Sally says, "that the lumbermen didn't make it all the way back here. It's why there are some sentinels left."

After another mile or so along the cliffs, we cut in and find ourselves in a forest of giant trees. This is the grove of the sentinels, but it feels like we're in a cathedral.

"What do you think?" Sally whispers, her voice low, as if we're in some holy place.

"It's amazing," is all I can say. It truly is.

Chapter 15

An army of tall straight trees—yes, like sentinels—surrounds me. The foliage only begins about halfway up the tree, far above where we stand, so what I see is an array of trunks, large, maybe five feet in diameter. Gazing skyward, I see dense clusters of long needles filling branches curved upward like arms raised in praise. The top of the canopy sways slowly in a breeze that cannot be felt down here at ground level, and a soft whispering is the only sound. The sunlight is merely a flicker through the undulating branches.

I step up to the nearest white pine and trail my fingers over the bark, rough and corrugated like primitive battle armor, a spectrum of soft browns, greens, and silver. At the base of the tree, moss covers the north side, and around the tree the understory is primarily pine needles and a few seedling pines.

There is a musty smell, the odor of decay. Several fallen trunks are green with moss and riveted with holes that I guess were made by woodpeckers or insects. Sally says, "Those are the critter condos. The dead trees make a home for all sorts of life, and the decaying wood replenishes the soil."

I've seen the California redwoods, which are larger, but these trees are just as magnificent.

The trunk of one fallen tree provides a good place to stop for lunch, which Sally produces from her pack. Apples, trail mix, and a couple of rough-cut slices from that homemade bread.

For a while we eat in silence, taking it all in.

"How old are these trees?" I ask.

"Some may be five hundred years old. That's why people should think twice before they cut one down."

"And the second growth?"

"Most of that was planted back in the thirties by the Conservation Corps. You saw how small those whites are, even after eighty years."

"These guys must be, what? Two hundred feet high?"

"I wish I knew. I read that the largest living white pine in the U.S. is about a hundred and ninety feet tall. But stories from the old days tell that there were trees well over two hundred. They're all gone now."

"Have you got a piece of paper?" I ask. "And a pen or pencil, too?"

She rummages through her pack—while I continue to gape at the huge trees—and finds a letter-size sheet and a pencil. "Making some notes?"

"Give me a sec," I say. I walk to the base of what appears to be the tallest of the nearby trees. From there I step, toe to heel, through the understory, counting my steps, to a place about fifty yards from the tree, where I can see its top. Then I align the edge of the sheet perpendicular to my eye and sight along it. I make a mark on the paper where it intersects with the tree top. What I'm doing is simple geometry that will give me the height of the tree. I return to where Sally sits and do some more calculation, then look at her with great satisfaction. "Sally, you're going to like this."

She has a smile of anticipation. "What are you doing, silly man?"

"I just measured the height of that big tree using a poor man's triangle."

"Huh?"

"It's easy actually." I show her the paper. "You see, the mark on the paper defines a triangle, which is a similar triangle formed by my distance from the tree and its height."

She gives me a blank look, so I continue.

"The point is, that tree, give or take about five feet, is two hundred and ten feet high."

Sally's jaw drops, then she shoots a quick look up at the tree, as if needing to verify that it's still there, before turning back toward me. "Oh, my ..." She shakes her head and exhales a big breath. "So we're sitting under the tallest known white pine in North America. Thank you, Wil. It's kinda handy having a physicist around."

"Thank you," I reply. "I can't remember when I've seen anything so beautiful." I pause, then add, "These trees, I mean." I think I see a little rosy blush in her face, so I continue quickly. "Are you going to report this finding?"

"And why would I do that?" She sits up straighter now, as if bracing for an argument. "This pine is perfectly happy living here all by itself. The pines have already been through enough. No need to build a road into this place, maybe make it a park, so we can bring thousands of belching automobiles back in here." She sags. "Okay, sorry. End of speech."

I certainly don't want to argue about it. So I ask, "How many big trees are in this grove?"

"Probably only a hundred or so. Pretty sad. There are some more over in the Sylvania Wilderness west of here, but that's about it."

"So, was it your dad who got you excited about all this stuff?"

"Yes, and also my time up at Michigan Tech. That's where I became something of a radical about saving the environment."

I'm sitting mere inches away from Sally now. Her bare knee is nearly touching mine. Her face has a look of fresh exuberance. She wears no makeup, but her smooth fair skin doesn't need it. Her eyes flash with life. Sally hardly looks like a radical to me. I have to clear my throat before I reply, because I'm thinking some pretty radical things myself right now. "What happened up at MTU that turned you into a radical?"

"I've always had a passion for the wilderness. But at Tech I got involved with a pretty wild advocacy group, which wasn't sanctioned by the university. We'd do protests at local lumber and mining companies and shipping companies that navigate the lakes. We'd write irate articles that the newspapers wouldn't print. We had a website where we talked about the irreversible damage they are doing to the planet. Nothing illegal really, but kind of far out there." She shakes her slowly, then smiles and adds, "I've mellowed a bit since then, but only a little."

"Sounds like exciting times."

"It was. I remember ..." She stops in mid-sentence, then stands. I watch as she paces back and forth, taking quick nervous steps.

"What's wrong?" I ask.

She stops and turns toward me. There's trouble all over her face. "I think I know. Oh God, I think I know who he is."

"Huh?"

"The man that Mrs. Verlander saw. The man who was coming to see me."

Chapter 16

Sally finally sits back down next to me and begins. "I guess I don't really know for sure, but this seems right." She's quiet for a few moments, and I wait patiently while she thinks this through. Then she continues. "When I was in that group at MTU, we had a mentor spend some time with us—"

"Mentor?"

"Sven Norstaad. He was a disciple of Aldo Leopold. You've heard of him, Wil? The famous conservationist? Anyway, Norstaad was one of his last students down at Madison back in the late forties. Later, Sven became a professor at Madison, made a name for himself for his contributions to freshwater ecology. Then suddenly, at the peak of his career—probably twenty years ago—he resigned from Madison. Moved up north, up here somewhere. Nobody knew for sure where. Sort of dropped off the face of the earth. Wrote some fiery letters before he left, saying he'd had his fill of modern culture and was going back to nature."

"Sounds like quite a character. He must be really old. How did you run into him?"

"Yeah, he must be in his eighties. Every now and then Sven would surface, just appear unannounced. There was a time, over a period of several months, when he would show up at Michigan Tech and meet with PAWN—that was our advocacy group, Protect All Waters Now."

"He would just show up?"

"That's right. Some of our members thought he was crazy. He would babble on and on about things that didn't seem to make sense. Sometimes he'd talk in riddles. But then he'd come up with some observation that was amazing. I don't think he's crazy. I think he's a genius. A very strange genius."

"How long ago was that?"

"A year ago, right up until my mother got sick. After that I sort of left all that stuff behind, at least for a while."

"Why do you think he was the man?"

"Well, he sort of fits the description. I never saw him when he didn't have a plaid wool shirt on."

"But that's not enough to—"

"I told you Sven was an unusual man. When he left Madison, he totally rejected all modern technology. He told us he didn't have a phone, didn't have a computer, so he never sent email or texts. He did have an old truck. I remember seeing that up at MTU."

"So that's why he would come looking for you, instead of picking up the phone or sending you an email."

"Exactly. That's why I think it's him. I need to contact him, but I don't know how."

"Can't you just go see him?"

Sally shrugs her shoulders helplessly. "I wish I could, but like I said, nobody knows where he lives."

"Why do you think he'd be looking for you?"

"That's a good question." She purses her lips, as if focusing her mental energy, then looks straight at me. "I don't know."

For most of the walk back our conversation is minimal. Sally seems deep in thought since her revelation about Sven Norstaad. But by the time we're back to Warren Lake, she's talking again. "I'm sorry I'm such poor company, Wil. There's not much I can do about this, so I just need to let it go. It was just a hunch, anyway, about it being Sven. I don't really know anything for sure."

A clap of thunder catches us by surprise, and we both jump. Then we laugh. Our attention is drawn to the far side of the lake, where a heavy downpour is nearly upon us. We dig furiously for our raingear. "I say let's get out of here," says Sally, still laughing.

"You won't get an argument from me," I agree. I'm still laughing too as we pick up our pace to outrun the storm. But we are no match, and within minutes we are caught in drenching sheets of rain. Even with our ponchos, we are going to be soaked. It doesn't help that my poncho is made for someone Sally's size.

A half-hour later we make it to the car, wet and cold, but we are pumped with adrenalin and panting hard. Inside the car, we peel off our ponchos and wait out the torrent. Sally removes her cap, undoes her ponytail, then shakes out her long hair, spraying me in the process. "Oh, gosh, I'm sorry," she gushes, "I'm worse than having a wet dog in the car." This causes us both to laugh again.

Within fifteen minutes the storm has blown over, and already the afternoon sunlight is streaking through the trees. Almost giddy from our soaking, we watch through steamed-up windows as the storm recedes. I look at Sally, wet and radiant, and I want to kiss her. But instead, I buckle my seat belt and prepare for the drive back to town.

Back in White Pine, the streets, glossy from new rain, sparkle in the bright sun that's just emerged from the dark clouds headed east. The wet maples glisten, and as I study their leaves up close after we stop, I'm delighted by the water droplets, like little spherical mirrors, that cling to each yellow leaf. I wish I had my old macro lens, which I sold off with all my Nikon gear after I left UCLA and couldn't get a job for a year.

We're just inside Sally's house and ready to head for the showers when her cell rings. After the call, she says, "That was Mrs. Grabowski."

"How's she doing?"

"Not so good today, but she asked if you might come over and see her."

"But I'm leaving in the—"

"You could go right now. There's plenty of time." Of course I know there's plenty of time. It's just that I'm not really up for a visit with a terminally ill person I don't know. But Sally's eyes are expectant as she waits for my response. As I hem and haw, she adds, "I'm happy to go with you."

"I guess I could go for a few minutes." I shake my head as I climb the stairs toward the shower. "Sheesh, I can't say no to her," I whisper.

Mrs. Grabowski sits in her recliner, with the colorful quilt pulled up around her, just like yesterday. An array of puzzle books fills her side table. She beams when she sees me. "Wil, why don't you pull up a chair and sit down close, so we can have a good talk."

I move one of her padded dining room chairs in next to her recliner and sit. "So, how are you feeling today, Mrs.

Grabowski?" I remember Sally asking this yesterday, and it seemed like a good intro.

"Oh, I've been better." She looks over at Sally. "On top of everything, I think that urinary tract infection is flaring up again."

Sally says, "I'm sorry to hear that, Hazel." She's stayed on the other side of the room, on the couch, paging through a *Ladies' Home Journal.*

Great, now we're having a discussion about her urinary issues. Mrs. Grabowski turns back to me, "But you didn't come over here to listen to me complain." She gives me a deep look, her penetrating blue eyes like searchlights behind the thick glasses. "I wanted to get to know you better, Wil. Didn't have much of a chance to talk yesterday. You said you teach physics?"

"That's right."

"Tell me about what you teach."

I go into a little overview of the Physics 101 course, how it's designed for non-science majors and how I think it's important that everyone has some grasp of physics. She nods with interest as I go on. At some point I realize I'm babbling on too long, so I shift gears. "So do you have a husband, Mrs. Grabowski?"

"Please call me Hazel. Yes, I was married. Forty-seven years. That's Arthur over there." She nods toward the large painting over her fireplace. Arthur looks like a jovial and honest sort of guy. "And that's also him," she says, continuing to nod toward the fireplace.

"You mean the urn?"

"Those are his ashes. He's been gone six years now."

"I'm sorry." I shift uncomfortably in my chair.

"Wil, I was wondering why you didn't take communion with us yesterday."

"No offense intended, but I'm just not into that kind of thing."

Her eyes are prodding me for more information. "Oh?"

"Well ..." I pause, picking my words carefully. "I guess I just wasn't brought up that way."

"How were you brought up, Wil? What is it you believe?" There's no judgment— which I would be very sensitive to—in her question. Just honest curiosity.

"Uh, I guess I believe the universe is a vast, complex system, and we humans should try hard to be good people." That's about as much philosophy as I'm willing to get into.

"So you don't believe there's a God?" Out of the corner of my eye, I notice Sally look up from her magazine, as if interested in my answer to this.

"I don't disbelieve there's a God either, so I guess you'd call me an agnostic." That pretty accurately covers it. Maybe we're done now. I'm ready to go, but she's clearly just gearing up.

Hazel looks troubled by my words. "You're ridin' the fence, huh?"

I glance over at Sally, who hasn't missed a thing. I don't want her thinking I'm the kind of guy who rides the fence. "I guess I just don't think about the subject very much."

"I hope you get around to thinking about the subject sometime. For me, it's the most important thing the world."

I nod, my mind busy, thinking not about God, but about how I can steer the conversation onto an exit strategy. I look down at her puzzle books. "So, have you worked on any interesting puzzles lately?"

Hazel politely allows me to shift the conversation. "Oh, I've done all those. I'm waiting for another batch."

"I've got a puzzle for you," I say, realizing that this might be a good diversion. "Sally and I found a slip of paper, and it could be important, but all it had on it were the words 'HOME Skill,' the first word written in all caps. What do you think it means?" This should give her something to chew on for a while.

"I'm guessing you've already considered that it might be a home repair or a construction company or maybe a house sitter?"

"It could be that."

"You say the first word was all caps? So it could be an acronym."

"Yes, that's possible," I say, "or the writer just wrote that word in all caps."

"Yes, maybe. But let's just assume for now that it is an acronym. What could that stand for?" She pauses, then asks, "And where did you say you found it? That could be a critical clue."

I don't want to tell her the whole story. For one thing, she's an old lady living alone. This could frighten her. So I say, "A man who we don't know dropped it, then disappeared. Like I said, we think it could be important." Sally has put the magazine down now and has come over to stand near me.

Mrs. Grabowski rubs her chin. "Hmm, I'll have to think about that one. I'll let you know what I come up with." She looks at me without speaking for a few moments, then says, "And Wil, I need to say one more thing. I don't mean to be impolite. I really do appreciate you coming today. But the reason I asked you those other things is that you just don't seem very happy, and I hate to see that."

I open my mouth to speak, but then don't say anything.

Sally must sense my distress, as she asks, "Hazel, is there anything you need today? Anything we can bring you?"

"I'm fine. The visiting nurse is coming in about an hour. I hope she'll have something for that UTI."

"We'll mention you in our prayers tonight at Bible study." Sally leans forward and rests her hand on Hazel's shoulder. I feel like maybe I should too, but I don't.

Back at the car, Sally says, "I'm sorry, Wil. I hope that wasn't too awkward for you. She really does mean well."

"It's okay," I say. "She's a nice—"

Sally's cell rings. "Don't tell me that's Hazel again," I say.

Sally says, "Hello." After a pause, she says again, "Hello? Huh. No one there." She checks the call history. "Call came from a 414 area code. That's down where you live, isn't it, Wil?"

"Yeah, what's the number?"

A shaft of fear jolts through me as she reads it to me.

"What's wrong?" she asks.

"The number. It's my cell phone."

Chapter 17

We stare at each other, speechless. Sally's mouth hangs open. Mine, too, probably. "Call it back," I say.

She does. "I'm just getting your recording," she says.

"Let's try the lost-phone app again."

Back at Sally's house, we bring up Find My Phone on her laptop. This time a map appears, and a blinking blue dot shows the location of the phone.

We lean in closer to examine the map. "Oh dear God," gasps Sally. "It's just a few blocks away. Let's go." She's already bolting towards the door.

"Shall we take the car?" I holler from behind.

"No, let's run." She leads me on a sprint down Sixth, then pointing toward a stretch of grass between two houses shouts, "Let's cut through here."

My mind is racing. What will we find when we arrive at the phone's location? Or whom? The man with the shaved head?

We hop a low picket fence, skirt a vegetable garden, make it across another yard before a barking dog can reach us, and emerge onto another street. Just short of the next intersection, Sally stops, then holds up a hand. "It's just around the next corner," she pants. I'm out of breath, and I think she is too.

We move out of the street and ease up next to a garage, trying to keep out of sight. We slide along the wall of the garage until we can peer out onto the next street. "It should be right here," she whispers.

I see nothing. We're at an intersection. On two of the corners are vacant lots. On the other corners sit old homes, far back from the road. We see no cars or people.

"Maybe it came from one of those houses," I say.

"From the map, it looked like it was in the street. Those GPS signals are pretty accurate, so I'm guessing the call came from a car. But let's check with Mr. Pokorny." Sally leads the way up to the front porch of the nearest house, a stately Victorian, and rings the doorbell. After a long time, an elderly man comes to the door, bald except for shaggy white hair at his temples.

"Sally, it's good to see you. What are—"

"Mr. Pokorny," Sally interrupts, "we need to know if you've seen anything suspicious in the last half hour, like a car parked around here or a person walking by, or—"

"What's this all about, Sally?" He has a worried look.

"Not a big deal. We're trying to find a stolen cell phone."

Mr. Pokorny shakes his head and says, "Afraid I haven't seen anything. I've been in the back giving Angie a bath."

"Angie's his Lab," Sally says to me.

Back at Sally's, we try the Find My Phone app again, but the map hasn't been updated since we last tried. Apparently the phone is now offline or has moved to a place with no signal. I call my cell provider and deactivate the phone, chastising myself for not doing this as soon as the phone was stolen.

We bat our thoughts around, trying to be objective, but we can't seem to get anywhere.

"Why would they have your number?" I ask.

"I don't know." She looks away.

"And why would they want to call you?"

"I don't know!" she says, obviously unhappy with my grilling.

"Look, Sally, I'm thinking this is serious. I'm thinking that—"

"And I'm thinking it's just a local caller. The best explanation is that it's a bored teenager having fun. Nothing more. Wil, this is White Pine, after all, not Milwaukee."

I shrug. Maybe she's right. But other questions haunt me. Does this mean the break-in at the church is related to Sally and not me? Or does it mean that the break-in now connects both of us in this, whatever *this* is? What does the call tell us, if anything, about the relationship between the break-in and the body I saw in the hedges? And what about Sally's revelation that the man in the hedges might be Sven Norstaad? How might a radical recluse living off the grid be involved? And, for that matter, just what does "HOME Skill" mean, or is that unrelated to any of the other questions?

And the biggest question of all: What should we do now?

Finally, Sally pronounces, "Well, there's no point hanging around here freaking out. I'm going to the Bible study. You want to come?"

I let out a loud sigh of exasperation. "At a time like this, how can you be—"

"Wil, I'm not going to stop living just because I got a crank call." Then her voice softens. "Anyway, I think you'll enjoy it. Why don't you come? There'll be nice people there and good food too."

"But I don't really know anything about the—"

"You don't need to know anything about the Bible. Just hang out. It's only an hour." She looks at me with those big eyes, and my resolve melts.

"Sure. Okay. I'll go, but—"

"Good. The potluck starts at six. I better put something together for that."

While Sally's scurrying around in the kitchen, I go out to the front porch and crash in one of the rockers. Fortunately, Mrs. Verlander is not outside, so I don't have to deal with her condemning glares. I continue to stew about the phone call.

The late afternoon sun flickers through fluttering maple leaves, stirred by the soft breeze that followed the quickly moving storm. While I rock, trying to quiet myself, a brown hare darts across Sally's lawn, freezes midway and gives me a cautious look, then disappears into bushes next to Mrs. Verlander's yard. High overhead, a V-shaped formation of raucous Canada geese passes across my field of view. The scene calms me. Maybe I'll skip Sally's Bible study after all and just stay here in my rocker, watching this beautiful evening unfold.

Tomorrow I'll be on that bus headed home to Milwaukee. As dismal as my life there has been, it will be a huge relief to be away from the disturbing events of the past two days. I feel guilt, like icy fingers on my neck. Will Sally be okay? Am I leaving her in a dangerous situation? Truth is, I don't really know what the situation is.

I do know that these problems only surfaced when I made my fateful stroll down Eighth Avenue on Sunday night, so it's likely that when I leave, the string of disturbing events will leave as well. Or am I just rationalizing that Sally is safe? But this seems right, and as I accept the reality that I will be going home tomorrow, a peace settles over me, something I really need right now.

Sally appears in the doorway, holding a foil-covered casserole dish in both hands and with a thick book—her Bible I assume—tucked under her arm. "We need to hurry or we'll be late."

I begin to offer my new plan to stay put in the rocker, but then think again. She took me out to the white pines today, so this is the least I can do. I stand and offer to carry the covered dish. It's just a two-block walk to the church. Along the quiet street we skirt large, rain-filled puddles, which will likely be gone by tomorrow. Like me.

As we approach the church, I see a figure standing in the shadows near the parish hall entrance. Sally hasn't noticed him. A slender man wearing a purple muscle shirt. His hair is tinted a bright red and waxed to stand up straight. His strong arms bear multiple tattoos. A cigarette dangles from his lips. I've seen him somewhere before.

I stop, then reach out to take Sally's arm. "Do you see that man?" I whisper.

"Which man?"

"The one by the parish hall." The man sees us now.

"That's just Lander. He's in the Bible study."

As we draw nearer, the man stomps out his cigarette and turns toward us. "Hey, Sally," he hollers, then looks at me.

"Lander Rawlins, this is Wil Weathers. He's joining us tonight."

"Hey," says Lander, turning toward me and extending a hand, which I shake. He has a narrow face, pale in complexion, that sets off wide blue eyes that seem perpetually squinted, as if he's focusing to see better. His eyebrows, like the waxed spikes on his head, are dyed red. A silver ear ring dangles from his left ear. I now remember where I've seen him—working in the kitchen at Danny's Northwoods Café.

The three of us enter the parish hall up the same steps I used on Sunday night. Inside, several others are already gathered around a large table, where dishes sit on a white table cloth. They're laughing and having a good time, like they've known each other their whole lives, which they probably have. Small-town fellowship. I really don't fit in here.

I place Sally's dish among the others and try to look relaxed, while Sally makes introductions. Hans Gerhardt, the principal's dad, who's peeling foil from a platter of deviled eggs, gives me a nod. A burly rough-skinned man named Ed, who looks like he works outside lifting heavy things, stretches out a meaty hand for me to shake. I wonder if he is the same Ed Officer Darby referred to when he mentioned the wolf sighting at Ed's place. Next to him is a skinny, leathery-faced woman with bleached hair, wearing tight pants and a tank top intended for a woman half her age. I assume she is Ed's wife. Sally introduces her as Tracy, and I learn that she works at Irene's Hair and Nails. I nod, recalling the old bank building on Main.

A heavy-set man with a red face and large warm eyes looks familiar. He's standing next to Lander and seems almost as out of place as me. I learn that he is Danny Piper, owner of Danny's Northwoods Café, and I remember seeing him in the restaurant back in the kitchen with Lander. I also learn that tonight is his first time at the Bible study, so I won't be the only awkward one here.

A short, thin woman with fiery eyes and hair so short I wonder if she's been in chemo wears a clergy collar atop a light blue shirt. Sally introduces her as Deacon Ellen Radcliffe, who I learn is also the town's veterinarian.

We all bow our heads while Deacon Ellen says a short prayer, then we get busy loading up our plates. I take my plate, piled with green salad, several of Hans's deviled eggs, a scoop of scalloped potatoes and a couple slices of ham, then head for the center of the room, where several folding tables have been pushed together for supper. I find a place between Lander and Ed, while Sally's across the table, busy chatting with Deacon Ellen.

Lander and Ed are attacking their food, so I try to make some small talk, even though my mind's still churning on the call from my cell phone. "So, Lander, I recall seeing you working at Danny's." Danny, who's sitting on the other side of Lander, takes note.

Lander finishes chewing a piece of ham, then says, "Yeah, Danny's good to give me a job. Keeps me going during the summer."

"You're the best worker I got," says Danny.

"During the summer?" I ask, "What about the winter?"

"I'm usually in Colorado or Wyoming in the winter, as soon as there's snow on the slopes."

"Lander's our resident ski bum," laughs Ed from my other side.

"Pretty close," says Lander. "I fish all summer and ski all winter."

"Tell him about that muskie you got last week," says Danny. "Really made me jealous."

"Forty-eight inches, but I've caught bigger." Lander spreads his arms to show how big the fish was.

The table banter goes on like this for a while, and I'm doing my best to be on good behavior as Sally's guest. Then Deacon Ellen cuts in and tells us it's time to begin the study. "So ..." She clears her throat and laughs. "Last time we left off at the beginning of chapter three. Sally, why don't you read the first six verses of that chapter for us?" Then Ellen looks over at Danny and me and says, "We're looking at the Letter to the Philippians," and already Lander has edged his Bible over in front of me, so I can follow along.

Sally reads the passage—something about the apostle Paul, whom I've heard of but don't know much about. Same guy they named this church after, I'm guessing. Paul is telling people about his accomplishments, and I must say that to me he sounds like quite a braggart, hardly a guy who should be writing something in the Bible. But I'm paying little attention to the text. Sally's reading gives me an excuse to stare at her, this woodsy girl I wanted to kiss in the car this afternoon. Her long dark brown hair is still undone from the ponytail she wore earlier today and hangs to her shoulders, framing the soft skin of her face. Her skin is pale, well not really pale but delicately white like a baby's, strange for a girl who spends so much time outdoors. It looks like if you pressed on it, you'd leave behind a pink spot. But I'm fixated on her full lips and how they move, as she reads the words with an educated precision. I don't hear the words, only the lively lilt of her voice, and I half expect that she'll break into her little-girl laughter in the next moment. When she finishes, she lays her book down and stares straight at me. I look down at my deviled eggs.

Deacon Ellen asks, "So, what do you make of this?" She looks around the room, and everyone is quiet. Danny is poring over the text, looking lost. Hans scratches his chin and takes a swig of coffee. Tracy's looking down at the table, like a student afraid to lock eyes with the teacher because she might get called on.

Finally Ed speaks up. "Well, it seems Paul's had a lot of accomplishments, I guess." He shrugs his shoulders. "All I did today was haul a load of fertilizer."

Everyone laughs, which causes Danny to chime in. "Ed, everyone says you're full of BS, but I never took it literally." More laughter.

"Watch it, Piper," Ed shoots back, feigning offense. "It wasn't ... uh ... manure, anyway," he says, looking uncomfortably at Deacon Ellen. "Chemical stuff."

Deacon Ellen tries to redirect the people back to the reading, but I see that Sally is appraising Ed with a serious look. "Chemicals?" she asks. "What kind?"

"Okay, Miss Smartypants," Ed retorts, "do I look like the kind of guy who'd know about stuff like that? Maybe it was kryptonite, for all I know. Some guy wants fifty bags of crap dropped off at some intersection in the boonies, I just do my job."

Sally frowns and looks down at her Bible as Deacon Ellen cuts in again, still trying to get us back on track. "So Paul has a lot to be proud of, a lot of accomplishments. Lander, why don't you read the next two verses?"

Lander clears his throat, clearly nervous about reading, and launches in. "Yet whatever gains I had, these I have come to regard as loss because of Christ. More than that, I regard everything as loss because of the surprising—" He's stumbled on a word and goes back to correct it, "... because of the _surpassing_ value of knowing Christ Jesus my Lord." Lander pauses and inhales a big breath, like he's loading up for the home stretch. "For his sake I have suffered the loss of all things, and I regard them as rubbish, in order that I may gain Christ."

"Nice job, Lander. Speaking of fertilizer," Deacon Ellen says, then pauses while there is a smattering of laughter, "the word _rubbish_ that Paul uses in this passage literally means 'dung' in Greek. What do you make of that?"

Everyone's looking over the text, trying to figure out what to make of it, but I'm not following closely, as I'm more interested in just watching these people. Why do they care about what this Paul thinks? I mean, the guy lived two thousand years ago. But Lander pipes up. "It sounds like, in spite of all of Paul's accomplishments, the most important thing in his life was his faith."

Heads around the room nod, and Deacon Ellen smiles and says, "Exactly. But why do you think that is?"

Lander purses his lips like he's pondering this, then says, "Well, maybe he realized that having a big fancy job wasn't really so important." As one who no longer has a fancy job— or any job, for that matter—I pay attention to this comment.

"And why would that be?" Ellen asks. She clearly knows how to draw people out.

Hans clears his throat and says, "Well, I look at how Paul started out. He was a pretty bad guy. Wanted to see people killed. And then he was totally changed, and I guess he probably knew it." He clears his throat again and adds, "And I also guess that his being changed was all God's doing."

Ed is quiet and looks confused like Hans's comment flew right past him, but now Tracy looks like she just woke up. Me, however, I'm still working on the last of my deviled eggs.

Deacon Ellen continues. "As we saw earlier in this letter, Paul is in prison, probably chained to a wall, perhaps awaiting execution. How could he be so confident?"

"Seems to me," Lander says, leaning forward, getting into this, "Paul has finally figured out what's really important in his life. And maybe when you do that, then there's nothing to be afraid of anymore." I stop chewing my deviled egg as Mrs. Grabowski's words about me riding the fence come back and don't feel so good. I look over at Sally, but she's watching Lander, who apparently isn't riding the fence.

As we're leaving the parish hall, Deacon Ellen approaches me. I'd been trying to avoid her. Her clergy collar makes me nervous, and I'm in no mood for more grilling about my religious views.

But she says, "I was sorry to hear about your things getting stolen. That shouldn't happen in a church."

"Yeah, well ..." I don't know what to say to her.

"It was nice of you to come tonight, Wil." Oh boy, here it comes.

"Thanks," I say, continuing to edge toward the door.

"I hope you come around again. You're always welcome here." Her intense eyes project such sincerity that I'm tempted to believe she really means it.

"Uh, so you're a deacon. Is that like a reverend or a priest?" I blurt this out awkwardly, as her eyes make me feel like I have to say something.

"Well, yes." She lets out a laugh. "I am ordained and I did go to seminary for a while, but I'm a volunteer here, helping out with services and home visits. The congregation's too small to afford a priest." There's nothing at all snooty or pompous about this minister, and that makes me more comfortable.

Later, when we're back at the house, Sally says, "Now that wasn't so bad, was it?"

"I guess. It wasn't quite what I expected." We're standing in her living room, and I'm feeling a bit awkward with her. "You know," I say, "Lander's a great kid, but he sure doesn't fit my image of what a religious person looks like."

"And just what does a religious person look like, Wil?" There's an edge in Sally's response.

I know I'm digging myself in deeper, but I say it anyway. "For that matter, you seem to spend an awful lot of time at that church."

"It's very important to me," she says, almost in a whisper, and I can tell she's working hard to project calmness.

I try to explain. "It's just that you're healthy and young and educated. You don't seem like the kind of person who'd need that religious stuff. I mean—"

"Is that true?" Her dark eyes, now on fire, penetrate into mine. She stands straight and purposeful, hands on her hips, then leans in toward me. "So tell me, Wil," she says with obvious disdain, "just what is it that you need?"

Without missing a beat, I lean forward and kiss her. I pull back briefly and see her startled look, but she doesn't move. Then I take her face between my hands, cradling her, and kiss her again. This time she moves into my arms. When we finally separate, we are both gasping. Then she backs away and folds her arms across her chest. With her head down, she says, "You're leaving in the morning. We should get some rest." With that she marches off toward her room.

I start to follow her, but stop as her bedroom door closes with an authoritative click. I'm left standing there still exhilarated from our kisses, but feeling utterly alone.

Chapter 18

Fog has moved in off Lake Michigan, dropping the temperature of what would normally be a warm September day by twenty degrees and requiring me to pull on an old sweatshirt for my morning walk down to Starbucks. It's quiet along Brady Street on this Thursday, but it's still early. A few energetic joggers pant as they pass me. A local shopkeeper sweeps his small patch of boulevard frontage. A garbage truck progresses slowly down the street. At each stop its whirring lift rattles green trash bins, penetrating the silence.

Starbucks is about half-full, not as busy as it will be later, when the late commuters stop by for a latte before strolling into the office at nine, when the housewives and their girl friends order their chais on their way to the mall or tennis lessons, or as a respite after getting the kids off to school. There are just a few folks like me—alone, hunched over laptops to give our persona a busy professional air—and several street people lounging on the well-worn chairs in the corner, no doubt seeking refuge from the chilling fog.

It's much earlier than I'm usually out and about, but the trip home, which was uneventful, really messed up my sleep pattern. I napped on the bus most of yesterday, then couldn't get to sleep last night. I'll probably crash later and need a long nap, but right now I'm alert and ready to roll. With no place—other than Starbucks—to roll to.

With my small house coffee in hand, I find a good spot in the rear, with plenty of privacy, yet with a good view of the unfolding action of the morning. I've got on chinos and a nice sport shirt, still trying to project the image of someone with someplace to go and something important to do.

Before booting up my laptop, I review my plans for the day. I'll need to go pick up a new phone, maybe later in the afternoon. When I talked to the rep on Tuesday, she informed me that a replacement for my stolen iPhone would cost me a hundred bucks, which I can't afford right now. But I can get a free phone—one of those cheapies without all the high-tech bells and whistles. What a bummer. But I can no longer afford the iPhone's data plan anyway.

I haven't looked at the online academic job postings for a few days, so I should check into those this morning. But I'm not holding out a lot of hope for anything new on that front, and I can't bring myself to look yet. Instead, I check my email. Nothing. Then I launch into my usual surfing routine. ESPN has a good analysis about why the Brewers will miss the postseason playoffs yet again. The Weather Channel site informs me that the fog will burn off by noon, and it will be a warm, partly cloudy day. CNN has the usual collection of disturbing headlines about violence in the Middle East and political infighting in Washington, plus more gloominess about the jobs outlook. I avoid all these.

One posting near the bottom of the CNN page catches my attention though: "Algae Bloom Kills Record Number of Manatees." I do a brief scan of the article, which reports the alarm in southwest Florida that 173 manatees have been killed this year by a red tide, an unusually high concentration of a one-celled organism. In the article, Fish and Wildlife officials assure the public that such red tides are naturally occurring and are not due to pollution. I don't really care about manatees or even know much about them, but I wonder what Sally would have to say about that.

Sally. I should send her an email and see how she's doing. Our farewell yesterday was a bit frosty. I offered to take her down to Danny's before catching my bus, but she said she wasn't hungry. She did walk me to the bus stop, though. She had her game face on as I boarded the bus, and she wished me good luck, but we didn't even shake hands before I left. She stood with her arms crossed, then headed home before the bus pulled out. She didn't look back.

There was one other odd thing at the bus stop. While we were waiting, Dennis Yardley walked by, no doubt heading to the bank. He said to me, "Finally leaving, huh?" Then he looked hard at Sally, but said nothing. Sally looked away. The whole thing lasted no more than a few seconds, and then my bus came. Probably nothing but more small-town drama.

I take a sip of coffee and survey the room. Very quiet. Even the two girls behind the counter seem subdued this morning. Maybe it's just early. I continue my aimless internet surfing, and I decide to see what I can learn about Sven Norstaad. A Google search brings up nothing recent, just some old accolades about his work on freshwater ecology when he was a prof at Madison, a reminiscence about his early days studying under the famed conservationist Aldo Leopold, and a twenty-year-old article from the *Capital Times* reporting Norstaad's sudden resignation in protest of what he called "man's rape of the environment." But there's nothing recent about him and nothing that Sally had not already told me. I pull up the Google images of Norstaad. All of them are old. Could this be the person I saw in the hedges? It's impossible to tell.

I don't send Sally an email. Don't know why—just not sure what to say to her right now. Instead, I send a note to Del Behrens to see if he's up for a beer tonight. My list of friends is pretty short. Since I was only an instructor at UWM and not one of the tenure-track profs—and even among the instructors, I was the only one without a Ph.D.—I was always a bit of an outsider. Del once told me that was just in my head, and my lack of friends was my own doing—that I just needed to reach out to others, that I would find all kinds of good connections if I did. Maybe he was right. In any case, as I review who I might get together with tonight, the list is short. Sure, Megan and I had friends we hung out with, but she was the social planner, and they were her friends.

I've had enough of my web ramblings, so I gulp down my coffee, pack up my laptop and head home. I need to go get that new phone, but maybe that can wait until tomorrow.

Back at the Bali Hai, I'm not ready to go up to my apartment yet. I take a seat in one of the web chairs around the small patio, empty at this hour. The fountain in the corner that normally bubbles away is broken. That dreaded sense of despair, which has renewed itself these past five months, is welling up inside me. Maybe I should give my parents a call. But that doesn't help much these days. Last time I called, I broke down and started crying, which was just what I didn't want to do. I could hear them worrying about me—trying to be sympathetic, but unable to resist giving me advice I didn't want to hear. "Wil, you just need to snap out of this," my mom said. "You're young and healthy. You have your whole life ahead of you." She paused, then added, "Son, I worry about you. I don't want to see you go through this again."

That was where I broke in and told her that I'd be okay, that this wasn't like the last time. But she came back at me, saying, "Maybe you need to get some help."

Even if I had a phone I wouldn't call them. Not now. Not until I'm feeling better. There's a growing pressure behind my eyes, the pressure of tears, and I fear that sobs might pour out of me if I don't head them off. I make eye contact with one of the silly plastic flamingos nearby, peering at me from behind a bush. Even in my state, it's hard to suppress a chuckle. This helps.

Chapter 19

Del said to meet him at Zilly's, over on Water Street, at eight. The place is loud and hopping when I walk in, which I find surprising for a Thursday night. Zilly's is in an old building that's been refurbed but still retains a sleazy warehouse-district ambiance—which, judging by the crowd, cool young professionals seem to love. It's a long, narrow room, with exposed heating ducts and rough ceiling rafters. A bar runs the length of one side, fronting a wall of colorful back-lit bottles beneath rows of huge flatscreens. The other side of the room is lined with dark-wood booths, dimly lit to guarantee that clandestine liaisons will remain just that.

Del has already claimed a booth and waves me over. He wears a red Wisconsin Badgers hoodie and a green Packers logo cap and looks to be in good spirits tonight. I'm doing better tonight, after my earlier pity party. Those things have been running their course pretty quickly for me, and that fact is the key piece of data telling me that this isn't like the last time.

"Good to see you, Wil," Del beams, spreading welcoming arms like he might jump up and give me a big hug. Which I'm glad he doesn't do. "Hey, they've got the mother lode of drafts here. I'm going for one of the Central Waters brews." He pushes the draft beer menu over for me to review, and I select a Bell's Oberon.

"Been a while, Del. How are things in the department?"

"How the hell would I know?" He lets out a big belly laugh and hoists his glass, as if making a toast. "Only three weeks into the fall term, so most of the kids are still actually coming to class, and the midterm isn't for two weeks, so everybody's feeling good." Del takes a big slug from his frosty glass. "So how's the job search coming? I'm guessing you've landed something really juicy by now."

I look up at one of the flatscreens, as the barmaid brings me my pint. Some guy just lined one off the centerfield wall, but no one in the bar is paying attention. I turn back to Del, whose eyes are glued on me like I might be about to explain the Higgs boson. "Not yet," I say. "Still got a few irons in the fire, though."

"Well, we sure could use you around the department. Letting you go was a bad call. I know I've said that before, but it's true." Del's referring to my glowing student reviews. Yes, the students did love my classes; I made the intimidating world of physics less daunting for these business, art, and English majors. That's what their reviews said. I was also an easy grader. The reviews never said that. Students are smart enough not to kill that golden-egg-laying goose by commenting in a survey the administration will see, but I know it was true.

"Thanks for the vote of confidence, Del." What Del doesn't know is that while my student reviews were good, I got called on the carpet more than once for not getting through the course syllabus by the end of the term. It was the same old problem I had back at UCLA. No matter how hard I tried not to, I'd get carried away with the subject matter, and I couldn't move on to the next topic. Then before I knew it, the term would be over and I would still have two course modules that I hadn't covered.

"Hey, so what've you been doing for fun? Not still moping around over that student chick, I hope." Del gives me a sly smile like he's waiting to hear about some titillating scandal.

I hardly think of Megan as a student chick, and I don't want to talk about her anyway. "Well, I went on a backpacking trip up north. It was pretty great."

"Yeah, I remember you said you used to be into that stuff," he sneers. "FYI, my idea of hell is to spend a night sleeping on the hard ground, swatting mosquitoes and waiting for a bear to sink its fangs into my butt."

This makes me laugh, which I need. "Ah, Del, you have such a way with words. Actually, it was fun." I pause, then add, "I met a girl." I add that last part, only because I know it will get Del's attention big-time.

He leans forward now and looks at me with raised eyebrows that say, "Tell me more, lover boy."

I'm making this up as I go, but whatever I say will make his evening—and it'll help dispel my image as the pathetic, unemployed loser. Gotta admit, I'm kinda loving this. "Yeah, up in the boonies." I sit back, manufacturing a self-satisfied look, then add, "I spent a couple nights at her house." I let this marinate for a while in Del's dirty mind, but while he's savoring it, I feel a pang of guilt. I shouldn't be telling stories at Sally's expense, but geez, it's not like Del's ever going to meet her.

My last comment is almost too much for Del. He pulls off his horn-rims and wipes his sweaty forehead with the sleeve of his hoodie. Then he looks around suspiciously, like a national security breach may be in the making, and whispers, "You rascal, I want to hear every juicy detail."

I'm not going to tell Del any juicy details, mainly because there aren't any. Well, there were those kisses, but that's not juicy enough for Del. So I say, "Yeah, she's a pretty classy lady. An environmental biologist." I see the red go out of Del's face as he leans back, disappointed.

"You mean like a save-the-planet type?"

"Actually, that pretty well describes it. She's interested in saving the Great Lakes—"

"Save them from what?" Del looks annoyed and suddenly uninterested, as it now appears he won't be hearing any red-hot tales about small-town lust.

"From a lot of things, I guess. Pollution, invasive species, outsiders trying to—"

"If you ask me, that's all a bunch of crap. The lakes are doing just fine. You've got these huge industrial cities like Chicago and Detroit and Toronto sitting on the shores of these lakes for centuries, and the lakes are still doing all right, as best I can tell. Sure, there's a few tree huggers crying about zebra mussels and BS like that, but they're the same crack-pots that want to shut down all our factories, blow up all the dams and let wolves wander through the city streets." Del's smug smile heralds his parting shot: "So let me ask you then, this isn't one of those macho broads that doesn't shave her legs, I hope?"

This gets me laughing again, as I shake my head no. I know for a fact that Sally does shave her legs. I spent quite a bit of time checking out those shapely limbs. And, I must admit, thinking about them now is a bit of a distraction. Now

Del's laughing too. The barmaid shows up at our table, and it's time for a second beer.

Back at the apartment, I'm ready to crash. I suspect I'll be able to sleep tonight. I stand for a while in the open doorway and survey my drab living room, which also serves as a dining area, and the tiny connected galley kitchen. The white walls and popcorn ceiling are stark. I haven't hung one picture in the four months I've been here. The beige carpet is worn and stained from past abuse. But there's more than enough space for my futon, which is loaded with clean laundry that still hasn't been put away, and a small dining table, piled with papers and books, with only a spot cleared for my laptop. The place has only two small windows, one over the sink and another in the adjacent bedroom. Both look out on an alley, which only seems to enhance the claustrophobic feel.

I make my way to the kitchen to check the fridge for a snack. Not much there. Half a quart of out-of-date milk, three shrink-wrapped pieces of string cheese, a few pieces of fruit and a head of lettuce that's seen better days. I grab one of the string cheeses and begin to peel the plastic away, while I turn to the sink for some water. When I first see it, it doesn't quite register. My initial response is relief, like you'd feel at finding your misplaced wallet. Then slowly, as all the implications sink in, my relief is replaced by horror. There on the kitchen counter, carefully placed in a prominent location where I couldn't possibly miss it, is my iPhone.

Chapter 20

With my back pressed against the fridge, I scan the room, holding a broom—the only weapon within reach—in my hand. The intruder may still be here.

I edge into the living room, my ears straining to detect any sound. A shuffling coat hanger in a closet, a bump against the toilet seat, breathing. Nothing. I check the coat closet off the living room. It's clear. I move into the small hallway toward the bathroom and the bedroom then stop. What am I going to do if I find someone? My broomstick is a pathetic weapon for a confrontation with someone who is likely armed with a real weapon. I visualize the man with the shaved head waiting behind my bedroom door. This isn't a good idea. Backing into the living room, I abandon my search.

I need to call the police. I start back toward the kitchen, to get my phone, then stop, remembering the phone has been deactivated. I ponder my options for a moment, then step into the empty hallway that runs the length of the apartments on the second floor and knock on the door next to my apartment. It's late, but I hear the TV going. I've never met this neighbor before, but then I've never met any of my neighbors at the Bali Hai. The door opens as far as the security chain will allow, and a dark face peers out at me. "I'm Wil, your next-door neighbor," I pant, barely holding my hyperventilation in check.

"Someone broke into my apartment and I need to call the police. I don't have a phone." The door swings open, and a woman stands aside so I can enter.

"What happened?" she asks with a worried voice. She's an African-American in her thirties, slender, with short-cut curly hair dyed a rust color. She wears a terrycloth bathrobe.

I give her my abbreviated version of the story, then she points to a phone next to the TV, where Jimmy Fallon is doing his stand-up. After I've made my call, the woman says, "I'm Starla Reynolds." Her voice is deep and steady. "Sorry about your troubles. That kind of thing happens in this neighborhood, I'm afraid. You got a deadbolt on your door?"

"No, but I guess I need one." Starla has a warm smile and a strong presence that helps me feel better. I thank her, then head down to the entry door, where I can buzz in the police. My brain is about to melt down. There are too many questions. How did the intruder get into my apartment? Why is he after me? Is there a real, ongoing threat, or is someone just trying to scare the crap out of me? What do I do now?

After minutes that seem like hours, a black-and-white police car pulls up out front. Two uniformed Milwaukee cops, a slender young Latino woman and a portly middle-aged white man with a sad face, follow me up to the apartment. They remove their caps as they enter the apartment and introduce themselves as Officer Ramirez and Sergeant Williams. After I've described what happened, they do a thorough walk-through of the apartment and find nothing suspicious.

Sergeant Williams, who looks about fifty, scratches his graying head and says, "So you say your phone was stolen up north, then someone brought it back tonight?" He looks weary, like he's been doing this hard job too long.

"That's right. I think it was placed here to frighten or threaten me."

"Could it just be someone returning it?" asks Officer Ramirez. She has dark penetrating eyes and is all business.

"I don't think so," I say. I go through the whole story again, but my words are met with questioning looks, and, hearing my story out loud, I realize it doesn't seem that serious.

Officer Ramirez looks at Sergeant Williams. "Thomas, this doesn't sound like a crime to me. Or at most not very much of one. Someone took his phone, and now they've returned it." She shrugs her shoulders, as the sergeant nods in agreement.

Sergeant Williams gives me a fatherly smile, like he's getting ready to let me down easy, then says, "Look Mr. Weathers, we don't see any sign of a break-in—no jimmied locks or busted windows, just this phone you lost. Have there been any threats or anything else that might indicate that someone is trying to harm you?"

They obviously think I'm a nut case. "Just what I've told you." I notice the wooden box that Officer Ramirez is carrying. I'm guessing it's a fingerprint kit. "So, are you going to dust the phone and the door handle for fingerprints?"

"Sure," the sergeant sighs, "I guess we could do that." He nods at Officer Ramirez, who places the box on my dining table and removes a small bottle and several fine brushes. Their hearts are clearly not into this. Officer Ramirez puts on a pair of thin surgical gloves, then dusts the phone, the front door handle and, after I insist, my laptop. They also take my prints, so they can eliminate those from their analysis. Though I'm pretty certain that no analysis will ever be done. The good officers are just doing their job in humoring an eccentric citizen.

"So, have you checked the call history?" Sergeant Williams asks.

"I didn't want to touch the phone until you got the prints," I say. Williams nods toward the phone, as if saying I should check it now. I pick up the phone and turn it on. There hasn't been any service since the call to Sally's home, but the call history is still there. The call to Sally's house is the only call from the phone since it was stolen. But as I switch back to the home screen a reminder message pops up. "Welcome home, Wil," it reads. A chill shoots down my spine.

I show the message to the police, and both of them shrug. Officer Ramirez says, "So, I guess this proves that whoever returned your phone wasn't malicious. That should make you feel better, Mr. Weathers. Now, is there anything else we can do for you tonight?" She finally manages a faint smile, but her eyes flash skepticism. I'm sure they'll be laughing about this one when they meet their buddies for coffee later on. I could have done just as well with Officer Darby.

"No, I guess not," I say with a sinking feeling.

After the police leave, I lock the door, then brace one of my dining-room chairs under the handle. Now what? I must think this through. I have to stay focused and disciplined. Not yield to panic. Fight off images, which threaten to overwhelm me, of the man with the shaved head lurking in the bushes outside my apartment right now.

I have to call Sally. Clearly, this situation, whatever it is, is not over yet. She may be in danger, and she needs to know. But my phone is deactivated. I'll have to call her in the morning.

I look over at my laptop, now coated with a sticky-looking black dust from Officer Ramirez's handiwork. I'm guessing the intruder checked out my laptop, if he could get past my password protection, which I have to assume he was able to do. And just what would anyone find on my laptop anyway? My mind does a quick inventory. A bunch of old PowerPoints from my physics lectures. Copies of online job applications. All my bookmarked websites. All pretty harmless stuff. My search history. That's pretty harmless, too. Or is it? This morning I was Googling Sven Norstaad. If Norstaad was the man in the hedges, then the intruder, who may be Norstaad's murderer, now knows that I am more than an ignorant bystander. I am no longer just some harmless dude who can be allowed to disappear into the crowd.

I can't wait until tomorrow. I need to contact Sally tonight. Maybe she's still up and reading her email. That's worth a try. I boot up the laptop and send her a quick email that avoids details: "Are you still up? We need to talk ASAP. Wil."

A half-hour later, there's been no reply, so I step outside to see if I can use the neighbor's phone again. But when I press my ear against her door, I no longer hear the TV. It's 12:40. Starla's no doubt gone to bed. I decide to walk down to the boulevard, just a block away. I'm pretty sure there's a pay phone there.

The street is quiet and nearly deserted. Not even any drunks stumbling home from the Brady Street bars. I'm still jumpy, and half expect an assailant to jump out at me, but my rational side keeps saying that having that black-and-white MPD squad car in front of my building would have driven away anyone bent on causing me more trouble tonight. And so far, my intruder seems more intent on frightening me than harming me.

At the corner there is a pay phone. I call Sally's home number. Fortunately, a numbers guy like me remembers such things. No answer. After four rings, her answering machine picks up. Why wouldn't she be home? Of course, Sally's an outdoor girl and could be out in the woods. I tell her machine that I'll call back in the morning. Then I call her cell. No answer. I try not to let my mind run wild with this. I've got to analyze the situation, but not over-analyze, not obsess, not go off the deep end. Which is exactly what I'm fully capable of doing. I've probably watched too many TV crime shows for my own good.

Back at home I again brace a dining-table chair under my door handle, then stretch out on the futon—amidst the laundry—cradling the broomstick like a sentry napping at his post with his rifle at the ready.

Chapter 21

It's amazing how sunshine streaming in the window can brighten up almost any situation. And a few hours of sleep don't hurt either. Last night's near-panic over the iPhone incident has subsided, and I'm determined to force myself back into my normal routine. Anyway, I rationalize, there's not much I can do about any of these crazy events right now.

My '95 Fiesta springs to life on the first crank, and I tell myself once again how I don't miss the Acura at all. It was fortunate that the lease was up right after I got laid off, so I was able to dump that big payment and get a great deal on this little gem. Without Megan to impress, what did I need that cool car for anyway?

My morning is focused on errands. First stop is to reactivate my iPhone. Then I'll make a stop at the Coinstar machine at the Piggly Wiggly, where I'll convert a jar of loose change into some folding money. I'm guessing that'll be good for maybe forty bucks, which will really help. I'm pretty much out of other options for raising cash. Last month I sold off my mountain bike and Bose headphones on craigslist. Never used the bike much, but I do miss those cool headphones.

That next unemployment check is also my next-to-last unemployment check, so if I don't land a job pretty soon, it'll be Domino's or throwing myself on the mercy of my parents.

It's probably time to abandon my hopes of landing another teaching job and look for any kind of job, but I just can't face that yet. The last resort would be going to my parents, because that would be one more confirmation for them that their son, the one who failed them and himself, the one who couldn't hack it at UCLA, the one who took a year to find a job after being tossed out of UCLA, the one who got laid off at UWM, the one who's broke at thirty-three… well, you get the idea. That's why I don't call them. That and the fact that I haven't even told them yet about losing my job at UWM.

At the phone store, I tell the tech that my phone had been stolen. After her inspection, she assures me that it has not been tampered with, but that the GPS is turned off. "Do you think the thief might have turned it off?" she asks. "Find My Phone will work anyway, but I suggest we turn your GPS back on."

"Sure, turn it back on," I say. But it wasn't the thief who turned it off. It was me. It was right after Megan left and I was out with Del Behrens. I was in a real funk. I told him about cancelling my Facebook account because I couldn't stand seeing all of Megan's posts about the breakup. That was all Del needed to launch into a lecture about identity theft. "Dumping Facebook was a good first move, Wil," he said. "But it's only a start." It didn't take long for him to convince me to turn off the phone's location services for all my apps. That seems silly now. Seems like another world.

The trip to the Coinstar is a great success, netting me a little over thirty-seven bucks, which more than offsets the wad I blew at Zilly's last night with Del. I'm feeling pretty good.

I decide to skip Starbucks and work at home. The morning worries about money focus my brain on getting more job queries out there. But I wind up surfing the net for awhile instead. Finally, after I've run out of ways to avoid the search, I bring up the *Chronicle of Higher Education* website, which I've done so many times before. I used to use the job-search box on the home page, where I could limit my search to physics jobs in four-year institutions in the Midwest. Now I just click the link that says ALL JOBS.

The doorbell rings and I jump. It's Starla from next door. Her gray jogging outfit hangs loose on her skinny frame. She carries a large dish. Leaning casually against the door jamb, she says, "How'd it go with the cops last night?"

"Not very good. They didn't think it was a real break-in."

"Well, that sucks. I say, get yourself that deadbolt and don't worry about it anymore." Starla has a big, easy smile.

I nod.

"So I was feeling bad about your situation, figured you might need a little somethin' to lift the spirits." She hoists the dish toward me. It smells heavenly. "It's a meatloaf I just made."

"Thank you." I hold the door open for her, and she takes the dish into the kitchen. In my current situation, I'm not going to turn down any free food. Plus I'm starving, after having finished off the string cheese and an apple for breakfast. I pull down two plates from the cupboard. "Why don't you join me?" I push aside some of the mess on my dining table and pull out a chair for her.

The meatloaf is huge. I'll get a couple of days out of this.

"You got some veggies to go with this, Wil?"

I find a can of green beans in the cupboard, shake them into a dish, then zap them for twenty seconds. Now we have a balanced meal.

"So how did you wind up at the Bali Hai?" Starla asks, her huge brown eyes radiating a motherly concern, even though I'd guess she's barely older than me.

I take my first bite of the meatloaf and think I might pass out. It's that good. "I got laid off."

"I'm sorry to hear that. And you haven't found somethin' else yet?"

"No, but I'm okay." I'm so busy chewing that my sentences come out in short bits. "What about you?"

"I've still got my job, thank the Lord, but me and Sam— that's my boyfriend—are trying to save some money. That's why I live here. I'm an adjuster."

"You mean like a chiropractor?"

She lets out a big laugh. "No, not that kind. I'm a claims adjuster for Northwestern Mutual downtown."

"That sounds like an interesting job." Isn't that the kind of thing a friendly neighbor should say?

"It is," she says, and I see a pleased smile appear. "Worked my way up through the system." She finishes chewing a bite, then says, "So tell me, Wil, you got a girl?"

"Not right now." I pause. "We broke up after I lost my job."

"I'm sorry to hear that. You still feelin' tore up about it?"

"Not too bad anymore."

"So why aren't you out meetin' somebody new, a good lookin' young guy like you?"

"Well there is a girl I met ..." I trail off. Not sure why that even came out.

Starla leans forward. "You met a girl? Say more."

"Well, I hardly know her. So I guess I'm not sure where, or even if ..." I trail off again.

"Gotta say, Wil," Starla laughs, "you seem kinda flustered about this. I'd say that's a good sign."

I feel myself turning red. "Oh, I really don't—"

"She live around here?"

"No, she's from up north."

"Then what're you sittin' on your butt here for?"

Just then my phone goes off, which causes me to jump again. I grab it and hit the Accept button, expecting to hear Sally's voice.

"Wil, it's Megan."

Chapter 22

When I hang up—the call lasted no more than a couple of minutes—Starla's eyebrows are raised in concern. "By the look on your face, I'd say that was either some loan-shark thug sayin' he's comin' over to kick your ass, or that was the old girlfriend."

Even with my brain addled from the call, Starla makes me laugh. "The latter," I say. "Did I look that stressed out?"

"Don't know about stressed out, but you sure didn't look like some starry-eyed lover gettin' ready for a big rendezvous."

Megan's call took me by surprise, although I'd been waiting for it for five months. There was such a sloshing in my brain of anger, sadness, hope, and joy that I was nearly speechless. Which was okay, because Megan did most of the talking anyway. She didn't say much, though. Didn't say she was sorry. Didn't say she shouldn't have left with just an email, didn't say she missed me. In fact she didn't even say why she had called. Just said she'd like to meet me for a drink. "Well, I really wasn't expecting to hear from her," I say to Starla, trying to justify my awkward behavior.

"I think you did just fine, Wil. It isn't easy hearing from an old flame." I don't feel like I did just fine at all. This was my chance to let Megan have it, to serve up all the potent responses to her rude good-bye that I'd been rehearsing for months. But I didn't say any of those things. "Sure," is all I said, with as much nonchalance as I could muster. So I'm meeting her tomorrow night at a bar down on Brady Street, a loud place that'll be packed on Saturday night. Which is perfect.

I turn my attention back to the meatloaf, trying to eradicate the dark cloud that Megan's call has suddenly produced. "So, if you're an adjuster, Starla, how do you have time to be making meatloaf on a weekday?"

"I don't work on Fridays. And I love cooking, especially when I can help feed some starving soul who got his place broke into." Her big smile is not one of pity. I guess you'd say it's more like compassion. "So what did those jerks take?"

I sigh. So far, my version of this story has been met mostly with either disbelief or downright disdain. But I tell her anyway. The whole thing, starting with the hand in the hedges.

Starla chews her meatloaf, while her big eyes are glued on me like she's watching the season finale of NCIS. When I've finished, she delicately dabs her mouth with her napkin, then says, "Holy shit, Wil, that's an awful story. What are you gonna do now?"

I run my hand through my hair, then let out another sigh. "To tell you the truth, I haven't got a clue." I poke my fork at my meatloaf for a bit, then set it down. Reliving this mess, then getting Megan's call on top of all that, has thoroughly ruined my appetite. "I thought this thing was behind me, that once I got home I'd never have to think about it again. Now I don't know."

Starla ponders this for a moment, looking as if she's choosing her words carefully, then says, "Here's what I think. Someone's screwing around with you. Not sure they really want to hurt you, otherwise they'd have just been waiting for you here last night when you got home, and you'd have never gotten to eat my meatloaf, and there'd be all this yellow police tape shit wrapped around the murder scene here."

I offer a weak laugh, although the word *murder*, said out loud, almost triggers my old hyperventilation.

"No, I don't think they want to hurt you, at least not yet. I think they're trying to make sure you stay away. You and that girl both. I think your theory is right, Wil. They don't know how much you know, but they want to make sure you're so scared you won't be nosing around in this mess anymore."

"That's why I'm worried they may have looked at the search history on my laptop. If this guy Norstaad really is tied up with this thing, then they might not be able to risk leaving me alone."

"And what about the girl up north? What does she think about your little break-in?"

I lean my chair back on two legs and rock slowly. "I haven't been able to reach her."

Starla's mouth falls open just a bit. "Oh," she says softly. "You probably need to reach her, Wil." Her eyes carry admonition that I cannot ignore.

"I know."

"Look, Wil, I say, get that deadbolt today and be careful. And get ahold of that girl. Soon. If you need somebody to help you, you can call me anytime. And I can get Sam to help too. He was a linebacker for the Badgers. Nobody's gonna mess with him."

I start to say something about not worrying and that I'll be okay and that I shouldn't have bothered her with all this crap, but I don't. I see a solemn steeliness in her eyes. "Thank you, Starla," is what I say.

Chapter 23

I never got back to the *Chronicle of Higher Education*. Instead I try to reach Sally several more times, but get no answer. Mostly I relive the phone call from Megan over and over, and, each time, I have an improved version of what I should have said. At the least I should have gotten some idea about what she wants to talk about. Does she want to get back together? Does life with me suddenly look better after a few months out there on her own again? And how would I respond if that is in fact what she wants? I concoct several Saturday-night fantasies, but my favorite goes something like this.

The bar is packed and loud as I walk in, a few minutes late. Megan is already there, looking anxious, her hands cradling a glass of white wine. She looks up at me as I approach the booth, her eyes wide and helpless-looking, as fetching as always. She manages a weak smile as I slide into the booth.

"Megan, it's good to see you," I say with calmness, even flashing a warm but self-assured smile. She wears that light blue cashmere sweater that was always my favorite, and I suspect she remembers that. I can tell she's surprised at my presence, my lack of anxiety, my poise. I order a pint from the young barmaid, who's shamelessly checking me out and causing Megan's mouth to fall open.

Megan looks me in the eye and says, "Wil, thanks for coming."
Then she looks down, and it seems for a moment that she might be about
to cry. Though I don't recall ever seeing Megan cry. Still looking down,
she says, "These past few months have been hard." She pauses again, then
looks up, her lower lip trembling. "Oh God, Wil, I've been so wrong."

I say nothing, but I don't look angry. I look in control. Strong.
Above it all, yet caring, that's me.

The fantasy usually dissolves at this point, as this is about
where I start chastising myself for being so pathetic.

In the afternoon I get a deadbolt from a small hardware
store down on Brady. Paid a couple of bucks more than I
would have at Walmart, but I didn't have to drive. When I get
back, I toss the plastic-wrapped deadbolt on the dining table.
I'm sure I've got the tools I need to install it somewhere out in
the storage locker, but I just can't do this right now.

Instead I turn on the tube and am lucky enough to find a
Brewers game. After the game, I channel surf until I get
drowsy. I fall asleep on the futon.

After a restless night, but mercifully free of nightmares
and intruders, I'm up early and heading down to Starbucks for
my morning routine. I've got to get serious about getting some
more applications out this morning. After I'm settled in with
my coffee, I bring up my list of recently visited websites to get
to the *Chronicle of Higher Education*. But I mistakenly click on my
recent Google search for Sven Norstaad.

I'm just about to go back to the list when I notice a new
posting from the Topix local news for Iron River, Michigan.

Sven Norstaad, a former professor at the University of
Wisconsin, Madison, was killed in a single-car accident
east of Iron River. His car was found in a ravine near US
2 early Friday morning. No further details are currently

available. A spokesperson for the University said Norstaad was a former student of the renowned environmentalist Aldo Leopold and had been a leading researcher in freshwater ecology before his resignation in 1992. No information regarding next of kin or services for Mr. Norstaad is available at this time.

I read the article again. Everything is now clear. This is not just some coincidence. Norstaad may have been found in that ravine, but he didn't die there. He was murdered, and this was someone's way to dispose of the body. He died in those hedges in White Pine, and only three people know it: Sally and I. And the killer.

Chapter 24

By the time you're ten miles north of Milwaukee, the urban sprawl has been replaced by the kind of country for which Wisconsin is famous. Large farms stretch across low rolling hills rimmed by dense stands of oaks and maples that haven't yet started to turn, unlike the trees up in White Pine. Stately farm houses, century-old barns and tall silos look like they're straight out of an Andrew Wyeth painting. US 41, a freeway busy with big trucks and SUVs pulling ski-boats up north, cuts right through this region, skirting cities I've never seen—Fond du Lac, Oshkosh, Appleton and Green Bay—on its way to Michigan's upper peninsula, the U.P.

I wish I'd gotten an earlier start. After finding that article yesterday, I wasted too much time trying to figure out what to do. My first inclination was to wait until after tonight's meeting with Megan before deciding what action, if any, I needed to take to find Sally. Now I probably won't make White Pine before dark, and being unable to reach Sally after trying her phones almost hourly, I have nowhere to stay. It doesn't help that I have to keep the speed down on the Fiesta, which starts to vibrate over sixty. It probably needs a front-end alignment or something. I never was much of a car guy.

An hour north of Green Bay, I leave the heavy traffic of the freeway and take to a network of two-lane state highways slanting off to the northwest. According to Google Maps, which I'd consulted on my laptop back at the apartment, this is a shorter route than the one I took on the Indian Trails bus, which sticks to US 41 up to Escanaba, then cuts over to White Pine on US 2. Once I'm off the freeway, the scenery begins to take on a northwoods feel, only occasionally interrupted by a small town.

So what am I going to do when I get to White Pine? Go to Sally's house, sure, but I'm guessing she's not there. Maybe I'm making too big of a thing out of this. She goes away for a couple days and I get paranoid about it. Over-reacting again. Yet, the news about Norstaad's death has galvanized all my fears and legitimized my knee-jerk reactions to the events of the past few days into a realization that Sally and I are involved in something real and ugly and murderous.

I should contact the police, tell them everything. But what, really, do I have to tell them? That Norstaad was the man in the bushes and that his traffic accident was staged? "And how do you know that?" they will ask. And my answer is that Sally had a hunch that the man in the bushes was Norstaad? That the plaid shirt proves it? It's not hard to imagine Officer Darby's response. What I've got to do is find Sally first, then she and I will figure out what to do next. But as this scenario plays out in my mind over and over, I never get to the figuring-out-what-to-do-next stage. I'm stuck at the place where I first see her face.

And what about Megan? Twenty-four hours ago I was wrapped around the axle about our meeting tonight, torturing myself with silly fantasies about it, longing for it and dreading it all at the same time. I'd been waiting for her call for months, but now I'm headed up north, and I'll be standing her up tonight, and she'll be pissed. I called the number she used to reach me and listened to her recorded greeting, but then I didn't leave a message. Not sure why. And I'm also not sure why I'm not thinking about it very much.

At dusk I pass through the small town of Suring, where a marker informs me that I've just crossed the forty-fifth parallel, so I'm halfway between the equator and the North Pole. My life right now also feels like I'm halfway between two worlds, and I don't understand either one of them very well.

Everything in Suring looks closed up on this Saturday evening. Still a couple hours from White Pine, I pull into a BP station and top off my tank, which sucks thirty bucks out of my wallet. I try Sally's numbers again with no luck while I munch on a slice of Starla's meatloaf, which shares the front seat with me.

Another hour north I pass a sprawling Indian casino and hotel complex, a garish montage of bright flashing lights that almost hurts my eyes and seems wildly out of place after I've driven the last forty miles in darkness. The huge parking lot is almost full, an odd sight out here in the middle of nowhere. These places make me sad, as I imagine locals dropping their paychecks here in the hope of hitting a jackpot. The ones who can least afford to lose are the ones being hurt the most.

Just a half-mile up the road, I pull off and ponder where I'll spend the night. I'd like to drive through, make it up to Sally's house, but I'm sure she's not there. I could sleep in my car in her driveway, but I would run the risk of Mrs. Verlander spotting me, followed by an unwelcomed visit from my favorite member of the White Pine County Sheriff's Office. I check my mirrors, then make a U-turn and head back toward the casino. That parking lot is the perfect place to recline the thin vinyl seat in my Fiesta and try to grab a couple hours of sleep.

But I find it hard to sleep. The couple of times I start to doze off, some inebriated folks bring their loud revelry out to the parking lot. I pull out my phone and call Sally again. Nothing. I start to page through my apps, but quickly remember I no longer have a data plan. I bring up the photostream from my iPhone's camera and scroll through my pictures, mostly of my backpacking trip with Ron. I realize I haven't actually looked at them yet. There's a great shot of Ron across the camp fire from me. He's laughing, probably recalling one of our old adventures from graduate school. Another shot, pretty artistic if I say so myself, catches the morning sunlight streaming into the doorway of my tent. Several shots show off the beauty of Porcupine Lake, a blue-water jewel surrounded by pines beneath puffy white cumulus. Here's a shot Ron took of me, shouldering my pack, looking like some carefree mountain-man from the cover of *Outside*. This brings a smile.

The last picture in my photostream is a dud. At least that's my initial reaction. I don't recall taking this one. A small lake, which we could have easily passed and I just don't remember. But the exposure is way off. The water of the lake is a bright, almost iridescent green. Clearly I botched this picture somehow. Kind of pretty in a psychedelic sort of way, but also rather creepy. A sudden thought chills me. Perhaps the thief took this picture. But why? Is this a warning or a threat?

A single chime signals an incoming text. It's from Megan. I sigh. Short and, well, not so sweet. "You jerk. You jerk. You jerk." Okay.

What am I doing out here? I should have called Megan. I can't blame her for being angry. I could still call her and grovel, then turn around and head back home. I check my watch. Ten fifteen, not too late.

I call Starla instead.

"Let me get this straight," she laughs. "You're spending the night in a casino parking lot in the middle of the woods?" Then her voice turns serious. "It sounds like you're going up north to find that girl. Good move, Wil. But didn't you have a date with the old flame tonight?"

"Well, it wasn't really a date. I'm not sure what it was, maybe a … but yeah, I didn't go. Didn't call her either and now I'm feeling kinda crappy about that."

"Yeah, you shoulda probably called her. But the fact that you didn't says something, doesn't it?"

"Like what?"

"Like you're moving on to where you need to go, and not letting yourself get all beat up over the past. I say that's a healthy thing." I can picture Starla's warm eyes urging me on. "One more thing, Wil. It would seem like you're starting to color outside the lines. No tellin' what kind of amazing things might happen to you."

When we hang up, I'm feeling better. Somehow, images of my parents come into my mind. They have always lived such a cautious life, predictable and safe. Even though I haven't talked with them in ages, and Lord I really do need to, I know exactly what they're doing tonight. They're ensconced in their condo behind that locked gate, watching PBS. Not that

that's a bad thing. But Starla's words keep ringing in my head. My parents never have colored outside the lines.

I text back to Megan. "Something came up." That's all I say.

I switch on the car radio and scan to the only station that comes in, a country-and-western station playing oldies. I listen awhile to plaintive serenades from George Strait and Tammy Wynette until I'm drowsy, then switch off the ignition and finally drift off.

Chapter 25

I'm in a strange place, at the base of steep stairs down which I have apparently descended, but I don't remember coming down them. I do a slow three-sixty to take it all in. What is this place? Is it an illusion, a mirage? Am I asleep? Yes, there is beauty here, but I'm not sure I can trust it. I consider retracing my steps back up the stairs, back to where I sense things are more predictable.

But I don't. I close my eyes, then take a deep lung-filling breath. No, I'm not hyperventilating. It's something else. A peace—a strange unexpected peace. I reluctantly open my eyes and try to focus on my surroundings, but I'm in a mist. I glance over my shoulder at the stairs again. Maybe it's time to leave, but no, I'm not ready yet.

I'm drawn forward into the mist, where I come upon a table covered in delicate white linen. An assortment of items are neatly arrayed upon the table, but I cannot identify any of them. What are these things? Why are they here? I have to intentionally push away my tendency to over-analyze. "Just let it be," I say out loud, but there is no sound.

One item comes into focus: a sleek black pen. I can tell that it's an expensive pen, the kind one would use for delicate drafting or fine art work. I want to touch it, want to use it, but am I allowed to do this? What are the rules for this strange place anyway? Maybe it's best to just leave the pen alone.

But the pen pulls me forward, and now it's in my hand. I marvel at its elegance, its lines like something a Ferrari designer would fashion. The barrel is hard and heavy, polished like finished marble. I hold it up to the bright mist above me and study it in profile. I touch the point to my palm and make a short mark, a tiny wet black streak that looks like it will take time to dry. I must write something with this pen, but there is no paper, no notebook, no log into which I might make some scientific entry. There is only the fine linen upon which the pen has rested. I long to draw upon the linen, but surely it is not allowed.

A momentary flash of childhood misbehavior flickers in my mind: my mother scolding me for using my crayons to draw dragons on my bedroom wall.

I begin to put the pen down, returning it to its resting place on the table. But I stop. A great cathartic sigh is followed by my stepping forward, leaning down, and beginning to draw on the expensive linen.

At first they are tentative marks, meager streaks, but then they become wild sweeps of the pen. The linen is at the tearing point, but I do not slow. Images form and I burst into laughter. These are great. Huge. Dangerous. Dragons.

Chapter 26

Now it's cold. Frost has formed on the barrel of the pen, and the ink seems to be frozen inside the tip. I come awake with a shiver. It's first light outside and there is a patina of frost on the windshield. I pull my fleece from the back seat, wrap it around my shoulders, and try to reenter that peaceful dream world I do not want to leave. But it's no use.

After finishing off the meatloaf, I visit the john in the casino lobby, a low-budget attempt to replicate a flashy Vegas setting. The gaudy carpet looks worn in the overly bright illumination from a bank of spots high in a domed ceiling. In the center of the room, a gurgling fountain surrounds the tall statue of an Indian warrior with his hand shading his eyes, gazing off into the distance.

A sleepy clerk drooping behind an ornate counter, which I'm certain isn't really ebony trimmed in gold leaf, doesn't even raise his head as I pass by. An elderly couple, looking forlorn, stagger out of the gaming area, where they've apparently been hitting the slots all night.

In front of the bathroom mirror I splash water on my face and try to tamp down a cowlick. I pat out the wrinkles in my sportshirt and tuck it into my khaki chinos. Not that I'm trying to impress anybody, but I was a bit of a filthy slob last time I saw Sally. I've got some old Levis and my hiking boots in the car, in case I need to go out into the woods. I'm not really sure what to expect up here, so I've got to be prepared.

In an hour I'm cruising down the main drag of White Pine, asleep on this sunny Sunday morning. I pass Danny's Northwoods Café, also deserted, probably waiting for the big after-church rush, and turn down Sixth toward Sally's house. There's no car in the drive, where she parked when I was here last week. This gives me a moment of relief. If she's gone, as I suspect, then she took her car. This means that leaving was her decision. Or ... someone could have taken her and her car. I fight that thought off.

I knock on the front door and wait for a minute or so while I scan the neighborhood. Fortunately, there's no sign of Mrs. Verlander giving me a suspicious eye. Then I go around to the side door, which I recall Sally leaves unlocked. I knock again. No answer. I test the handle. The door is in fact unlocked, which sends a shiver up my spine as I picture Norstaad's murderer testing this same handle. "Don't go there," I say out loud.

I consider going in, but stop, realizing that the prying eyes of Mrs. Verlander may well be glued upon me, even if I haven't spotted her. I hop back in the Fiesta and head for the church, where I leave the car in the small lot behind the parish hall, which is still empty at seven a.m. I walk back to Sally's, taking a route that won't lead me past Mrs. Verlander's bay window.

In Sally's kitchen I stop and call her name. There's no answer. It's weird being here alone. I feel like some malevolent prowler, like I'm invading her private space. But I've come too far to turn back. I walk briskly through the house, looking for anything that appears out of place, but nothing looks suspicious.

At the plastic table in the living room, where Sally's papers and laptop sit, I thumb through a pile of reprints of technical articles on freshwater conservation and environmental protection topics and note how many passages have been marked with yellow highlighter. Several thick texts, all on specialized subjects in biology, are stacked on the table. I check out a couple of the titles. *Phycology*, a word which means nothing to me. *Algae and Human Affairs*. I recall the article I read the other day about the manatees dying in Florida from the red tide and think again how this probably interested Sally. But nothing looks amiss.

I flip open the lid of her laptop then pause. Now I'm really invading her privacy. I type in her password, *mitosis*, which I remember from my ordeal with the bus ticket the other night.

I look over the icons on her desktop. Nothing much of note there. I open her word processor and examine the documents she's recently worked on. All the titles sound like technical articles and notes, just a lot of biology gibberish.

I pop open her internet browser and see that her Gmail account is open, so I scan her recent emails. There's a long list of unread emails, highlighted in bold, dating back to Wednesday. So Sally hasn't checked her email since the day I left White Pine. I check her folder of SENT emails. Nothing sent in the last week.

Next I click on her folder of bookmarked websites and scroll through the list that pops up. Only one catches my eye. I click on the link to PAWN, the environmental activist group that Sally belonged to up at Michigan Tech. The background on the homepage is a blue panorama of a huge lake, with bold red lettering across the top that reads "Protect All Waters Now." The font is raggedly scrawled in red to look like blood oozing down the page and to give the title a cautionary, perhaps threatening, appearance.

I read through the first part of PAWN's mission statement—pretty much what Sally told me about the group. I scan through the list of officers. No name rings a bell. I click on the link that says NEWS and bring up a listing of recent events of the group. The item at the top snags my attention. "PAWN Mourns Jeff's Tragic Death." I read through the short note, which says only, "We mourn the loss of our dear compatriot Jeff, who died fighting for the cause." The note doesn't give Jeff's last name or say how he died. It's dated eight months ago, just a few months after I'm guessing Sally left the group. Interesting that this is the last news entry. I check the bottom of the page to see when the website was last updated. March, shortly after Jeff's death.

I lean back in Sally's office chair and let my eyes wander around the stillness of the living room, as my mind races to put the pieces of this story together. The room is like an exhibit from an American history museum, and a velvet rope across the entrance with a placard cautioning visitors to keep out and not to use flash photography wouldn't be out of place. I study the huge grandfather clock and notice that the pendulum has stopped. Don't these things run for eight days or so? Another indication that Sally has been gone for a while.

I decide to learn more about this Jeff, who was killed. Google leads me to the online version of the Houghton, Michigan newspaper—the *Daily Mining Gazette*—and I begin to scan the headlines and the obituary listings for anything about the death of a man named Jeff on the days surrounding that last entry in the PAWN website. My heart almost jumps into my throat as the silence is shattered by the ringing of the phone. For a second I stare at the ancient rotary handset, across the room on a small table next to a wingback chair. It could be that snoopy Mrs. Verlander. But it could be a call that offers a clue to Sally's whereabouts.

I cross the room and pick up the receiver, but wait for the caller to speak first.

A familiar voice says, "Sally, are you there?"

It's Hazel Grabowski. Maybe she knows something about Sally's whereabouts. "Oh, hi, Mrs. Grabowski, this is Wil." I work hard to sound relaxed and casual. "Sally's not here right now. Can I take a message?"

"Oh, of course, it's Sunday morning. She's at church. Actually I wanted to speak with you, Wil, but didn't know how to reach you. I would like to see you."

Oh Lord, not another lecture about riding the fence. I can do without that. "Gee, Mrs. Grabowski, I'm rather busy right now, I just—"

"I wanted to talk to you about that riddle you gave me, about *HOME Skill*."

"Did you figure it out?"

"I think I did, but I'd like to talk to you about it. Can you come over?"

"Can't you tell me over the phone?"

"I'd rather you come over." When I'm silent for a moment, she adds, "You wouldn't deny a sick old lady a visit, would you?"

"Uh, I guess I could come over. How about later this morning?"

After we hang up, I return to Sally's laptop and continue my search for information about the death of Jeff. But I've barely sat down when I hear a car pull up outside, and I freeze. I slam the lid of the laptop closed and jump up. Standing to the side of a large window, I use one finger to pull aside gossamer curtains just enough to see a police car in Sally's drive. Two cops jump out. One is Darby. They both have hands resting atop their holsters as they move quickly toward the house, Darby coming toward the front door, the other cop heading around the side.

Chapter 27

I'm frozen in place. My first impulse is to run, but I'm not sure where to run. No, that's a bad idea. It's best to greet Officer Darby at the door and explain things. Like how I'm in Sally's house, but she's not here, and I don't know where she is. It takes only a fraction of a second to realize that this is an even worse idea. Out-of-town drifter—that's how Darby sees me—is caught trespassing in the home of a missing woman. You don't have to be a genius to see how this is going to turn out. With panic welling up inside me like something is about to explode and a sudden desperate need for oxygen, I yield to my first impulse. Run. But where?

Darby's voice interrupts my analysis and makes it clear he's not here to discuss his latest wolf theory. "Weathers, open the door. We know you're in there." A second passes while I stand paralyzed. Then he growls, "If you don't come out, we're coming in."

I spin to examine possible escape routes, so quickly that I stumble and almost fall over. With Darby at the front door and the other cop around the side, my only chance is up the stairs, even though I know this route is a dead end. I bolt toward the stairway and bound up to the second floor landing, taking two steps at a time. I pause at the landing and listen. They're now in the house.

I hear them talking. The cop who came in the side door says to Darby, "You sure he's in here?"

Darby snaps, "Of course I'm sure. Old lady Verlander saw him with her own eyes. And she said Sally isn't home, hasn't been here in days." There's silence, then Darby says again, almost in a whisper, but loud enough that I can hear, "Be careful, Bart, this creep could be dangerous."

I'm hyperventilating like mad, but my lack of oxygen seems to be offset by an abundance of adrenalin. They'll be up here in seconds. Only one way to go. I continue up to the third floor, to my old dormer room, taking the steps quickly but as lightly as I can, so as not to transmit a creaking signal of my location.

In the bedroom I slept in just four nights ago, I stop to figure out my next step. I consider hiding under the small bed or in the shower stall across the hallway, but they'd easily find me there.

I hear the two cops coming up the stairs. They're on the second floor now. Out the window, that's my only chance. I part the wispy curtains, lift the bottom section of the double-hung window and remove the window screen, which is secured by two hooks. I'm not sure I can climb out onto the steep roof without falling, but I hear them on the steps now. I extend one leg through the window and try to get a good footing on the steeply angled shingles. But my foot slips on the slick surface, and I have to grab the window sill to keep from plummeting to the ground, a good twenty feet below. I try again, and this time get a tenuous grip. I ease my other leg through the window and find myself clinging precariously to the steeply-sloping edge of the dormer-window housing. I lean back in, pull the curtains closed, lower the window section, then lift the screen back into place. From the outside, I cannot fasten the hooks, so I just press the screen into the window frame, hoping it will stay there and that the cops won't notice the unfastened hooks.

I'm in a perilously unstable position, and I try not to look down. Fortunately, the huge maple blocks most of the view of my surroundings, so I'm hoping that Mrs. Verlander, who's no doubt watching this drama unfold, cannot see me. I consider climbing up over the peak of the roof to the other side of the house, which would be a better hiding place, but the pitch is too steep. I look down and consider lowering myself from the edge of the roof, then jumping the rest of the way to the ground, but I'm too high up. I would break bones for sure. The maple tree is my only chance. If I can make it onto the large limb a few feet out from my position, I might be able to climb down undetected. Of course, when I get to the ground, what I do then is another issue.

I extend a hand toward the nearest limb of the tree, but it's a good two feet beyond my reach. It will require a leap. My shortness of breath intensifies at this thought, and I fear I may pass out. But I cannot let this happen. There's no time to lose, and there is no other option. I drop into a crouching position like a third baseman getting ready for a hard grounder, then launch myself away from the roof and toward the tree limb. I hit the limb hard, having propelled myself farther than needed, but I hang on tight with arms and legs, as several birds are flushed from the tree.

Strangely, my first thought is that this is a beautiful morning. I'm bathed in golden light filtered through the turning leaves, fluttering in a light breeze. Maybe I could enjoy it more if I weren't fighting for my life.

The plan to get down is simple, but challenging. I'll slither my way along this limb in toward the base of the tree, then somehow shinny down the trunk to the ground. All this while not being spotted by Darby and his buddy. The question I'm pondering is whether I should get down as quickly as possible, even though the cops could emerge from the house just as I touch the ground, and I'd be a cooked goose. Or should I wait up here until they leave? Of course, the longer I'm up here, the greater the chance that someone will spot me.

Even if I get down from here and make my getaway, I'm going to be a fugitive, with everyone looking for me. Getting out of this mess will depend on me finding Sally and her setting the record straight about me.

I decide to go for it now. I was never a member of the gymnastics team or a great athlete in any sport, so getting down this tree will be no small accomplishment. But I have no shortage of motivation. I do a pretty good job of easing my way along the top of the limb, in toward the trunk. But just as I'm about to transfer my body from the limb and onto the trunk, I hear the front door open and see Darby and the other cop step off the front porch. They stop directly below me. I'm no more than ten feet above them. If one of them looks up, it's all over. I can even visualize Darby taking a shot at me, thinking that this is much more fun than shooting wolves.

"Where do you think he is?" Darby's sidekick seems puzzled.

"I'm thinking he left before we got here." Darby blows out a frustrated breath. "That Verlander broad saw what she saw, I'm sure of that. If he was in that house, we'd have found him. But I suspect he hasn't gone far." He pauses, then adds, his voice cracking, "If he's done anything to Sally, I'll … I'll …" He doesn't finish the sentence.

They get into the car and drive off, while I cling to the tree, trembling.

Chapter 28

After I've lowered myself down from the tree, keeping my body on the side of the trunk away from Mrs. Verlander's house, I sink to the ground to catch my breath. I consider slipping back into the house now that the cops are gone. But that isn't safe. I can't be sure that Mrs. Verlander's eyes aren't locked on me right now. I can't stay here.

Fifteen minutes later, after I've taken a circuitous route through several back yards, trying to stay out of anyone's view and doing my best to imitate a Navy Seal slithering along a foreign beach, I'm back at the church lot where I left the Fiesta.

I need to just get out of town quick. The buzz is no doubt spreading fast about this suspicious Weathers character. I won't go undetected for long. But I still haven't got a clue about Sally's whereabouts. A half-dozen cars now accompany mine in the small parking lot behind the parish hall, but Sally's Outback isn't among them. A service must be in progress. Could Sally be in there, as Mrs. Grabowski supposed?

I could enter through the side door to the parish hall, where I first saw Sally just a week ago. But that means I'd have to enter the church from that door down the hall, which would bring me into the sanctuary near the altar, in plain view of everyone. Eighth Avenue is empty, so I decide to slip up to the front door of the church to have a peek inside. The bright-red wood door is massive, but I pull it open just enough to glimpse the interior. Then I hear a car and turn to see it a couple of blocks away, coming up Eighth toward me. I can't tell if it's a police car from this distance, but I can't risk waiting until it gets closer. I pull the door wider and step inside, keeping my hands against the door to let it close quietly behind me.

I sag in the darkness of the church, breathing hard. It's quiet. As my eyes adjust to my dim surroundings, illuminated mainly from sunlight streaming through the two large stained-glass windows on either end of the sanctuary, I see Deacon Ellen up front, kneeling in front of the altar. No more than ten others are in the pews, and they are also kneeling. I slouch toward a pew in the rear, hoping to go undetected.

But one person looks up at me. It's Lander Rawlins. I try not to make eye contact, but it's too late. He flashes a big smile and waves me over. I ignore him, but he waves again. I shoot quick looks around the church, but apparently no one else has noticed me. I don't see Sally. I manage a weak smile as I slip into the pew next to Lander, who says nothing, but pushes an open book in front of me to share. I slide my knees down onto a padded board on the floor, kneeling next to Lander.

Deacon Ellen is saying some prayers that are printed in the book, and at various points, the small congregation reads responses. I keep looking over my shoulder, expecting the cops to barge in through that big red door. But somehow the dim stillness of this place begins to dispel my anxiety, even though this is where I spent the night hiding under a pew just last week. As the prayers are read by Deacon Ellen and the congregation in slow solemn tones, I study the dark wood and arched rafters of the high, peaked ceiling and try to think through my next moves. Should I abandon my search for Sally and just get out of town fast? But could I make it out of White Pine before the cops have an ID on my car, which I suspect won't be long? And it won't be long, I'm sure, until they find the Fiesta here in the St. Paul's lot. But what do I do if I stay here? I have no place to go.

I feel the old hyperventilation rising inside me. Just then, Lander gives me a gentle poke and whispers, "Dude, you okay?"

"Sure, I'm fine," I say.

"Here," he says, pointing to the right place in the prayer book. I feign interest and do my best to follow the words said by the congregation: "Defend us, your humble servants, in all assaults of our enemies; that we, surely trusting in your defense, may not fear the power of any adversaries ..." I'm not a religious guy, for sure, but I notice that my hyperventilation is beginning to recede.

Within moments, the service is over, and Lander stands. "Hey, how's it goin', Wil? Where's Sally?"

I look around the church, hoping no one else has noticed me. So far, so good. I turn back to Lander, who's wearing a tight-fitting black T-shirt, which says *Pray for Snow*, over old Levis. Do people really go to church dressed like this? I wonder. The largest of his many tattoos is a leaping trout on his right arm. "I don't know. I was hoping she might be here."

"Yeah, she never misses, unless she's out in the woods." He gives me a penetrating look, then a smile breaks across his pale face. "So, you wanna grab some coffee in the parish hall?"

"I really need to go." I edge toward the red door, although I haven't got a clue where I'm going to go.

Lander raises one eyebrow, dyed red like his spikey hair. "Crap, something's wrong, isn't it?"

"Well, actually, I … uh …" I realize I'm stammering. I look down.

Lander takes hold of my sleeve, then whispers, "Let's go back there, where we can talk." He leads me into a small side room off the main sanctuary, which holds several pews and a small version of the altar. "This is the chapel. No one will bother us here. Grab a seat."

We sit in one of the polished-wood pews. "So when did you last see Sally?" I ask.

Lander ponders this for a moment. "I guess the Bible study last Tuesday night. What's this about, Wil?"

I'm quiet for awhile, and Lander waits patiently for me to speak. He looks down, as if he thinks his gaze might keep me from speaking. He seems wise beyond his age, which I'd guess is no more than twenty-one. I'm not sure I can trust Lander, but I've got nothing to lose by telling him everything. Which I do. I go on for a long time, not leaving out any details about the man in the hedges, the scrap of paper with the words *HOME Skill*, the stolen-then-returned phone, the death of Sven Norstaad, Sally's possible disappearance, and my recent run-in with Officer Darby. When I've finished, I let out a huge sigh and say, "Okay, so tell me I'm crazy, but if I'm not, then I'm worried that Sally's in a lot of trouble."

"Holy crap, Wil, that's a terrible story." He stands and paces the small chapel area, one hand gently stroking his spikes of hair. Then he turns to face me. "So what's your plan?"

I shrug. "I'm not sure. Now that the cops are going to be looking for me everywhere, it's going to be harder to do anything. I guess I'll just—"

"Here's the first thing, I think. We've gotta find you some place to stay, a place that's safe. I think you're right that they'll be looking for your car, so we gotta take care of that. You can stay at my place, which will be safe. That's the first step, then—"

"I need to go see Hazel Grabowski. She may have a clue about *HOME Skill*, if that means anything. Maybe it's nothing, but maybe it's important. Do you know her?"

"Sure. We can stop by there on the way over to my place. Then our search will begin." Lander is becoming animated and looks excited. "Dude, a couple of smart guys like us will find Sally, no sweat." He gives me a sly smile, then says, "Hazel, huh? That gives me an idea."

Outside, he says, "You follow me over to Hazel's. No time to screw around, with the cops on the prowl." He climbs into an old VW van, which seems like a perfect fit for Lander. It's a Eurovan, probably about a '92, one of those models with a popup top for camping. Its exterior has faded into a pale gray from two decades in the sun, and there are rusted-out holes at the bottom of each door panel. It's easily the only vehicle in the parking lot that looks worse than mine.

Chapter 29

Hazel Grabowski looks more frail than she did even a few days ago. Her face, which seemed surprisingly full and healthy for a terminally ill woman, now appears sunken and there are new shadows around her eyes. I wish Sally were here to help me through this visit.

She sits in her usual chair, the quilt still around her, and I wonder if that's where she sleeps. She peers at us with those large blue eyes, her head tilted down slightly to see us through the tops of her thick bifocals. A magazine entitled *Original Logic Problems* lies on her lap. She looks tired.

But Hazel's spirit seems undiminished. "Wil, I'm so glad you came. And Lander, it's good to see you too, even though I see you've still got that crazy hair. Guess there are some things I'll never understand." She pauses then asks, "But where's Sally?"

"She couldn't come this morning," I say with a casual air. No need to alarm Hazel. "But it is really good to see you." While Lander positions himself on the couch, I kneel down next to Hazel, just as Sally would have done.

Her eyes question me. "So Wil, I'm pleased that you're still here, but I thought you'd be back in Milwaukee by now."

Where you supposedly have a steady teaching job, I remind myself. "I came back up this morning to see Sally," I say. I pause, then add, "By the way, Hazel, would it be okay if I left my car in your garage for a while? I'll be staying with Lander and won't be needing it."

"Of course," she says, which is good, since we've already stashed my car in her garage, which fortunately was unlocked. She says nothing more, but her curious eyes tell me that the wheels are turning in that quick mind of hers.

I change the subject, again mimicking what Sally would say. "So, how are you feeling today?"

"Oh, I'm fine," she says with pluck, but it's clear she isn't. "But Wil, you didn't come here to talk about me. I am glad you came. I hope I wasn't too hard on you the other day, putting you on the spot about faith." Her eyes expect an answer from me.

"Oh, no, that was okay," I lie, hoping the conversation isn't turning once again to God and my riding the fence.

But she's moved on. "And we've got a puzzle to solve, don't we?" There's now a twinkle in those tired eyes.

"Yes, that's right. So what have you concluded?"

Hazel looks first at Lander, who's leaning forward, paying close attention, then back at me with a coy smile. It's clear she's going to stretch this out. She's quiet for a few moments, then says, "So, let's review what you gave me."

I nod.

"You found a scrap of paper with the words *HOME Skill* written on it, in pencil. The first word was written in all caps. And you thought it might be important."

"That's correct." I try to appear patient.

"So what have you come up with?" she asks.

I sigh. "Well, I'm at a dead end. I checked home maintenance businesses, in-home nursing care, construction companies—things that might have that name—and came up with nothing. So I came up dry. Like I said, maybe it's not really important."

"But of course you think it's important." She gives me a gentle smile. "Otherwise you wouldn't have asked me about it, would you?"

"You're right, of course," I say almost in a whisper.

"So you didn't give me much to go on, but I've been doing some thinking." She pauses again, as I lean in a little closer. "First I have another question for you."

I nod again.

"You said that *HOME Skill* was two words. Are you sure about that?"

I try to retrieve the image of the paper scrap from my brain. I only saw it briefly before Darby snatched it away. I realize that it may not have been the two words *Home* and *Skill* after all. Perhaps I mentally broke them up that way because they formed two familiar words. "I guess I'm not so sure."

"It would be understandable to break up the letters that way, but I'm wondering if there isn't another way. Another question. Was the *S* in the word *skill* capitalized too?"

I struggle to recall the words on the scrap of paper. "You know, I think maybe it was."

Hazel smiles like she was expecting me to say that. "So then …" She pauses. "You know, I wish I could easily get out of this chair. Then I'd make us all some tea. Wouldn't that be nice?"

Lander jumps up from the couch. "I can go make some, Mrs. Grabowski, if you tell me where the stuff is."

"Why, thank you, Lander." Hazel gives Lander some instructions and he heads off into the kitchen.

"So, back to the words ..." I say softly, trying to get her to move along. She's clearly enjoying this social time and probably doesn't want to rush through anything.

"Yes, the words. Here's why I asked you those questions. If you group all the capitalized letters together and the lower case letters together, you get something entirely different from what you originally were thinking."

I scratch my head. "You mean *HOMES* and *kill?*"

She smiles but says nothing. I wait patiently, not wanting to be rude, but I am beginning to wonder if she has actually come up with anything.

Then she says, "Let's wait for the tea. We wouldn't want Lander to miss out on this."

I sigh, then hope she doesn't sense my impatience. Minutes later Lander brings in a tray with a delicate china teapot and three dainty-looking cups.

After her first sip, Hazel says, "So let's assume that *HOMES* is an acronym. Then there are five words or entities symbolized by *HOMES*, right?"

I nod again. Yes, of course.

"So what are the most obvious five entities around here?" Now she's giving us a puzzle.

I look at Lander, who appears clueless, then look back at Hazel and shrug.

"Oh, come on, you boys, you're an educated lot. You can do better than this."

"Hmm," I say, but then have nothing to add.

"Okay, here's what it means, fellas. The five big things around here are ... the Great Lakes." She smiles like this should have been obvious, and maybe it should have been.

"Of course," I say. "Huron, Ontario, Michigan, Erie and Superior."

"Exactly, Wil. Now, of course I could be wrong about this." She licks her lips in satisfaction. "But I suspect I'm not."

The Great Lakes. Then when you add the word *kill* to it, the message becomes menacing.

Hazel's solution suddenly glues together other parts of the puzzle. Sally's interest in saving the Great Lakes. Norstaad's expertise in fresh water ecology. Protect All Waters Now. Sally told me that day in the sentinels that Norstaad often spoke in riddles. *HOMES kill* must have been a warning, a warning from Norstaad to Sally about a threat to the Great Lakes.

But I'm struggling with this. If Norstaad was on his way to warn Sally, why the written message? Maybe he scrawled it after he was attacked and knew he wouldn't make it to Sally's.

And, even more mind-boggling, how could anyone kill the Great Lakes? They're enormous. Like Del Behrens said during his rant the other night, they've withstood many threats already. I'm at a loss for an explanation, yet the riddle of *HOMES kill* only deepens my conviction that I'm dealing with something very dangerous. Now Norstaad is dead and Sally is missing. I glance over at Lander, and his face mirrors my own: a look that mixes fear and helplessness.

Chapter 30

As the Eurovan sputters back toward Main Street, Lander says, "So where do you think Sally is?" A cigarette dangles from his lips.

"Two possibilities I can think of. One is that she set off to find Norstaad. The other possibility ... I don't want to consider that one." I can't allow myself to think of Sally being harmed.

Lander rubs one of his red hair-spikes between a thumb and forefinger and nods. "But now Norstaad's dead. So he's already been found, you might say."

I shake my head slowly, without any bright ideas to share.

Lander turns onto Eighth and then cuts into a small alley and parks right behind Danny's Northwoods Café. "Well, here we are," he says.

"Huh?"

"This is where I live," he says as he sweeps his hand in a panoramic arc around the interior of the van.

"You live in your van?"

"Sure, but don't worry, it's cool. You'll have your own digs, plenty of privacy. And there's a head in the back of Danny's that you can use. All the comforts of home." With this, he leans forward in his seat, twists a lever above the windshield, then stands and pushes the roof of the van upward. The popup section is now opened up, and I see a thin mattress in the narrow space above us. "Your new suite, sir. Climb up and check it out."

This is hardly the Ritz-Carlton, but it beats any other option I have at the moment. I stand on the front seat and climb up into the upper berth. Claustrophobic, yes, but there is enough room to stretch out. Plastic windows on the front and sides of the popup section provide a murky view of my surroundings. The van reeks of cigarette smoke, but I'm hardly in a position to complain. All in all, definitely better than the front seat of the Fiesta.

Just as I'm about to climb back down, a police car turns into the alley and pulls up next to the van. I slither back into the popup section as far as I can. I'm a total sitting duck here.

Lander says, "Hey, Darby, what's up?" He sounds upbeat and nonchalant.

"We're looking for a drifter named Wil Weathers. Broke into Sally Ladke's house this morning. Have you seen anything suspicious?" Darby is just inches away from me. I try to stay absolutely motionless.

"Weathers, you say?"

"Yeah, do you know him?"

"What's he look like?"

"Eh … fairly tall, but basically a nondescript guy. I think Sally kinda liked him, but she's always been the type who takes in stray dogs. They hung out together for a while last week. Now we can't find her."

"Doesn't she go off into the woods a lot?"

"I guess so. Not too worried about her whereabouts, at least not yet. But this Weathers guy—"

"I'll keep an eye out for him." Lander sounds like a model citizen, not a guy hiding a fugitive in his car.

"One more thing, Rawlins." There's a silence, and I imagine Lander giving Darby an innocent look. "I know Danny says you can park this old heap out here, but it makes me uneasy. I'm sure there's some ordinance against it. I'll have to look that up. Meanwhile, if I were you, I'd be thinking about finding a real place to live. This is a decent community, you know."

"I'll keep that in mind, Officer." There is a syrupy compliance in Lander's voice that makes me almost laugh out loud, but that I suspect Darby doesn't catch.

After Darby's car has left the lot, I drop down from the pop-top bed into the front seat of the Eurovan and let out a big sigh. "Thanks, Lander."

"No problem. That was fun." Lander's blue eyes have a twinkle that's pretty devilish for a guy who's just come from church. "Guess we should figure out some lunch, huh?"

"I'm probably not going to stroll into Danny's for some kielbasa."

"Not to worry. I've got everything here." He gestures over his shoulder. "You just stay put." Lander goes to the rear of the van and raises the hatch. Looking back through the interior, across a pile of stuffed plastic bags, cardboard boxes, numerous fishing-rod cases, and several tackle boxes, I see him fold out a table that's built into the van, then slide out a big cooler and a plastic bin. He's busy for a few minutes, looking like he knows what he's doing, then he returns up front with a platter of sandwiches and two Sierra Mists.

"Hey, this looks good," I say. The sandwiches, which look like chicken salad, are cut on the diagonal and nicely arranged between chips and two pickle spears.

"Don't sound so surprised. I do work in a restaurant, you know." He waits for me to take a sandwich before he digs in.

"So, not to sound like Darby, but how come you live in your van?" I chomp into the sandwich. It is chicken salad, with chopped celery and onion. I haven't had any breakfast.

"Keeping costs down. Working part-time in Danny's kitchen isn't exactly six-figures, in case you're wondering." He pauses to finish chewing a bite. "I don't want to spend all week slaving away at some office job just so I can retire in forty years and do what I'm already doing."

"So you really do fish all summer and ski all winter?"

"Pretty much. I haven't found anything yet I'd rather be doing."

"Do you have family somewhere?"

"Sure, my mom and dad live in Wyoming most of the year. Jackson. I'll see them when the snow flies. They're in New Zealand right now. Working the lifts and waiting tables. They're ski bums just like me. Only difference is, they ski all year. I head up here to fish all summer."

"Why Wisconsin?"

"My uncle in Eau Claire. He took me out muskie fishing when I was a teenager, and it wasn't just the fish that got hooked. I think these sandwiches need a little more mayo. What do you think?"

"Mine's perfect, Lander. These should be on Danny's menu."

"Actually they are. That's how I learned to make them."

"So, how'd you wind up in that church?"

"It was all Deacon Ellen's doing. I had this old dog, Abby. A few summers back she got sick and I took her to Ellen. She's the vet, you know. A really good one. But we had to put Abby down." Lander's eyes moisten. "She was fourteen, after all. Ellen invited me to come to that church, and the rest is history."

We finish off the sandwiches, then Lander says, "So, what are you going to do, Wil? I mean, I don't want to be a downer, but we don't have a lot to go on."

"I'd like to know more about that group Sally belonged to up at Michigan Tech. PAWN. We know that Sally and Norstaad shared that connection. And there was that strange death of one of the members. And the riddle that Hazel solved also points that way. It's a long shot, but there might be a clue to Sally's whereabouts up there."

Lander nods like this is a good idea.

I continue. "And I'd like to learn more about Sven Norstaad."

"Like what?"

"Not sure, but apparently he knew what's going on. If we could find his house—"

"You said nobody knew where he lived."

I nod. "But we do know where Norstaad's car crash happened."

"Near Iron River, right? If that's it, then I know where his car would've been taken. There's only one junk yard around there. The car could tell us something." Lander rubs his hands together with fake enthusiasm. "So we have a plan."

Yes, we have a plan. It's pathetic, not well formed, a complete shot in the dark. But at least we have a plan. And I also have—well sort of—a co-investigator.

Lander lets out a nervous laugh. "If the killers or the cops don't get us first," he says.

Chapter 31

I drive with the windows down, trying to air out the cigarette odor that permeates Lander's Eurovan. A beat-up Michigan roadmap, lying open across the passenger seat and kept from blowing away by my laptop, indicates it's a good hundred miles up to Houghton, up on the Keweenaw Peninsula that juts out into Lake Superior. With the van topping out at around fifty, even on the level stretches, the drive will take me at least two hours. So it's a good thing I got an early start.

Lander has to do his shift at Danny's this morning, but he was generous enough to let me have the van for the day—with a full tank of gas no less.

I've got plenty of time to figure out what I'll do when I get to Michigan Tech, but I wonder if any of it will lead me to Sally. At the very least, this will be my chance to learn more about PAWN and Sven Norstaad and maybe how these pieces of the puzzle fit together.

I was careful leaving White Pine, so I wouldn't be spotted, and I'm constantly checking the rearview mirror now, remembering a hundred old movies where the bad guy's car suddenly appears, complete with villains leaning out the windows, pointing their automatic weapons at the good guy (which would be me). But it's a quiet drive this Monday morning—only a few logging trucks headed south as I wind through endless stretches of thick woods, interrupted by a small village only every fifteen or twenty miles. Up here the trees are ablaze with brilliant yellows and reds, even more stunning than down in White Pine.

As I approach Houghton, my cell rings, causing me to jump. It's Starla.

"Thank God you finally picked up, Wil." Apparently I've had no cell reception until reaching the edge of the city. "What kind of mess have you got yourself into now?"

"What do you mean?"

"There've been cops crawlin' all over your place this morning, asking me if I've seen you. Wouldn't tell me anything. And I didn't tell them anything either."

I tell her about my run-in with Darby.

"So the cops are after you because they think you did something to Sally? Wil, I'm worried you've gotten in over your head now."

"Yeah, maybe I have. That's why I'm headed up north this morning. I've got to find Sally before the cops—or God knows who else—find me first." Just hearing my own words sends a chill up my spine.

"Look Wil, if you need some backup, you call. Understand? Sam and I can be up there fast. Somebody needs their butt kicked, you call. Okay?"

Starla's strong words buoy me up a bit. My team: Lander and Starla. Against unknown killers, while trying to avoid the cops. Even in my state of mind, I have to suppress a chuckle. "Thanks, Starla. I'll call if I need you."

After I hang up, I finally absorb what Starla said. The cops in Milwaukee are looking for me now too. I let out a loud, desperate gasp, then turn my attention back to the driving.

The campus of Michigan Tech University takes you by surprise after you've been driving through mile after mile of U.P. wilderness. You round a curve on US 41, approaching the little city of Houghton, and there it is, spectacular modern glass and sandstone-colored buildings, stretched out along both sides of the highway. Almost instantly, my spirits begin to rise. A modern college campus. I'm in my element.

It can be a nightmare finding a place to park on a university campus, but fortunately I spot a visitor's lot almost immediately. My plan is to find the library or some other place where I can connect my laptop to Wi-Fi, bring up a campus map, then plan my next moves. I want to check out the biology department to see if there are any clues about Sally there. Then I want to learn more about PAWN. There has to be an office that handles campus organizations, and even though PAWN wasn't a sanctioned group, this should be a good place to start.

But right outside the van, my plans change. Several large white-peaked temporary tents sprawl across a broad lawn, with a crowd mingling underneath them. I've been around universities enough to know this is probably a parents' luncheon or some other guest activity. Mainly, I know there will be free food there, and among a horde of folks who don't know each other, I may be able to slip right in. So far today, I've only had two Clif bars, which was enough at the time—but now I'm starving. And I don't want to ransack Lander's cooler.

It's easy to slip into a buffet line among chattering families and cheery student helpers. I load up a plate with scrambled eggs and brats and find the least-occupied table I can.

I keep my head down, minding my own business, but a woman down the table won't leave me be. "I'm Cheryl," she beams. "And you are?"

"Uh …" I pause. I'd better not say my name. Who knows how widespread the manhunt for me might be? "Uh … I'm just here visiting the campus. I'm being considered for a faculty position." Well, I did send in an application to Michigan Tech, I think, and I haven't heard from them. So maybe they are considering me.

"Oh my," Cheryl says, seeming impressed. "What department?" She scoots along the bench a few inches in my direction, apparently ready for a good visit.

"Physics," I say in a soft voice. It would be just my luck if someone from the physics department were sitting nearby.

"Ooh, physics," Cheryl says. "That's way over my head. But Franklin's going to be an engineer, got all his brains from his dad." She nods toward a sullen kid across from her, who doesn't look up.

But someone else does look up. A young man at the next table shoots a quick, inquiring look in my direction, then averts his eyes. My paranoia can do a lot with that little event. I quickly finish off my meal, nod a farewell to Cheryl, then make my departure.

I find my Wi-Fi hotspot at a student gathering place nearby and bring up a campus map. I decide to make my way over to the Memorial Union Building, where the campus website says I can learn about student activities and where I'll see what reactions I get when I ask about the outlaw organization PAWN. It's a warm cloudless autumn afternoon, and I should enjoy this stroll across a beautiful campus. Students recline under golden maples with text books on their laps. Two guys toss a Frisbee across a wide expanse of lawn. Others stroll hand-in-hand or with faces glued to their smartphones. Bicyclists sail in and out between the walkers.

But the pleasant scenery only reminds me of UWM and UCLA, and that stirs the unhappy awareness of my failures. Overwhelming that, however, is the sense that someone may be watching me. Sure, I'm just another anonymous face on campus, and no one would be expecting me to arrive in an old Eurovan. But then again, someone made his way into my apartment without leaving a trace, so whoever I'm dealing with may be one step ahead of me.

The Memorial Union Building, a traditional red-brick structure that must be one of the early buildings on campus, is bustling with students. I pass the campus bookstore, then find the Student Activities office. From behind a counter, a bored middle-aged woman gives me a game smile like she's glad I stopped in. Her raised eyebrows silently ask, "May I help you?" Behind her, several people, who I guess are students, talk around a cluttered desk.

"I'm trying to find information about a campus organization. PAWN, Protect All Waters Now." I don't expect her to know about the outlaw organization, but this is at least worth a stab.

The woman looks puzzled. "Not familiar with that one. Let me check. PAWN, you say?" She types a few keys in front of her monitor. "I'm afraid I can't find anything about a group with that name. You sure it's an official campus organization?"

"No. Thanks anyway," I say. I turn to leave, but notice a girl looking at me from the group at the desk behind the counter. I smile, but she just stares at me, like she's trying to figure out something.

I ponder my next move as I head back toward the entrance of the Memorial Union. As I'm about to push open one of the glass entry doors, I stop in my tracks. Through the glass I see a man heading toward the entrance. A man with a shaved head and glasses. I can't be sure, but he looks like the man I saw on the bus. He's striding with purpose in my direction. Suddenly it's hard for me to breathe. I look around for another way out. There probably is one in back, but I can't tell from here. I decide to take refuge in the campus bookstore, just off to my left. I dart behind a tall rack of MTU sweatshirts and ball caps and peer out through the gap between the XLs and the XXLs. I see the man move past the entrance to the bookstore. Then, as I'm letting out a sigh of relief, he stops and does a quick one-eighty. Then his eyes settle on the bookstore, and he heads in my direction.

I back away from the rack of clothing and move farther into the store, back behind low shelves of textbooks. I don't think he's seen me yet, if in fact he's even looking for me and this isn't just another one of my fits of paranoia. I crouch so fast behind the shelf that I almost bring a mountain of massive Psych 101 textbooks down on top of me. Slithering along behind the low shelf that blocks the man's view of me, I have no plan. Just an urge to escape.

Then I realize I've allowed my panic to cloud my reason. Sure, on some empty side street in Florence or in my apartment he could take me out, but here with a dozen other students around me, why am I running? I'm not a stare-danger-in-the-face type, but this is a time when I've got to let reason control my actions. If I'm going to find out who this guy is, if I'm going to find out where Sally is, this may be my best chance.

I stand and take a deep breath. The man with the shaved head stands near the entrance to the store, casually scanning the place. When he sees me, our eyes lock for an instant, then the man shifts his eyes to the other side of the store. As I approach him, he turns toward me with a questioning look.

"Are you looking for me?" I ask. I do my best to appear calm and unafraid.

He opens his mouth but says nothing. He looks straight at me with cold eyes. Then I say, "It seems you've been following me."

The man continues to stare at me. I cannot read what's going on in him. Surprise? Anger? What? Then, without saying a word, he turns and leaves.

I'm not certain this is even the man I saw on the bus. Nor do I have any real evidence that this man was looking for me. If he wasn't, I've just made a complete ass out of myself.

But if this is the man I saw on the bus, if this man was looking for me—perhaps informed by the girl in the student activities office or the guy from the tent—then my confrontation has served a purpose. He now knows that I am not fleeing in terror. That I will push back. That I must be reckoned with. And if this is the man from the bus, with the eyes I saw in the hedges, the eyes that looked upon the corpse of Sven Norstaad, then I am in extreme danger.

Chapter 32

The biology department is on the third floor of the Dow Environmental Sciences and Engineering Building, a beautiful eight-story blend of modern glass and traditional brick architecture. Although the department office is right in front of the elevator, I decide to walk the halls and get a feel for the place. As I peek into the rooms along the hallway, I see nothing unusual, certainly not to a science teacher. Undergraduate teaching labs, offices, a lecture hall, several research labs filled with electronics and racks of glass tubing.

I jump at the tap on my shoulder, then turn to see a young woman looking up at me. It's the girl I saw at the student activities office. She's Asian, pretty, with soft, round features framed by straight black hair, probably no more than five feet tall. She wears a white turtleneck over blue jeans and has one of those one-strap packs—a sling bag I think they call them—over one shoulder. "I'm Minji," she says. Her brown eyes are large and inquiring behind frameless glasses. "You were asking about PAWN."

She may have been the person who tipped off the man with the shaved head. "That's right. Can you help me?"

"Depends on what you want to know, Wil." A shiver jolts up my spine as she uses my first name. She smiles.

"How do you know my name?"

"Sally told me about you, of course." There's a twinkle in her eyes. "I wasn't sure, but I figured it might be you. Took a shot."

"Oh?" How do I go about dealing with this? "Sally?" I ask.

"Sally Ladke. Come on, Wil." She raises an eyebrow.

"And how do you know Sally?" A dumb question I know, since we're standing in the biology department, where Sally did her studies and where everybody probably knows her, but I'd rather have Minji do the talking at this point.

"Sally was my TA for a while." She pauses, never taking her eyes from mine, then says, "And of course we were in PAWN together."

"So you've talked to Sally recently?"

"A few days ago. Why?"

I decide against telling her that Sally is missing. Maybe she already knows it, but I'm not letting on—at least yet—that I know it. "Oh, just wondering. I just met Sally a week ago."

"So if you want to know about PAWN, why don't you just ask Sally?"

I avert my eyes from hers. If I'm going to concoct some tale here, I can't do it locked into that stare. "Sally's gone for a few days, and I just thought I'd take a drive up north for the day. Never been up here before." I realize I'm stammering. "Thought I'd just check out the places Sally told me about and—"

She cuts me off. "Sally said you went back to Milwaukee, that you thought some guys were after you. So what are you doing here?"

My mouth has gone dry. What's the downside of telling Minji the truth? If she's in cahoots with the bad guys, she already knows that Sally is missing. If she's not, then maybe she can help. What have I got to lose? "Look," I say, "I think Sally's missing. No one's seen her for several days. I came back up here to—"

"Is it possible she's out camping? She does that a lot, you know." Her wide eyes are skeptical.

"Well, maybe." I'm not going to tell her about Norstaad's death and the danger Sally may be in, not yet, although she may already know that. "Just want to be sure." I pause, searching for my next words. "And ... and to maybe learn more about the work she was doing. We're both scientists." *Geez, that sounds hokey,* I think as I inwardly cringe.

Minji's skepticism seems to melt. "Why don't we go sit down?" she says. She leads me to a lobby area near the department office, where she gestures toward some soft chairs arranged near coffee pot. She plops into one of the chairs and pulls her legs up under her into the chair. She's so tiny, the chair seems to swallow her up. "So how can I help you?"

Minji radiates big-eyed innocence, but if she didn't tip off the man with the shaved head about my whereabouts, then who did? On the other hand, I'm starting to have doubts as to whether the guy in the bookstore actually was the same man I saw on the bus.

Finally I say, "Tell me what happened to PAWN. There hasn't been an entry on the website for eight months."

She looks like she's thinking this over. She sighs, then says, "The group disbanded."

"After Jeff's death?"

"Yes." Now she looks down, but only for a moment.

"What happened?"

"Sally didn't tell you?"

"No."

Minji shifts in her chair. "Would you like some coffee?" She nods toward the urn on a table behind her, then stands and walks toward the urn.

"Not now, thanks. What happened that caused the group to disband?" I'm not sure any of this has anything to do with all the mystery of the past few days, but it's worth pursuing. Sally and Norstaad were connected through PAWN, and now one of them is dead, one of them is missing and PAWN closed down because of a death.

Minji returns to her chair, cradling a cup in both hands. She looks off towards a bank of windows behind the receptionist's desk for a few seconds, sighs, then looks back at me. "The accident occurred on private property. Police were called in. There was an investigation, a lot of negative things printed in the local papers about it. Several members had had enough and quit. The group just sort of disassembled."

"Did you see the accident?"

"We all did."

"What happened?"

"We were demonstrating at a local sawmill. We'd climbed over a fence and were trespassing, which wasn't a good idea to begin with, but we were trying to make our points to the employees at the mill."

"Your points being?"

"That cutting our timber must go hand in hand with reforestation and intelligent forest management, that kind of thing. The mill owner had made a statement about the good old days, when entrepreneurs could cut down anything they wanted. We couldn't let that go, so we—"

"How did Jeff die?"

Minji licks her lips, then swallows, as if her mouth has gone dry. "It all happened so fast. He and another member of the group climbed up onto a stack of cut logs. Must have been thirty feet high. That wasn't part of our plans, so no one knows why they went up there."

"There was another student up there as well?"

"Yes. Lucas. Lucas Tanner. He was a part-time student, I think, but he was a member of the group. Didn't know him well." She stops and looks around the lobby area, like she's concerned someone may be listening.

I wait quietly for her to continue.

"Lucas and Jeff climbed up onto the log pile. Next thing we knew the logs apparently shifted or something—that's what Lucas said—and Jeff fell." She opens her mouth and exhales a loud breath. "He died instantly. We all saw it."

"Did you know Jeff well?"

Tears form in Minji's eyes. "Yes." She pauses. "He was my boyfriend. So yes, I guess you could say I did know him well."

"I'm sorry. I had no idea that—"

"There was no finer person than Jeff Yardley."

"Yardley?" That name rings a bell, but who ... ? Wait. That's the same name as the suspicious banker in White Pine.

She must notice my strange look. "What?" she says.

"Oh, nothing. It's just that I met a man, a banker down in White Pine, who—"

"That's Jeff's father." She wipes her eyes with the back of her hand.

I decide to shift the subject. "So what happened to Lucas Tanner?"

"I don't know." She seems suddenly disinterested in the direction our conversation is heading. "Haven't seen him much since the accident. I think he might have dropped out of school."

"He left town?"

"No. I think he's still around. Heard he works at the Downtowner. That's a bar near here." Then those laser eyes lock on me again. "So why are you really here?"

I don't answer the question. "Did you know Sven Norstaad?" I ask.

She's quiet for a moment. "Of course. Everybody in PAWN knew him. Crazy guy." She pauses another moment. "Look, I heard he just died in a car crash. Why are you asking about him?" Her eyes are full of questions.

"It's just that Sally knew him ..." I trail off. Time to change the subject again. "So this is where Sally did her work?"

"Sometimes. But mostly over at the Center. The Great Lakes Research Center. It's down by the water, not far away."

"Who would I talk to over there if I wanted to learn more about her research?"

"You are one nosy guy, Wil. I'm not sure I should be telling you so much." She cocks her head, like she's still sizing me up. "Look, I've got to run. I hope you—"

"I just want to see where she worked. How can that hurt?"

Minji sighs. "Ethan Ross was one of the professors she worked with. His office is over in the Center." She places an index finger against pursed lips. "I'm not sure what to make of you, Wil. But I'm going to assume you're all right. So I want to say this. I don't think you have anything to worry about. I'm sure Sally's okay." Then a slight smile comes across her face. "But I gotta admit, it's kind of cool that you're concerned about her."

Chapter 33

The Great Lakes Research Center is a stunning building—modern, yet blending into the environment, with metal and stone in muted earth tones of buff, oxidized copper, and gray. It sits at the edge of the water, a wide blue channel that my map shows cutting across the whole peninsula. Several boats, probably research vessels, are anchored out front.

I'm not sure what I'm looking for here, but I might as well start by cruising past the office of Sally's old professor. With the help of the directory just inside the entrance, it's easy to find Ethan Ross's office. His door is closed, and he's posted no schedule that mentions when he'll be back.

I peruse several research papers tacked on the cork board next to his door. Apparently his research has focused on blue-green algae in fresh water. Is this what Sally was working on? One colorful photograph from a NASA report catches my eye. It's a satellite view of Lake Erie, with the western third of the lake so contaminated with algae blooms that it's visible from space. I skim the article enough to learn that these algae blooms thrive because of pollution by fertilizers, sewage and industrial outflows. That photo was taken in 2011. Right below the article is a clipping from the *Cleveland Plain Dealer*, from August 2013. The first line reads, "Harmful algal blooms are growing once again around western Lake Erie, threatening fishing and boating." Allegedly this new bloom was caused by the dumping of partially treated sewage into the lake. "As we flew over," one eye-witness reported, "the algae bloom seemed to be growing by the minute."

Yet another article tells how certain toxic forms of this algae can cause death in mammals in as little as an hour.

Creepy stuff. I always thought of blue-green algae as just pond scum, a seasonal nuisance. I wish Del Behrens could see this.

I almost jump out of my skin as I realize someone's standing right behind me. I turn to see a tall, slender man in the doorway of the office on the other side of the hallway. He looks no older than me but is already losing his hair. His thick, frameless glasses accentuate the curious look on his pale, narrow face. I check the sign beside the door. This must be Professor Larkin. I can spot a teacher a mile away, especially a science teacher. "Looking for Ethan?" he asks.

"Uh, yes. A friend of mine was one of his students."

"Afraid you've missed him. You're welcome to wait here, but it might be a few months. He's on sabbatical in Australia." He gives a slight wry smile that shows he appreciates his own humor. His short-sleeve shirt and faded blue jeans look so wrinkled, I wonder if he slept in them last night. "Who was the student?"

"Sally Ladke."

"Yeah, I remember her. Smart kid. Dropped out, I seem to recall."

I nod, thinking that a teacher probably shouldn't be mentioning confidential student matters to total strangers. I look back at the posters next to Ethan Ross' door. "This stuff looks scary. Seems like it could be a real threat."

"I guess I wouldn't worry about it too much. Ethan's one of our resident nuts. He has this theory that some new strain of blue-green algae might be developed that could take over the freshwater systems of the world. Pretty far out, if you ask me. Hey, I'm not an expert on that kind of stuff like Ethan. I'm a fish guy. You want to know about yellow perch populations, I'm your man. But Ethan's a bit over the edge. It would take some kind of exotic algae that doesn't exist, something that could survive cold water and low nutrients. A little too much sci-fi for my tastes." Again the wry smile.

"Unlike fish."

"Yep. Fish. Something you can sink your teeth into." This guy's a barrel of laughs.

"So Professor Ross left for Australia?"

"Yep, lucky guy's going to miss the legendary Houghton winter this year. He lost his only two students, so I guess he figured it was a good time to get out of Dodge."

"Sally. Who was the other student?"

"Hmm, don't remember his name. A part-time student, I think. Was doing a bunch of lab work with Ethan. Wait. It's Lucas. Lucas something. Nice guy."

"Maybe Lucas Tanner?"

"Yeah, that's it. You know him too?"

"Not really. Just heard his name mentioned around campus." I give Larkin an appreciative smile and leave.

I pause at the entrance to the center, next to a large student bulletin board, with the usual offers of free puppies and announcements of upcoming concerts and group meetings. But one note catches my eye. A plain sheet of white paper features one word typed in a large font: "QUEEN." Underneath, in smaller type, appears "The QUEEN always takes the PAWN."

I decide to return to the biology department and find out what Minji knows about this QUEEN. In the lobby area, adjacent to the chairs where Minji and I talked an hour earlier, a young man behind the counter concentrates on his computer monitor. When he sees me approach, he looks up with a big smile.

"I'm looking for a student named Minji. Don't know her last name."

"Minji? Don't know anyone by that name."

"But she's a student here."

He shrugs. "I'm just filling in this afternoon. I really don't know anyone here." His eyes return to the computer.

I turn to leave, then turn back. "One more thing. Have you ever heard of a group called QUEEN?"

Now he seems interested. "Well, duh. Who hasn't? We are the champions of the world. That was their greatest—"

"Not that Queen. But thanks." I head for the elevator, while the receptionist hums "We Are the Champions" behind me. I'm not feeling much like the champion of anything.

Chapter 34

I'm more confused than ever. I've just about run out of leads, and so far I've come up with more questions than answers. How do Jeff and Dennis Yardley fit into all this? I now understand how Dennis Yardley might bear resentment toward Sally, if his son died during an illegal demonstration for a group that Sally once belonged to. And if the loose-lipped Officer Darby talked about Sally taking me in, then that might explain his suspicion about me. Yet, that doesn't mean that Jeff Yardley's death and the demise of PAWN somehow connect to Norstaad's death and Sally's disappearance. And was that guy in the Memorial Union Building the same shaved-head guy I saw on the bus? For that matter, who, really, is Minji? Can I believe anything she told me? And what is QUEEN?

I also have bouncing around in my head the disturbing facts about blue-green algae that I learned outside Professor Ross's office, and I cannot help but wonder if this, or some other ecological nightmare, is related to Norstaad's strange message, *HOMES Kill.* Lots of data—the kind of stuff a numbers guy like me should chew up and spit out. But I can't piece any of this together, and I certainly am no closer to finding Sally.

I head into town to the Downtowner to see what I can learn about Lucas Tanner, who knew Sally and was on that log pile when Jeff Yardley died. I realize this could be dangerous. Especially since I'm making this move based on Minji's information, and I might be a complete fool for trusting any of it. But I have no other leads, and I've come too far to turn back now. I'm surprised that my tendency to panic is not overwhelming me. Despite my growing urgency to find Sally, I'm strangely calm now, maybe because all of this seems too unreal. On this beautiful autumn afternoon on a bustling college campus in a seemingly tranquil small town, it's hard to be anything but calm.

Following the map I pull up on my laptop, I head down Shelden Avenue into the heart of town. The Downtowner looks to be no more than a couple miles away. A nice walk. I also prefer not to have prying eyes spot me driving the Eurovan, my getaway vehicle.

Walking north from the university, I'm in downtown Houghton within ten minutes. It's a striking old city, and if it weren't for the modern cars, you might believe the main street had time-traveled you back into the nineteenth-century. Commanding the downtown stretch of town is an imposing four-story brick and buff-stone building, with a lavish façade, towers at the corners and gold cupolas on the street-side roof line. A sign identifies the building as the Douglass House. These old buildings were built when people no doubt thought Houghton was going to be the next big city out west, not a nearly forgotten town a million miles away in the north woods.

At the far end of downtown, just before US 41 cuts to the right and crosses the blue-water channel that slices across the Keweenaw Peninsula, I come to the nondescript building which is the Downtowner Lounge. I make my way into the darkened interior, which looks like any other Midwestern bar and grill, and as my eyes adjust, I realize that the place is dead. It is mid-afternoon, after all. But then, through a glass door at the rear, I see a large wooden deck in the sunshine. That is where the action is.

About twenty patio tables are arrayed across the deck, affording a commanding view of the channel, which looks more like a lake, and a massive steel lift-bridge spanning the water. Plastic palm trees and several tall propane-powered heaters, which will soon be needed as the nights cool down, adorn the seating area. The deck is about half-full, mostly with college-aged kids, and is noisy with laughter and clattering glasses. There is a good feel here.

I take a seat at one of the unoccupied tables, and right away a young woman in a bright green smock is before me.

"I think I'll just stick with water for now," I say, buying myself a few minutes to figure out how to approach Lucas Tanner. I'm not sure what he can tell me. Not sure he's even here. Not sure this isn't dangerous. My best move is to get back in the Eurovan and split. But when the waitress passes by my table again, I flag her down and say, "I was looking for Lucas Tanner. Heard he works here."

The waitress nods. "Sure. I'll send him out."

Moments later, a young man, also wearing a bright green smock, is heading toward my table, wiping his hands on a towel. "I'm Lucas. You were asking for me?"

Lucas Tanner is an earnest-looking guy, with green eyes that look sad and straight blond hair combed to one side. "I'm Wil Weathers, and I'm here for the day. Sally Ladke's an old friend, and I just wanted to get a feel for where she went to school." I'm making this up as I go along, and I sense I'm not doing a very good job of it. "I heard you worked with her."

I'm expecting Tanner to be guarded, maybe refuse to speak with me. I could be anybody—a lawyer preparing a lawsuit over the accident or a reporter looking for a juicy exposé about a campus tragedy. But that's not the case. "Yeah, I knew Sally," he says, "Sorta. We both worked for Professor Ross for a while, but we never talked much. She left because of a sick parent or something. Is she okay?"

"Fine," I say. I hope that's true. "Anyway, Minji, this girl I met down at the Center, said I should look you up." I wait to see how he responds to this.

There seems to be a mistiness building in his eyes. "Why would ... look, you mention Sally and Minji. It's clear you're interested in PAWN somehow. That's the only connection those two had in my life. And PAWN's something I can't really talk about right now. Okay?" He begins to back away. I think he might cry.

"I'm sorry," I say, "I really don't know much about that organization. I don't mean to make you feel uncomfortable."

Lucas looks left and then right, as if expecting someone to accost him. He pulls out a chair and sits down. "I'm on break, so I can take a few minutes. You say you're friends with Sally and Minji?"

I nod. I'm still not sure why he's willing to speak to me.

"God, I wish I'd never heard of that group. My life's been a living hell since ..." He pauses and swallows. "Since the accident."

"Yeah, I heard about that. Must have been terrible, to be up—"

"It was worse than terrible. It was the worst moment of my life. I tried to stop him from going up there. God, I wish I'd tried harder. Now I have to live with that awful …" His voice trails off.

"I'm really sorry." I hadn't brought up the accident, but it appears that Lucas is looking for a chance to let it out.

He shakes his head, like he's trying to dispel a bad dream. "I didn't mean to go all crazy on you. You didn't come here to see me cry."

Obviously, Lucas is carrying a fair amount of guilt. His story strikes a sympathetic chord with me. I know something about guilt. And I know something about dropping out of school too. I try to shift the subject. "It must have been exciting working for Professor Ross."

"It was." Now he seems a bit calmer. "He works on cutting-edge stuff. I was only a part-time student, but he was very kind to allow me to help out in his labs." Then he turns glum again. "I guess I really let Professor Ross down, leaving so suddenly. But I was toast. I had to quit."

"You've been through a lot, Lucas. Why do you hang around Houghton?"

He shrugs. "If you know where there's a better job, I'm all ears. I'd really like to get out of here, but I need a job, and this is about all I can handle right now, until I get my act back together."

I try to make my conversation casual and chatty. "Do you have family somewhere?"

"I'm from out west around Superior. My dad died of a heart attack three years ago. Way too young." He pauses and chokes up a bit. "My mom left years ago. Haven't see her since I was a kid. What about you?"

"I'm originally from Los Angeles, but now I live down in Milwaukee."

"Big-city guy," he laughs. I laugh too.

We talk a while longer. Lucas Tanner is a pleasant sort, but there's not much for me to learn here. As his break comes to an end, he stands and says, "Well, I hope you enjoy your time in Houghton." He gazes out to the channel for a moment. "This really is a nice place."

As I leave the Downtowner, I pass a student kiosk where all kinds of notices are posted. There I see another poster about QUEEN. This one has more information: "If you think things have gone too far, if you want to regain the control we've lost, support the QUEEN. Quietly Undoing Excessive Environmental Nuisances. The QUEEN always takes the PAWN." There is no information about who runs QUEEN, no information on how to contact them.

I decide to take an alternate way back to the university, staying off the main street, in case someone might be waiting for me. Down the hill from the restaurant, a less-travelled road parallels the main street, following close to the channel among warehouses, parking lots, boat docks and open space. Boats motor out in the channel, their dull engine roar a pleasant sound. Raucous gulls circle overhead. I pause to watch, and I smile as I'm tantalized with a brief fantasy of Sally and me spreading out a picnic lunch along this shore.

From out of nowhere, something hits me hard and knocks me over.

I try to turn toward the assault, and I see two men and a flurry of fists. Now the three of us are tumbling. I spin frantically to get away, but I take a hard one to the jaw. Twisting and jerking, I go down on one knee, then hit the ground. I cannot see their faces. They may be wearing ski masks. It's all happening too fast.

One of them is lifting something black toward my face. I realize it's a bag he's trying to get over my head. If he succeeds, I'm done for. I thrash even more furiously, and as I do, he turns his body towards me to gain more leverage in pressing me down. This gives me my only chance. With all that I've got left, I plant a knee in his groin and hear him grunt. The other man comes up on my side and I see a flash of silver—a knife, I think. But I whirl in his direction with an elbow that meets his nose just as he swipes the blade toward my body. The collision with the man's nose makes a sickening crunching sound, and he leaps back for a moment. Just a moment is all I need to twist free. Adrenalin drives me to my feet and into a sprint up the alley toward the main drag. I do not pause to look behind me.

At the corner I turn left toward the university and keep going. But in a half-block I feel light-headed. I cannot allow myself to pass out now. Then I look down at the front of my shirt. It's bright red, soaked in blood. Then everything goes black.

Chapter 35

I'm not sure how long I'm out, but when I come to, there's a small crowd gathered around me. A woman, who's kneeling beside me, says, "Just remain still. We've called an ambulance. They'll be here in a minute."

"What happened?" asks someone.

Another person comes down beside me. "I saw it. Two guys attacked him back down on Lakeshore. I was trying to get to him to warn him, but I was too late." It's Lucas Tanner. He still wears his bright green smock. Then he says to me, "I'm so sorry I didn't get there in time, Wil. I saw two men follow you from the Downtowner, so I thought I'd better tag along. But you're going to be okay. It doesn't look too bad." He rests a hand on my shoulder.

I hear the siren approaching from down the street. I cannot let them take me to the hospital. That could take me straight into the hands of the cops. I try to rise to a crouching position, but Lucas holds me down with a gentle hand. "You'd better stay down, Wil, until the ambulance gets here."

"But I need to sit up," I say. "I can't breathe," I say louder.

The crowd backs away a bit, which allows me to get to my knees. I stay there in a crouching position for a few moments, as the siren grows louder. It must be just a couple of blocks away now. I bow my head, like I'm about to pass out again. Keeping my head down, I scan my surroundings and pick an opening in the crowd through which to make my escape. "I wonder if someone could find me a drink of water," I say.

Then, as several of the people exchange glances, pondering how to respond to my need, I make a run for it. Quickly, I'm on my feet and pushing through the crowd. I'm not sure where I'm headed, but I've got to get away from here fast. And I cannot allow myself to pass out again.

I push open the door of the nearest storefront and race in. It appears to be a quilt shop. Two women standing near a counter turn and gasp as I run by them. One holds a pair of scissors, and the other a length of cloth. I pause only for a moment to grab the cloth from the woman's hands, press it against the blood on my shirt, then sprint toward the back of the store. There had better be a rear entrance.

I stumble as I crash through a narrow hallway at the back of the shop, knocking over a shelf that sends items rattling noisily to the floor, but then I find a door. In a moment I'm in a narrow alley. I turn right and keep going. When I make it to the next street I cut left, back down toward the street where I was attacked. No sign of my attackers, no sign yet of anyone following me. I make another turn, then in a narrow gap between two buildings I sag against a brick wall, gulping for air. I slowly unbutton my shirt to survey the damage. A thin slice cuts across my chest, but it doesn't look deep. My elbow to the attacker's nose must have prevented the knife from making a fatal plunge. The bleeding is in fact now subsiding. I press the cloth harder against the wound.

I have to keep going. Somehow, I've got to make it to the Eurovan and get out of this town soon. I should be swaggering a bit, I realize, getting the best of two attackers. After all, I haven't been in a fight since junior high. But I'm in no condition to swagger. With the adrenalin wearing off, all I can do is shake.

Who were those guys? Not the cops. They were not very good fighters, so they weren't professional thugs, or I wouldn't have been able to break free. But it's clear they meant to do me harm. This was not a random mugging. Kidnapping or murder was their intention.

Who told them about me? Lucas Tanner? The man with the shaved head? Minji? She is the one who told me about the Downtowner. That could have been a trap. I can't make sense of anything. Lucas Tanner said he got a look at them. His description of the two men may be important, but for now it will take everything I've got just to get back to the van. My mind in a whirl, I just now notice a throb in my jaw, and as I touch it gingerly, I find more blood on my fingers.

Chapter 36

"Holy crap, are you okay?" Lander is shaking my shoulder. I come to, slumped over the wheel of his van. I'm not sure how long I've been here, or how in fact I actually made that long drive back. As my head clears, I can only recall brief snippets of my ordeal in getting back to the van and my drive to White Pine. "Oh my God," he stammers, "you're hurt."

"I think I'll be okay," I manage to say. I'm already starting to feel better, just knowing I've made it back. It's amazing how quickly a place, even one as unlikely as the alley behind Danny's, can start to feel like home. I try to get out of the car. "I think I just need to—"

"No, don't move. Not yet. Let's get you checked out." Lander opens the driver's side door and leans in to look over my bloodied shirt and the quilt fabric that apparently succeeded in stopping the blood flow. "You look okay, but what happened?"

I tell him the whole story while he shakes his head in disbelief. "So all this stuff you've been telling me is not just some paranoid crap."

I nod weakly. "What I'm really worried about now is Sally. If those guys who got me have gotten to—"

"We can't worry about that right now. We've gotta get you some medical attention first. I guess we can't go to urgent care. Look, there's some first aid stuff over at the church. I know where they keep it. Scoot over, we'll go right now."

I'm feeling better and don't think I need any medical help, but Lander's probably right. I do need something on these wounds that'll prevent infection.

I reach into my duffel in the sleeping space above me and pull down a sweatshirt, which I put on over the bloody shirt that makes my wound look a lot worse than it is. As Lander climbs in behind the wheel, he says, "I'm not sure how you made that drive home, Wil. You must have tapped into some inner strength."

I say nothing. One thing I'm not is some kind of inner-strength guy.

In two minutes we're parked in the empty lot behind the church. "Won't the church be locked?" I ask.

"The front door's always open," Lander says. "You can just sit here if you want."

I've already been sitting too long. "I'm feeling better, really. I'll come with you." But once inside the door, I'm feeling woozy. "Maybe I'll rest here while you go get the first aid kit." I lean against one of the dark wood pews as Lander heads off to the parish hall.

I look up at my old buddies, the four grumpy men in the stained glass window at the rear of the church. The afternoon sun has brightly illuminated the huge window, and while I could do without the grimaces of the men—the Gospel writers, I think Sally said—the colors of the window are astounding and, yes, beautiful.

I jump at the tap on my shoulder. I turn, expecting to see Lander, but it's Joe Gerlach, the high school principal I met at Danny's last week. I recoil slightly. Surely he knows that the cops are looking for me. But if he does, he doesn't let on.

"Wil, it's good to see you again," he says.

I nod.

"You know, I tried to reach you last week, after you left. Wanted to hear some more about your teaching ideas."

I nod again.

"But funny thing," he says, his intense eyes now locking into mine, "I tried to call you down at UWM, but the person I talked to there said you didn't work there." His raised eyebrows judge me like he's just caught me cheating on a midterm.

"Look, I didn't get around to mentioning last week that I—"

"But there's something else, Wil." Joe Gerlach is bearing more and more of a resemblance to the four guys in the stained glass window. "I was confused when the gal at UWM didn't know you. So I Googled your name."

I begin to back toward the door.

"It's amazing what I found. At first I didn't believe it, but then I found an old newspaper article and it had your picture. And I realized that it was, in fact, you."

His eyes are piercing now, and I have to look away. I say nothing, but continue edging toward the door.

"Wil, it said you started a forest fire back in California. It was a real bad fire, burned thousands of acres. It said that you were arrested, that—"

"Look," I say, "it wasn't …" but then I trail off, with nothing to add. My mouth has gone dry.

"I suppose you've told Sally about all this," he says. But of course he's certain that I haven't. And I suspect that he will tell her.

I glance up at the men in the window again. Their glowers seem even more intense now. "I need to go," I say, heading toward the door.

"Wil, wait, I'm not finished yet."

I hurry out of the church, not looking back. Maybe he's not finished yet. But it does seem that I am.

Chapter 37

There are some things that happen in our lives that are better forgotten, some things that have caused so much pain that there's no good reason to talk about them. No good reason that doesn't run the risk of opening up old wounds, wounds that may still not be completely healed.

Like Joe Gerlach said, there was a fire, and it was awful. And of course I haven't told Sally about it. Why should I? Or maybe, how could I? I don't even know her that well. I'm sure she's got a few juicy little secrets of her own. Or maybe not. Anyway, something that happened all those years ago doesn't really matter now. It's important that I move ahead with my life. I lie on my back in Lander's Eurovan and stare at the claustrophobic camper top, just inches above my face. But of course I haven't really moved very far ahead at all, have I?

I roll over onto my stomach and peer out through my plastic window at the back of Danny's Northwood's Café. It's just getting light. The only sound is Lander's snoring below. Joe Gerlach has no doubt told the cops he saw me, so they know I'm still in town. I'm sure he saw Lander on his way out of the church and probably told him about me, although when Lander came back out to the van, he didn't let on that he knew anything. At the very least, Joe Gerlach now knows that I'm with Lander, so he'll be able to tell the cops where to find me.

What do I do now? I know I will not be able to avoid the cops or the men who attacked me in Houghton much longer. Running is not an option. I have no place to run to, no place that is safe. My only choice is to charge ahead and not let myself get derailed by self-pity or thoughts that the men who attacked me may have already gotten their hands on Sally.

Lander has suggested going to the junkyard where Norstaad's car was taken. I don't know what we could possibly learn there, but what else are we going to do?

Chapter 38

Lander and I pull into Iron River Auto Salvage just after ten. Danny's allowed him to take the morning shift off. I'm feeling a lot better, but still a little banged up and grateful not to have to drive. On the way over, the subject of Joe Gerlach never came up, which gives me hope that maybe Joe didn't say anything to Lander.

I say, "What makes you so sure that Norstaad's car will be here?"

"Not too complicated, Wil," he says, "this is the only junk yard for miles. It's gotta be here."

I visited a junk yard once, back in high school, when a friend of mine was looking for a used carburetor, or some such part, for his old Impala. This place looks pretty much the same. A high chain link fence surrounds a huge treeless lot, with banged up cars, all lined up in rows with their hoods open, looking like hungry baby birds waiting to be fed.

We park in front of a small shack with a sign that simply reads "Office." Inside, a woman working with a calculator and a stack of papers says, without looking up from her desk, "What can I do for you boys?"

I have my speech prepared. "A man named Sven Norstaad was killed in an accident last Friday night, and I was hoping to see the vehicle. If you have it here."

Now the woman looks up. She's surprisingly well-dressed for someone who works in a junk yard, wearing a white sweater over dark slacks. Blond hair that doesn't look natural surrounds a round, brown face that's obviously spent a lot of time in a tanning salon. "And just why would I show the vehicle to you? You family or somethin'?"

"Yes, I'm his nephew. I haven't seen Uncle Sven in years, but I read about the accident and wanted to come over and just see, you know, the car he was last in. I don't even know where he lives. Maybe you could help me out with that too."

"You probably oughta be talkin' to the cops about that. They're the ones who know about the deceased."

"Well, maybe if we could see the car ..." I say.

"There's not much to see, I'm afraid. Burned to hell. And Mr. Norstaad too." She shakes her head like she's trying to forget an unpleasant image. "But I guess you can take a look."

"Do you know what happened?" I ask.

"No witnesses to the accident. Some drivers saw the fire, though. Vehicle apparently went off the road, somehow ruptured the gas tank and the whole thing just torched."

Lander asks, "So if the car is burned so bad, how do you know that the person inside was Sven Norstaad?"

The woman gives Lander a suspicious look, scanning his tattooed arms and the red spiky hair. "He's my friend," I offer.

"Well, I just know what I heard the cops say. There was the serial number on the car, for one thing."

Lander says, "But it could have been anybody inside the—"

"Then there was the ring. You're right, the body was ... well, the cops said it was unrecognizable, but it had a ring from the guy's university and his initials inside the band. If you want the ring, you'll have to talk to the cops. They're over on Genesee Street. They have anything that was found in the vehicle, and there wasn't much."

"Guess we'd still like to see the car, if possible. We've come this far already," I say.

"Okay, I guess." The woman reaches up behind her and pulls a key from the wall and hands it to me. "The locked lot right behind the office here. It's where we keep the vehicles still under investigation. The cops are done with it, but we haven't moved it yet. It'll be the first vehicle on your left as you go in, the only one burned black. You won't miss it. Prepare yourself, though. If that was my uncle's vehicle, not sure I'd want to see it."

Lander and I thank the woman and head out to the small fenced yard behind the shack. Like she said, it's impossible to miss the vehicle. It's a pickup—an old Ford, as best as I can tell—and the whole thing is charcoal black. The tires are gone, probably burned off. Both doors on the cab are open, so it's easy to peek in, but there's a strong burnt-plastic smell inside. I'm growing queasy just standing near the truck, thinking that here is where the guy in the bushes wound up. The guy who had reached out to me for help. And I couldn't help him.

"This is gross," gasps Lander, who seems to be reacting the same way I am.

"Not much to see, but let's look inside anyway." I lean into the cab on the driver's side, as the seat cushions have been burned away, leaving only blackened coil springs. The glove box door lies open and charred. Nothing inside. There seems to be no clue of any sort that might tell us more about Sven Norstaad.

I go around to the passenger side, so I can better examine the glove box. As I raise the glove-box door, I notice a tiny flake of ash protruding from the area where the door is hinged onto the dash. I lean down for a better look. I flex the glove-box door hard and pop it out of its mount. I set the door aside and see that, in the area where the under-surface of the door met the smooth metal of the dash, a fragment of paper seems to have been partially preserved. Part of it is burned, but the part pressed between the two metal surfaces is intact.

I gently lift the paper, and Lander and I study it together. It's a receipt for four tires, purchased at Crossroads Mobil in Iron River. The date of the purchase has been burned away, but I can make out that the bill is signed by someone named Russ. It doesn't have the customer's name, and it was paid with cash. It's not much, but it's a clue.

Chapter 39

Crossroads Mobil is just a couple miles away in downtown Iron River. The door of the service garage is up, and from the curb we see a guy working underneath a car on the station's only hydraulic lift. Lander says, "Okay, Mr. Genius, what are we going to ask these guys? Even if they remember him, which they probably won't, why would they tell us anything just because we've got an old receipt for tires? This is the north woods, after all, and folks up here respect privacy."

As if I have an idea how to proceed. I ponder this for awhile, and then I get an inspiration that just might work. "Come on," I say to Lander. As we approach the service garage, the mechanic, a thin red-headed man in his twenties, gives us a nod, and we wait for him to finish tightening some bolts with a large box wrench. Then he turns toward us with a grin, while wiping his hands on a greasy rag. "What can I help you with?"

Okay, here goes. "This is a kind of a strange request, but I wonder if you could help me out. I'm doing a graduate project up at Michigan Tech in the psych department, an experiment on memory. I'm trying to determine how well people remember information about people they've only met briefly. So my uncle, who lives around here, is one of my guinea pigs."

I manufacture a chuckle. "My Uncle Sven gave me several names of people he's had brief interactions with over the past few months, and I'm interviewing these folks to see how much they can remember about him. One of the people he came up with is Russ, who he says he bought some tires from recently." I notice Lander looking at me with some awe.

"Well, that sounds like fun. I'm Russ. What did you say your uncle's name was?"

"Sven Norstaad."

Russ ponders this for a moment, then says, "Not sure I remember that name. Guess I struck out, huh?"

"Not yet," I laugh, doing my best to sound like a carefree student. "I can give you clues until you remember. First clue: he bought four Cooper tires for his Ford pickup."

"Sorry, that doesn't help much. Do a lot of work on Ford pickups."

"Okay. How about this? He usually wears a plaid wool shirt."

"Not ringing a bell."

"Okay, we'll ramp it up a bit. Hope he won't mind me saying this, but he's kind of crazy. Talks strange."

"Hmm. Okay, okay, maybe I do remember who you're talking about." Russ scratches his head. "Yeah, in fact I do remember him, I think. Yeah, just a few days ago. It was funny. He had these old tires, real banana skins, that haven't been made for at least ten years. Big tall guy. Sandy hair. Really old. Right?"

I jot down the words Russ is saying on a notepad Lander had in the car. A student has to take notes, right? I have no idea if Sven Norstaad was tall or had sandy hair, but I know he must have been old if he studied with a Madison prof in the late forties. "You've got it! Excellent! In fact you've already answered two of the questions, what does he look like and how old is he. Very good. Ready for the final question?"

Russ seems pleased with his accomplishments. "Yeah. Shoot."

Moment of truth coming up. "Okay, Russ, one final question. Let's see if you can handle this. Where does Sven Norstaad live?"

Russ is silent for a bit, then shakes his head. "Guess I don't know that one. Sorry. Wait a sec. Jerry, that's my partner, was joking with Mr. Norstaad about mackinaws."

"Mackinaws?"

"Yeah, Jerry was kidding him about there being no mackinaws in Mackinaw Lake." Russ pauses, then announces proudly, "Yes, he lives on Mackinaw Lake. Not that I ever heard of Mackinaw Lake, but that's what the man said."

"Russ, I must say I'm very impressed. Three for three! You nailed it. In fact, out of all the folks I've interviewed, you've done the best. Would it be okay if I mention your name in my report?"

"Of course." Russ gives me his full name and I write it down. As we're leaving, Russ hollers out, "Be sure to say hi to Mr. Norstaad for me."

"Will do, Russ. Have a good one."

Back in the van, Lander turns to face me. "Dude, you were freaking amazing."

I think we're starting to enjoy our new lives as undercover sleuths.

Chapter 40

Lander's never heard of Mackinaw Lake either, but he knows someone who probably has. Tony's Sporting Goods is just down the block from the Mobil station. Lander says, "Okay, let me do the talking this time. I go into this place a lot. I know these guys."

As soon as we're in the door, a voice bellows, "Hey, Lander, how goes it? Got any big lies to tell us today?"

Although there is a hunting section in the rear and some outdoor clothing, Tony's is clearly all about fishing. At least a hundred fishing rods stand against one wall. Another wall is covered with tackle boxes. Several aisles of shelves contain nothing but lures, and several more appear dedicated to flies. It's hard to imagine there is a fishing accessory made that Tony doesn't stock.

"Lies?" Lander feigns insult. "Lies? You know I always tell the truth about my fishing."

"Sure, Lander, sure. I heard you got a forty-eight-inch muskie last week. Am I supposed to believe that?" Tony stands behind a long glass counter in which dozens of fishing reels are displayed. He looks about fifty, with lean weathered features and silver hair. He fits the description of a northwoods fishing guide who's been portaging canoes all day.

"Well, come to think about it, Tony, it could have been a little bigger than that." They both laugh. Then Lander says, "Tony, I need a couple Williams Wablers, silver, ounce and a half."

"Sure, Lander. Going for some lakers?"

"Well, I hope to get up to the big waters before the warm weather's over."

Tony pulls a couple of large fishing lures from a rack behind him and lays them on the counter.

"Say, Tony, this is my friend Wil. He's new in these parts, and I'm showing him around a bit this morning." Tony gives me a friendly nod.

Lander says nonchalantly, "Ever hear of a place called Mackinaw Lake around here?"

Tony rubs two forefingers over the gray stubble on his chin as he ponders this. "You know, Lander, there are fifteen thousand lakes in these parts, don't you?" He shakes his head slowly, as he extends his hands, palms up, as if he has no clue. But then a grin breaks across his face. "But of course," he laughs, "I know every damn one of them."

"Dang it, Tony, one of these days I'm going to stump you."

"Good luck with that, Lander. Lot of guys would have bit the dust on that question, though. Mackinaw's not on any map. It's not an official name or anything. Just a place a few old salts like me know about. I hope you're not planning to try your Wablers there."

"Why's that?"

"Well, Mackinaw Lake is only about twenty acres. A few bluegill and smallmouths in there, that's about all. 'Mackinaw' is a bit of a joke, isn't it?"

Lander turns to me to explain. "A mackinaw is a lake trout. They're only found in the big lakes, can get to be fifty pounds or more. That's why you need stuff like this." He dangles one of the big silver lures in front of me. His eyes twinkle with obvious pleasure at the contribution he's made to our quest.

Chapter 41

Lander's Eurovan bounces down a spider web of rough gravel forest-service roads and unmarked tracks, where I wish we had four-wheel drive. It bobs and tilts along the bumpy, pot-hole-pocked surfaces like a punch-drunk fighter trying in vain to dodge another jab.

I'm not certain Lander knows where he's going. "Are you sure we're heading in the right direction?" I ask. We have no map that shows any detail back in these woods, and we're going solely on the instructions that Tony gave us.

"I think we're almost there," says Lander in a confident way, although I can tell his confidence is faltering too. Then he comes to a stop, where two equally rutted roads—if you can call them roads—fork off into the trees. He runs his hand over his red, stiff-peaked hair and says, "Hmm. I don't recall Tony mentioning a fork, do you?"

Actually I do, and my spirits are buoyed a bit. "I think he said keep left at the fork, and you're almost there. The clearing should be just ahead."

Lander aims the old van off to the left, and in a few minutes we're in a small clearing. "We made it," beams Lander, like he's just reached the summit of Everest. "Dang, this place really is in the middle of nowhere. Good place for a hermit to live." He looks off to the left. "The lake should be just over there." A narrow set of tracks, barely visible, disappears into thick foliage. "We'd need four-wheel for sure to get up there. I think we walk from here."

We leave the Eurovan in the clearing and begin up the rocky tracks into dense woods, hopefully toward the lake. It is encouraging to see evidence of tire tracks, perhaps indicating that Norstaad's truck has been up this way. In about a quarter mile, we catch a glimpse of a small lake through the trees. Here the tracks curve off to the right, and we follow them to the far side of the lake, no more than a few hundred yards, to the front of a log cabin. The wood is so grayed with age that you can barely see the cabin at all unless you are standing right in front of it. We step up onto a creaky porch that is in great need of repair. Several of the floor boards threaten to give way as we cross to the door.

"Do you think this is the place?" Lander asks.

"We'll know soon enough, I suspect," I say, as I grasp the rusted handle on the door. It's unlocked and pushes opens easily. "Anybody home?" I call out, but there is no sign of life. Lander and I step inside. My first instinct is to reach for a light switch, but I quickly realize that there is no electricity here. For a while we stand just inside the door, allowing our eyes to adjust to the darkness. A few shafts of sunlight seep in through the dirty glass of two windows, and soon we are able to make out our surroundings. A strong musty smell is almost choking. I leave the front door ajar, so a little fresh air might flow in.

There is a wood stove in one corner of the single room and an unmade bed against the adjacent wall. Old tools, including an axe and a shovel, lean against the wall next to a door that apparently leads out back. Several tables around the cabin are buried under piles of books and papers. Some of the papers are scattered across the floor. Has the cabin been ransacked, or is this just the result of a messy tenant? This place makes the Bali Hai look like the Taj Mahal.

I find some matches and light the wick of a kerosene lamp, then begin looking through some of the papers, mostly old articles about ecology and conservation. This must be Norstaad's place. I'm not sure what I'm looking for here, just any kind of clue that might help me find Sally or shed some light on the mystery that now enfolds us.

I come to a stack of ledger-sized journals and open one, while Lander looks around the cabin. Some of Norstaad's entries are technical, some are nonsensical—the work of a lunatic. Others seem to be the work of a poet. Crazy but a genius. Isn't that what Sally said about him? These entries seem consistent with that appraisal of Sven Norstaad. A number of his scrawlings are like mini-essays, snippets that alternate between anger and detachment, melancholy and joy. They make me sad.

> *I used to be an optimist. Then I became a pragmatist. Then I became a pessimist. Then I became angry. But now I am nothing at all. Just one who waits silently, waiting for the owl to send his evening cry across a twilight meadow.*

I try to recall the lettering of *HOMES kill* on the scrap of paper. Could that have been Norstaad's writing? I'm not sure.

Another entry in Norstaad's journal paints a picture of a man still concerned about the environment, perhaps enough to alert someone about a perceived threat to the Great Lakes:

> *What will we have lost when the last trout dies? When the brooks choke with detergents? When the lakes gag with sewage and fertilizers? When the sweet pure coat of water that bathes our planet has been sullied?*

But I see nothing here that brings me closer to finding Sally. I slump with the heavy ledger in my hands and sigh.

I pace the perimeter of the room. One wall contains a large yellowed map of northern Wisconsin and a few faded black and white portraits that look like they're from the early days of photography. Leaning against another wall are several fishing rods and a snow shovel.

In the poor light I almost stumble over it before I see it. "Oh, my ..." I almost choke on my words. There, leaned up against the wall, is my backpack.

My knees grow wobbly. Why would my backpack be here in Norstaad's cabin? Could he have taken it? That seems unlikely if he was indeed dying in the bushes. There also is no motive for him to have taken it. This must mean that the intruder, who is likely Norstaad's killer, has been here. I look through my backpack. Everything seems to be intact.

As I wrestle with what this means, Lander says, "Wil, you might want to look at this." On the inside of the door, carved fresh and deep and ragged, is the word QUEEN. "What do you make of that?"

I tell Lander about the posters I saw in Houghton. So someone besides Norstaad has been here, as it seems unlikely that Norstaad would have carved this himself. I remember the line "The QUEEN always takes the PAWN." The adversaries of PAWN, the group that Norstaad mentored. I'm guessing they are connected to his murder. They are likely connected to the attack on my life. They are likely connected with Sally's disappearance. The only problem is, we have no idea who QUEEN actually is. Or why they would view us as such threats that murder is their goal. The more data we accumulate, the more confusing all this seems.

"What do we do now?" Lander asks.

"I'm not sure this tells us anything that helps much." I'm going to need time to put all these pieces together. Surely, the intellect that had been so keen at solving those classical mechanics problems back in the physics department at UCLA should be able to assemble all the data we have and figure out what's going on. But I still seem to be in a fog. I sigh. "Let's take a look out back before we go."

Lander follows me out the cabin's rear door. We freeze in our tracks. There, with all its doors standing open, sits Sally's Outback.

Chapter 42

An hour later we are still gathered around the Outback. It has been an hour of panic, grief, and fury. We ventured into the surrounding woods as far as we dared without getting lost, searching for any clue of Sally's presence, calling out her name. We went through her car. Some of her stuff was scattered around the car on the ground. Sally's base camp was a mess to begin with, so it was impossible to determine what might be missing. Her key was still in the ignition.

Now I sit near the car, cross-legged on the ground, weeping. Lander sits next to me, an arm around my shoulder. "God," I wail, "I should never have gone back to Milwaukee and left her."

Lander tries to be consoling. "Look, Wil, I know this looks bad, and I'm really upset too. But let's not jump to conclusions. Maybe she—"

I push Lander's arm away. "You can't sugarcoat this, Lander. Two men tried to kill me yesterday. Probably the same men who killed Norstaad. Now, Sally's car abandoned out here. She would not have left it here. How else can we interpret this?"

I stand and pace, throwing my arms into the air as if imploring some deity, but there is no one to help me. My life has brought sorrow to everyone who has ever cared for me. And now this woman who I barely knew, this kind and beautiful woman, so full of life and hope and joy, this woman who wanted me to stay with her. This woman I could love—maybe already do. This pure woman is gone. And maybe I could have saved her. But once again my neglectful ways have brought tragedy to the innocent.

"Wil, I'll stay here as long as you want, but I don't think there's any more that we can accomplish here."

"I know you have to get to work, Lander. You're already—"

"That doesn't matter." His normally pale face is red, and I realize that he's been crying, too.

"I'm sorry, Lander. I just don't know what to do now. It seems like there's no hope."

Lander looks me in the eye. "One thing I know for sure, Wil. There's always hope."

Chapter 43

The ride back to White Pine is mostly in silence. For a long time I stare out the window, watching the woods fly by. These woods I now hate. Dark, infinite, cold. Indifferent.

We had considered locking Sally's car and taking the keys with us, but then thought better of it. There is a slim chance she could return, so we put her base-camp paraphernalia back into the car and closed the doors, leaving the key in the ignition, as we had found it. We grabbed my backpack, threw it into the back of the van and left.

As my grief plateaus, I begin to think more clearly. Sally was almost certainly kidnapped. Perhaps she discovered Norstaad's cabin on her own and was kidnapped there. Or she was kidnapped elsewhere and taken there along with her car. If she was kidnapped, I do not hold out any hope that she is alive. The tears threaten to return, but I am able to push them back. But what if she got away? What if she fled into the woods? She is a skilled outdoorsman. She could survive.

But where would she go?

As we approach White Pine, Lander says, "What are we going to do about the police? We need to tell them about this."

He's right, of course. But I'm already the number-one suspect. Small-town justice would be served by just throwing me in prison and pronouncing the case closed. Darby wouldn't have to blame anything on wolves any longer. "Yes we do, but let's wait just a bit. Maybe we need another day or so to sort this—"

He looks at me, with one hand extended, palm up, toward me, as if pleading. "But they could be looking for Sally and the—"

I avoid his eyes. "I'm pretty certain they'd just grab me and be done with it."

"Maybe you're right. But what are we going to do now?"

I look over at Lander. "Where would Sally have gone if she fled on foot from Norstaad's cabin?"

He gives a slow shrug. "I have no idea. Somewhere she'd feel safe, I guess."

I have an idea. "I know a place where she would feel safe, but I'm embarrassed to say I don't how to get there. A place she calls the sentinels. She took me there last week. Have you heard of it?"

"No. She's never mentioned that to me. You think she might go there?"

"I don't know. I don't even know where it is. It might be too far away from Norstaad's cabin."

"Do you remember anything at all about the place?"

I'm silent for a moment. "I remember you travel west on 2 to get there. Turn up a forest service road." I pause, searching my brain for the number. "1277. That's it. 1277."

"Maybe up by Lake Warren?"

"You know about Lake Warren?"

"Yes, Sally told me how to get there. Told me about the great brookie fishing at the inlet. She was right. She only told me because I always do catch and release. But I don't know about any sentinels."

"You know how to get to Lake Warren?"

"Yeah. Been there a couple times. It isn't easy to find, though. You've got to know exactly where to stop along the road, and you've got to have the exact compass bearing. Then you can find it."

"The sentinels are beyond there. How far do you think that is from Norstaad's cabin?"

"Just guessing, but I'd say maybe fifteen miles cross country. Sally could do that for sure."

"Could you drop me off at the right spot, maybe tomorrow morning?" The sun is already setting, and, in spite of the urgency of the situation, I don't want to attempt that hike in the dark. I review my equipment. I now have my backpack. "One more thing," I say. "Can we stop by the church and get my sleeping bag? I'm not sure how long I'll be out there."

"Sure. You want me to go with you tomorrow?"

I think about this. I need to go alone. Sally showed me this special place and perhaps has shown no one else. I need to honor that. I realize that my trek may be as much a memorial, a time to remember, as it is a search. "I think I'd better go alone. If you could drop me off at the right place and show me the direction into Lake Warren, I think I might be able to make it from there." I pause then add, "If she's not there, then we go to the police."

Lander nods, as he lets out a sigh.

Chapter 44

It's dark by the time Lander pulls in behind the church. There are no other cars, but I'll be keeping my eyes open to avoid another encounter with Joe Gerlach.

I enter the front door and pass the big stained-glass window with the four glowering men, determined to not look up and again see their disapproval. I go straight into the parish hall and don't turn on any lights. There's still enough sunset-light coming in through the windows for me to see. My sleeping bag lies draped across a chair near one of the bookcases in the corner. I take it under my arm and beat a hasty retreat.

On the way out I cannot resist a look up at the four guys. So what made them tick? A feeling of superiority over guys like me? Guys like me who've screwed up and certainly don't belong in a stained-glass window like they do? Is that what kept them going? I always thought that was what kept the church going too. A feeling of superiority, a confidence that they have all the answers, they have all the virtues, and they have a strong desire to disassociate themselves from losers like me. But what about Sally? Or for that matter Lander? Or Hazel Grabowski? They don't seem that way at all. Maybe I need to rethink some things. But not tonight, when—

A tap on my shoulder causes me to jump. I turn quickly, expecting to see the accusing face of Joe Gerlach again. But it's Deacon Ellen. How did she come up on me so quietly?

"I was just picking up my sleeping bag," I say. "Have to get going."

"Yes, I was wondering when you would get that thing." Deacon Ellen looks up at me with gentle eyes that calm my anxiety. "Staying for Bible study tonight? Starts in about an hour."

"No, I can't stay. Sorry."

"No problem. I see you were studying our four grumpy guys," she says.

I laugh. So I'm not the only one who feels uncomfortable with these dudes. I wonder if she knows the cops are after me. I wonder if Joe Gerlach has brought her up to date on my failures. "Yes, they seem so stern."

"Why's that, Wil?"

"I don't know. It's just that they seem so holier-than-thou."

"Oh, I don't think they felt that way at all."

"They're in the Bible, aren't they? How can they not feel superior?" I edge toward the door.

"Well, let me tell you a little about them. If you've got a moment, that is. I don't want to keep you, if—"

I look toward the door, then back at her. "I guess I've got a minute." I take a seat in the pew closest to the windows.

Deacon Ellen remains standing, and even seated I am almost as tall as she is. She hardly looks like a minister right now: faded denim work shirt and blue jeans. No clergy collar. She puts a foot up on the pew next to me and leans forward. "Yes, these are four pretty interesting characters all right. But you might be surprised about them. Take a look at that first guy on the left. That's Matthew."

All four of them wear long robes and are barefoot, and each is writing in a book. Matthew looks like the oldest one, with a long white beard.

Ellen gazes up at the window as she speaks. "Matthew was a tax collector, who took money from the people and gave it to the Roman government, probably siphoning some off for himself. He was despised in his community."

I'm surprised to hear this.

"And the next one is Mark. He had an especially poor track record. It is believed that when Jesus was arrested, Mark fled, and he was in such a hurry that his robe fell off and he ran off naked. So humiliation was added to his cowardice. Then later, Mark went off on a mission trip with Paul, but bailed out when the going got tough. He let the whole team down, and it took a long time for Paul to trust him again."

"So why would these guys be celebrated in a stained glass window?"

"Let's go on before I answer that. The next one is Luke. He was an outsider, joined the ministry team late. He was the only one of the biblical writers, as far as we know, who wasn't a Jew. He wasn't a witness to the resurrection, never saw Jesus in person like the others did. Always an outsider."

Then our eyes turn toward the last figure. He looks younger than the rest.

"That's John," says Ellen. "He and his brother James were among the twelve apostles. But they had their issues. The Bible tells how they were ambitious, how they wanted special insider privileges with Jesus, how the other apostles resented them. John and James even picked up the nickname, which I suspect wasn't meant to be flattering, of "The Sons of Thunder."

I'm silent.

"So there you have it, Wil. A crook, a coward, an outsider, and one with self-serving ambitions. Quite a crew, wouldn't you say?"

I don't get it. "I thought they only put saints and people who lived perfect lives up in windows like that."

"Not at all, Wil. These are very imperfect people, some who messed up big time, some who had a lot to feel bad about, but they overcame it all because they got to know Jesus."

"But that's not enough to be a saint, is it?"

"Oh, those guys are saints for sure. You see, Wil, what this church is about is that everyone gets a second chance with God. And a third and a fourth one too if they need it. It's about realizing that we have all screwed up, many of us over and over again. But with God, you get to start over, if you choose to—get to be made new. Saint Paul, who had his own issues, said it's like being a new creation."

I'm quiet, unable to say anything, fighting hard to hold it together. I'm aware that my eyes are misty and I need to blow my nose.

Then Ellen steps a bit closer to me and says, "Wil, it looks to me like you're carrying the weight of the world on your shoulders."

That's all it takes for the flood gates to open. The tears I had experienced beside Sally's car return. Then huge wracking sobs. My mind is overwhelmed with images too great and awful to bear. Of wildfires sweeping down toward the homes of innocent people. Of my parents looking helpless as I sank deeper and deeper into the darkness. Of Sally's face that night I kissed her. Of that empty car and her things spread across the dirt.

Ellen puts a hand on my shoulder, and it feels comforting. I want to tell her everything, but the sobs do not let up enough for me to speak.

"It's okay to let it out here, Wil," she says gently.

Chapter 45

"Nine point three. This is it." Lander's been watching the odometer since we turned north onto Forest Road 1277. He angles the Eurovan onto the pine-needle carpet between second-growth white pines.

"Thanks for bringing me, Lander. I don't know what I'd have done without you."

Lander looks down and is quiet for a moment, but then takes a deep breath, pulls a compass out of his pocket, and holds it up for me to see. "Okay, so here's what you need to do. Lake Warren is about four miles in, and you'll come right out to it if you keep on a forty-degree bearing. That's northeast." I've used a compass before, so this isn't a new experience for me.

He hands me the compass, an old plastic Boy Scout model, with a long shoelace as a lanyard. "Yeah, I know it's pretty beat up," he says, "but it works. Just don't lose that baby or you'll be wandering around in these woods until you run into Sasquatch."

We laugh at that, which is much needed, given the solemn nature of why we're here. Then we're quiet while I lift my pack onto my back. Lander says, "So when do you want me to pick you up?"

"I'm not sure," I confess. "Sally and I made it in and out on a day trip, so that's what I'm aiming for. But I'm prepared to spend the night, if I have to. I'd call you when I got out, if there were any cell reception out here, so I say pick me up tomorrow about this time. If I get out early, I'll just camp here. I've got plenty of food and water." Well, I do have plenty of water, and I have a water filter. I can refill my Nalgene bottles at Lake Warren. But the food supply is maybe too modest. Two of Lander's chicken-salad sandwiches, several more Clif bars, and some fruit that Lander retrieved from Danny's.

I notice that Lander's eyes are misty, and I give him a little punch on the shoulder.

"I'm gonna be praying," he says, "that you find Sally."

I nod. Deacon Ellen said the same thing last night after I told her everything.

Lander shrugs, then climbs into the Eurovan, backs out from underneath the white pines, and rumbles down the gravel road, leaving a cloud of dust behind him. Then it's quiet.

I check the compass, now hanging around my neck from the shoelace, find the forty-degree bearing, then head into the woods. It feels good to be doing something, even if it's futile. I've got to keep moving. If I stop, I might just fall apart again.

Bushwhacking is even more challenging than I remember. But last week I had Sally's distractingly sexy legs leading the way ahead of me. The tree tops form an almost opaque canopy overhead, limiting the sunlight, and the understory of rocks, fallen branches, and thick patches of thorny ground vegetation makes every step difficult. I try to remember what Sally said these plants are called, but I'm drawing a blank. Every twenty yards or so, I check my bearings on the compass, pick a landmark—a particular tree or rock ahead—go for that, then check my bearings again. This is necessary because it's impossible to see more than fifty yards in any direction through the dense foliage. I'm well aware that if I lose my way, I could be in real trouble. And if there's even a sliver of a chance that I can find Sally, if there's any hope at all that she's alive, then my successful navigation is essential.

I've been going for a good hour, slower than I'd like. Lander said the lake is four miles in from the road, and it feels like I've gone maybe a couple, maybe not that much. I stop for a breather and drop my pack from my shoulders and lean it against a tree trunk. The trees whisper above me, stirred by a soft breeze. Otherwise, it's completely quiet and still.

I eat one of the sandwiches, take a swig from my bottle, and try to admire the beauty of these woods. But I cannot obliterate the recurring image of Sally's car out behind Norstaad's cabin, and despite my determination not to think about it, I am tormented by thoughts about what might have happened there. Did masked attackers like I faced meet her there? Tears threaten to return. I let out a long sigh, then a loud shriek, which feels good. Then I bellow out a stream of obscenities at the top of my voice and kick the trunk of a nearby tree as hard as I can.

Something moves in the trees beyond me. I come to a sudden stop and listen, my eyes glued on the place where I'm certain something moved. It could have been a deer; most likely it was. Sally said these woods are full of whitetails. I shoulder my pack, check the compass and continue on through the dense woods.

I've got to keep my mind focused on the job at hand. I try singing a song, but that doesn't last long. Never have been much of a singer. I try to retrieve some old physics problem that I once solved and discipline my mind to concentrate on this. I return to the classical mechanics problem of calculating the motion of a spinning top, a popular and intricate problem for physics students. The details require some pretty complicated equations, so I confine myself to outlining in my mind the steps required to solve the problem. This seems to help. When you're thrown in the lake, you look for a dock to swim to. Physics has often been my dock.

Another half-hour passes. I stop for another breather. I've got to be over half-way to Lake Warren. As I take a swig from my water bottle, I hear a sound, this time behind me, and I spin. Nothing is there. I'm certain that I heard something—footsteps shuffling through dry leaves—and it was something large.

Chapter 46

Now I'm spooked. Normally, I would discount what I heard as some animal or just my imagination. But too much has happened to me in the past few days. Threatening things that I don't understand. Now it is quiet. Although I can swear I hear my heart pounding.

Sure, it could be a deer, but a deer wouldn't be so loud, would it? A bear? Perhaps. A man? Could I have been followed? Could it be the men who attacked me in Houghton?

I reach down for the compass to check my bearings. My fingers grasp the shoelace and run along its length down to where the compass hangs and then slip off the frayed ends of the shoelace. The compass is gone. I look down to check, but I see only the ends of the shoelace dangling from my neck. The compass must have come loose when I spun to check out the noise behind me. "Stay calm," I say out loud, but already I feel the old breathing difficulties beginning.

The compass has to be nearby. I stand in place and survey the ground around me. The compass, a shiny plastic, should be easy to spot against the rusty pine needles. But I don't see it. I've got to think this through and not panic. I unshoulder my pack and lower it to the ground right where I stand, so that I'll be able to return to this spot. After all, this is still the most likely place for the compass to be. Then I begin a systematic sweep around the area.

An hour later, now one o'clock by my Timex, I abandon the sweep. I collapse to the ground near my backpack and hang my head. I must accept the fact that the compass is gone and that I am sunk. I try to judge the position of the sun, but through the dense foliage of the trees it's just not possible.

What now? It's best to stay right here, I conclude. When I lost the compass, I was on the route to Lake Warren. If I launch out without the compass, I will almost certainly wander off the route. Lander said he would be back tomorrow morning. When he finds I'm not there, he'll come looking for me. Won't he? Of course, I took his compass, so he'll have to find another one if he's going to head into the woods. Most likely, he'll conclude that something's wrong and he'll notify the police. So even if I'm found, that that will be the end of the story, the end of my search for Sally.

I'm lost.

I force my mind to return to the problem of the motion of the spinning top and breathe deeply. I remember a funny line we all learned in our classical mechanics class: *The polhode rolls on the herpolhode without slipping in the invariable plane.* We students used to get a great laugh out of these silly words. The polhode and herpolhode are actually mathematical curves that describe the path that the surface of an elliptical top will follow as it spins. That's not so funny—or I suspect for most people even very interesting—but right now it provides some comic distraction that I desperately need. *The polhode rolls on the herpolhode without slipping in the invariable plane.* I stand and say it out loud. "The polhode rolls on the herpolhode without slipping in the invariable plane." Now I shout it out. "The polhode rolls on the herpolhode without slipping in the invariable plane." Over and over again I shout it. Then I put it to music—to the melody of "Oh! Susanna," I think—even adding some accompaniment with my air banjo.

Now I'm quiet, and I'm aware of the stillness around me. Whatever was thrashing around earlier is also now quiet. Maybe waiting. It's strange how we react to quiet. Often we long for it, travel great distances to find it. I love quiet. In the city, there is seldom quiet. Sirens, a blaring radio, banging garbage cans, loud voices, the constant white-noise-din of the distant freeway.

But the quiet here, at this moment, is choking me. It's like the absence of oxygen. The cry of a crow, the scuffling of a squirrel would be welcomed, not to mention the cheerful morning chatter and clinking cups at Starbucks, which I always find soothing. This quiet doesn't allow pretense, it doesn't allow you to forget. It strips away everything. My own sounds, my silly preoccupation with old physics problems, my chattering, my keeping busy—these fail to mask the heaviness of the silence. I hear only my breathing, which heightens the awareness of how utterly alone I am.

I scoop up a handful of pine needles and study them. The long golden needles of the white pines are soft and smooth. They are a part of this quiet scene, like a bed the trees have prepared for a tired world.

I wasn't one of those passionate kids who always knew what he wanted to be—a fireman, or an astronaut or a scientist. My parents, especially my dad, are quiet people. They never pushed me. They encouraged me to do whatever I wanted. Unfortunately, I didn't know what I wanted.

In college I was an undeclared major in my sophomore year, pretty much drifting through school. It was there, when I was taking introductory physics courses, that I ran into Ned Kelly, who was teaching physics to undergrads. At one time, he'd been a big-gun research scientist at Fermilab. And it was through him that I discovered myself.

Ned Kelly pushed, mentored, and encouraged me into physics. By the middle of my junior year I had dived into physics head first. It was his influence that got me into the excellent grad department at UCLA.

I can see him now, on those afternoons in his office. "Or …" he would say, pushing his frameless glasses back up onto his nose and gazing up at the whiteboard filled with our scribbling of equations and diagrams from the past two hours. Ned Kelly was old and bent over, yes, and his white hair was thin, but when he got started talking about physics, he became energetic and animated. "Or … maybe you could solve it this way."

That would initiate another hour of furious scribbling. We each held a marker and would madly write down our approaches, often in opposition, like duelists fencing, with magic markers instead of swords.

I guess this is what got me started down the path of alternate solutions, which helped me to milk all the beauty out of a physics problem. Ned Kelly saw this as a strength, the hallmark of a creative, thoughtful scientist. An essential part of exploration.

Unfortunately, the professors who administered the exams at UCLA most often did not. One of them once said to me that, while it's great to explore all the beautiful scenic side roads of a physics problem, it is important—not just important but essential—to find the direct route toward its solution. "Physics is about results, not scenery. It's about solutions, not appreciation. Go be an art major if that's what you want."

But I just couldn't help myself. To me, physics is all about beauty. As one scientist wrote, "After all, music is nothing more than vibrations in the air." I guess when it comes to physics, I love the music more than quantifying the vibrations. And I make no apology for that.

Take the laws of electromagnetism. When some look upon the elegant equations describing electromagnetism, they see them as a mathematical tool. Yet, these four simple-looking equations are much more than that. Maxwell's equations, as they are called (after the great Scottish mathematician James Clerk Maxwell) are a thing of beauty. More than a tool.

I see them now, scrawled upon a page in my mind. I know them by heart. Just to gaze upon them is to gaze upon beauty. I recall a T-shirt that one student wore back in grad school. At the top it read, "And God said let there be light...." In the middle were the four Maxwell equations. And following those, the shirt completed the thought with "... and there was light." Yes, there is something almost holy about these things.

The Maxwell equations themselves are simple in appearance. Misleadingly so. Because the solutions of these four equations for most real-world problems involving electromagnetism are very difficult and can keep a smart grad student at work for days.

Is this how life is?

In principle, straightforward: be good, work hard, treat others fairly, follow the golden rule and all that, love, share, laugh, stop and smell the roses, make memories, don't forget to smile, have a goal.

But actually living life isn't so simple, is it? At least it hasn't been for me.

I stroke the white-pine needles in my hand. They are moist from recent rain showers, unlike the summer pine needles in the mountains of southern California.

It was back when I was at UCLA, back during that time I was getting ready for that weeklong battery of all-day exams—the written qualifiers—back when Ron and I were doing a lot of backpacking. I don't remember what day it was, but I needed a break, so I took an afternoon off and went camping by myself up in the San Gabriel Mountains, a high range that runs along the northern edge of the L.A. basin. It was a quick getaway—just an overnighter—that promised to clear my head and calm the anxieties that were already building about the qualifiers.

I found a good campsite in a forest-service campground up in the Angeles National Forest and got there in time to cook dinner on my camp stove. I had a campfire that night, as the temperature was dipping down into the thirties. I slept well, like I always did up in the mountains, but in the morning there was a layer of frost on my tent. I was shivering like crazy, so I threw a couple of logs into the concrete fire ring, got a warming blaze going, then began taking the tent down and getting my gear into the car.

I had an eleven o'clock quantum mechanics class back at UCLA, so I had to hurry. Once the car was packed, I spent a few more minutes around the fire, then doused it. Recreating that scene in my mind as if living through those moments again might change the outcome, I see myself spreading those coals so that they would cool, then sloshing water thoroughly over them until they were dark. My big mistake was not staying around to verify that the coals were cold before I left.

It was the next day when the police came to my door. They told me that a wildfire, now out of control, had started from a campsite they had traced to me from the registration form I'd filled out at the campground entrance. Then they arrested me. I hadn't even known about a wildfire until the cops told me.

My dad had to come down to the L.A. County Jail and bail me out. That night my face was plastered all over the local TV news. But that wasn't the worst of it. By the time the fire was out, it had burned almost ten thousand acres of prime forest. That's an area about four miles long by four miles wide. Worst of all, the fire had jumped from my campground over a ridge into Ponderosa Canyon and burned several homes. People could have been killed, and it's a miracle, for want of a better word, that all the residents were evacuated safely.

Much of what occurred during that time is just a blur to me now. But I've never been able to forget one event, no matter how hard I tried. The night my dad made my bail, I was watching the end of some TV show with my parents when a teaser for the upcoming news at ten popped up on the screen. There was a photograph of me, a shot taken as I was being led, handcuffed, into the jail. I'm giving the camera a frightened look, but on the tube I look like some psychopath. The caption under the photo reads, "Is this the face of a monster?" Even now I tremble when I remember that moment. That picture and that caption are engraved in my mind. Is that the image that Joe Gerlach saw in his Google search?

I scoop up another handful of pine needles. I note how the white-pine needles emanate from the branch in bundles of five—fascicles I believe Sally called them. These moist needles are safe from monsters like me. They will not be nutrition for the insatiable appetite of fire. I close my fingers tightly around the needles and look off into the thick woods around me.

Eventually my case came to trial, and I was convicted of a misdemeanor, which carried a fine of a thousand dollars (which my folks had to pay) and a hundred hours of community service work. I was lucky, the judge said. The fact that I had set the fire in an authorized fire ring kept it from being a felony, which would have meant a serious jail term.

The main thing I remember from the community-service work was picking up trash along the six lanes of the Santa Monica Freeway, ingesting the exhaust from a million cars and being leered at, and sometimes shouted at, by passersby.

The qualifiers came during that time, and I went ahead and took them. Big mistake, but I was trying to get my life back together and waiting another year to take the qualifiers would have just made things worse. Or so I thought. The tests were a disaster. Yes, it's true that my odd-ball problem-solving tendencies would have made the qualifiers hard enough, but that wasn't the real reason I flunked.

Driven by guilt, I was in full-blown depression and on antidepressants, seeing a therapist that my mom had set me up with. This went on for a year, during which I dropped out of grad school at UCLA—that's putting it nicely—and moved back in with my parents. It was the darkest time of my life. I would never be the same again.

Lander said he would pray for me. So did Deacon Ellen. I wonder what that really means. Talk to God? Isn't that just someone talking to the self? Having a conversation inside your own head and convincing yourself that some all-powerful being somewhere in the far corner of the universe is actually listening in? That this all-powerful being, the custodian over trillions of stars, is just sitting there waiting for some nobody in White Pine, Wisconsin, to check in? This seems ludicrous to me, but Lander and Deacon Ellen do not seem like ludicrous people who would be suckered in by a bunch of superstitious mumbo-jumbo.

So what would it be like to pray? Do I just say something and assume God will pick up the phone? *Hey God, this is Wil Weathers. Yeah, you know, the one who's been quite a mess, the one who has fallen short of just about everybody's expectations, the one who has no clue about the future. What, you've never heard of Wil Weathers? And you call yourself God? Okay, I understand. You probably do have more important things to worry about than helping out some loser, who, through his own stupidity, finds himself lost in the woods. In more ways than one.*

Even as I chuckle out loud at my clever cynicism, I feel my eyes tearing up again. The pine needles are still in my hand. I stroke them with my thumb, like someone would stroke prayer beads.

My phone rings. I jump, then lunge for my pack, where the phone's stashed away in an outside pocket. It's Starla. The phone shows one bar of signal here. I swipe the Accept tab, but there's no one on the line. The one bar has gone to no bars, and now it says NO SERVICE. Damn! I walk around in circles, hold my phone high overhead, but there's no signal anywhere. I don't take my eyes off the phone for another twenty minutes, waiting for the one bar to pop back up.

I'm just about to put my phone back into my pack when I notice the Utilities folder on my home screen. I tap it and it opens. There in the folder is the compass app. I had completely forgotten this was there. I wonder if it will work with no data plan. I tap the icon and a compass face pops up. In moments I have a working compass.

Hallelujah, I am back in business, I practically sing to myself. I notice, however, that my phone has only about a twenty-percent charge. No time to lose. I shoulder my pack and head off toward forty degrees.

Chapter 47

It's three o'clock when I emerge from the woods onto the shore of Lake Warren with great relief and a nearly dead phone. My euphoria at finding the compass app is short-lived. Although I cannot ignore the beauty of this small gem of a lake, this is a sad place today, a location that only heightens my awareness of Sally's disappearance and the grim prospects ahead. Without her enthusiasm, her stories of her parents and her love of the wilderness that brightened our time here just a week ago, I won't pause long. I see no loons today. They are gone too.

It's getting late, but I sit for a while anyway as a wave of hopelessness washes over me. Lander said that there is always hope. But what does that really mean? Someone once told me that the definition of hope is confidence built upon a promise. Maybe that's the way Lander sees it. But for me hope is no more than desperation, an unrealistic clinging to fantasy. It is self-delusion.

That year following my departure from UCLA is now a fog. Day after day, I would sit at my folks' home, in my bedroom or watching TV. Since my days back in Ned Kelly's office, sparring at the whiteboard over quantum-mechanical tunneling and Bose statistics and other tasty morsels, I had assumed my path would lead on through grad school to the acquisition of my Ph.D., and then into an exciting research career like Ned Kelly had at Fermilab. But that was not to be. A little thing like an overnight camping trip can change the course of one's life forever.

My parents were patient with me, and I really appreciate that, although I don't recall ever thanking them. My only requirement was a weekly visit to the therapist, a visit that usually consisted of adjusting my dose of Prozac. Slowly, I did get better, but the antidepressants took their toll. I had very few emotional valleys, like I had after the arrest and after I bombed the qualifiers, but I also had very few peaks. Life was numbness.

And yet, six months later, I was slowly emerging from the darkness. My therapist was weaning me off the antidepressants and had cut my dosage down to a quarter of what it had been.

Then Ned Kelly called and told me about the physics department at UWM, how they were looking for someone to teach physics to non-majors, how he thought of me. Would I be interested? Maybe he had seen my picture on TV or heard about my situation somewhere. He never said.

I said no, I wasn't interested. Good Lord, I wasn't really interested in anything. But with Ned, my therapist, and my parents all urging me to take the job, I finally said yes.

Through Ned Kelly's connections at UWM, and apparently based on his glowing recommendations, I was offered a job as a lecturer in the physics department. Because I didn't have a Ph.D., the usual requirement for university teaching, I would be hired on a one-year renewable contract, with no path toward tenure.

I wasn't enthusiastic about it at all, but in retrospect, it was one of the best things I ever did.

Those years at UWM were good. I kept busy doing my job, and I loved it. Slowly I crawled up out of the pit of depression. I didn't have much of a social life for a long time, and in fact, Megan was the first woman I was seriously involved with since before the fire.

I never told Megan about the fire. It wouldn't have been easy to tell her. But now I'm not sure she would have cared, one way or the other. She never was very interested in my past. And no one knew about it at UWM either, except the department chair.

With Sally, it's different. It's important that she knows. At some point I will have to tell her, if she's .... Even though it will mean she'll never talk to me again. I wonder if she would look at me and see the face of a monster.

Maybe I should have a bumper sticker on my car: "I don't just hug trees, I burn them down."

Enough of this. After a swig of water, an apple, and a bite from one of the Clif bars, I'm on my way, following the shoreline around the left side of the lake toward its headwaters. The bog lies ahead, and I'll be more careful this time. There is no one here to pull me out. I'd like to say that I remember the way around the bog, but I don't. Before crossing the small creek at the far side of the lake, the place where Lander fishes for brook trout, I locate a sturdy fallen branch that I can use as a probe and, if need be, a lever to push my way out of the muck. Taking one careful step at a time, then probing with the branch, I slowly make my way around the bog, like a soldier working his way through a mine field. At the far edge of the bog, I turn to appreciate my accomplishment, and for a moment I imagine that Sally is there, approving of my skills.

Ahead lie the rocky ridges we ascended on our way to the sentinels. It's now after five. Sunset is around seven, so I have a little over two hours of light left to reach my destination. I don't want to be climbing over these rocky outcrops, with their steep drop-offs, in the dark.

The late afternoon sunlight has turned these rocks golden. Photographers—like me, before I sold off all my Nikon stuff—refer to this time of day as the golden hours, that time of magical light, when everything glows. And up here in the northwoods wilderness, far from pollution and haze, the rocks and the trees seem to have a special radiance.

The route-finding is easier here, as the rocky terrain is open. I know I have to contour around and out onto the cliff edge, and there make my way for a mile or maybe two before cutting in toward the sentinels. Knowing where to cut in will be the difficult part, but I'm trusting that I will recognize the spot when I get there.

At the top of the first pitch, I stop for a breather and acknowledge how out of shape I am. I don't remember being so winded last week. That's the difference being with a pretty girl can make. I sit at the cliff edge, my feet dangling over the drop-off, which I estimate is at least a hundred feet, and take in the view while I catch my breath. Nothing but forest stretches before me for several miles. At least in this direction I see no signs of civilization. I hear the call of a raucous raven from somewhere far off, while high above me two vultures circle. If they're checking me out, they're wasting their time. I hope.

As I get up and ease my pack onto my shoulders, I see a motion back in the trees, or at least sense it. It's in the periphery of my vision, but I am certain that I saw something move. And though I can't be sure, I think it was something tall. I stay perfectly still, watching and waiting. If it's an animal, it may move again. But it doesn't.

I still carry the sturdy tree branch, which has been a useful walking stick as I've ascended the rocks. I clutch it more tightly now, realizing that it may become a weapon as well. After all I've been through already today, I take this pretty calmly. No hyperventilating. I need to make it into the sentinels, and I need to find my way there before dark. My sliver of hope for Sally depends on this, and if some assailant wants to confront me now, then I'm ready. It feels strange and good, this anger and determination that has replaced, at least for the moment, my fear.

The going is slow across the rocky cliff edges. There is no trail, so I have to carefully pick my way along. Several times I have to scramble up narrow cracks in steep portions of the rocks, as well as traverse narrow ledges, where a misstep could be fatal.

The sun has set, and a beautiful—but for me, melancholy—twilight stillness now settles over this world. The temperature has dropped with the sun, and I pull a fleece from my pack and slip it on. I'm not sure what to do next. The place to turn into the forest from the ledges could be anywhere along here. I'm certain that I'm close. If I could only remember some landmark, some identifying feature of where we cut in away from the cliffs before.

As I survey the evening shadows slowly spreading across the woods below, mother nature does me a big favor. I realize that the shadows I'm watching are actually the silhouettes of the trees behind the cliffs. One set of shadows stretches farther than the others. Could it be that these are the tall white pines, the sentinels? If so, the turnoff is just a short distance ahead, maybe a quarter mile. I pick up my pace and almost stumble but keep going. I'm almost there.

Immediately after turning in from the rocky escarpment, I'm enveloped in darkness and have to stop to let my eyes adjust. I have no flashlight, which would come in handy about now. As my eyes adjust, I become aware of shimmering shafts of moonlight scattering down through the dense pine canopy above me.

I continue on for several hundred yards, then stop. I'm in danger of becoming lost again if I wander too far away from ridges. I must be near the sentinels. This is probably as close as I am going to get tonight. I want to call out Sally's name, and I enjoy a brief fantasy of her answering my call. But I'm still concerned that I may have been followed, and the last thing I want to do now is signal my location.

I ease the backpack from my shoulders. This will be a good place to camp. I remove my tent from the back of my pack and unfold it. It pops together quickly, and even in the near darkness, I am able to latch the aluminum poles to the thin nylon fabric. In minutes my sleeping bag is stretched out inside my new home. I light my old WhisperLite backpacking stove and start a pot of water boiling for tea. I have no food to cook, but I'm not hungry anyway. I crouch beside the small stove, its sputtering the only sound in this quiet world.

From behind me I hear a shuffling and I jump to my feet, grab my branch and hold it like a spear, ready for an attack.

It's her. "Sally," I say. "Oh, Sally."

"You came." And then she's in my arms.

Chapter 48

There have been very few moments in my life like this: sheer joy like a flash of bright light dissolving the darkness of terror, rejection, uncertainty, and hopelessness. I know that a moment so transcendent is a mountaintop beyond which there will be only downhill and valleys and dark ravines. I savor this now, because I know I will never have it again.

And so it is, holding Sally in my arms. She is squishy in a puffy ski parka, with rays of moonlight—filtered through the pines—dancing off her hair, this girl I've known for only a week. She is alive.

We hold each other for a long time in silence, both of us shaking. Finally, I step back so I can see her face, holding her shoulders in my hands. "Are you okay?"

"Yes," she says. "I can't believe you're here. How did you find me?"

I take her hands, and we settle together onto the soft bed of pine needles, next to my camp stove. I brush her hair away from her eyes, now sparkling in the flickering light from the stove. Then I tell her everything, rattling it off in machine-gun fashion: finding my cell phone, my trip back to White Pine after learning of Norstaad's death, the run-in with the police, the solved riddle of *HOMES kill*, the attack in Houghton, how we found Norstaad's cabin and her car, how I came here as a last desperate attempt to find her. She listens intently, her eyes never leaving mine. "And when we found your car behind Norstaad's cabin, with all the doors open, we feared the worst. I just … I just … well, coming here was the only thing I knew to do."

"Oh dear God, Wil, I'm sorry for what you've gone through." She strokes my cheek with her hand. "Coming here was the only thing I knew to do, too. After you left, Mrs. Verlander told me about a car cruising slow past my house, then twice I saw it, too. A gray SUV. I tried to ignore it at first, rationalize that it was nothing. Then I heard about Sven's accident, which I knew was no accident, and I realized I had to do something. I decided to find Sven's house. Maybe there would be clues that—"

"You said you didn't know where he lived."

"After you left, I called Minji." I remember Minji mentioning that she had talked with Sally about me. "She said she remembered him babbling about Mackinaw Lake at one time, but she—"

"I ran into Minji up at MTU, she's—"

"Wonderful, right?"

"Uh, I guess." This isn't the time to share my doubts about Minji. But it's interesting that Minji told Sally where Norstaad's cabin is. Who else knew she'd be going there? She also told me about the Downtowner, and look what happened there.

"Minji didn't know where Mackinaw Lake is, but of course I did, being Warren Ladke's daughter and all." I hear that innocent childish laugh that I've missed and that seems so reassuring right now. "So I went. But after I'd been in the cabin for just a few minutes, I heard a car coming up the path.

From the window I saw that same SUV pull up. They must have been following me. So I ran out the back, where I had parked my car, grabbed what I could in a few seconds and hit the woods. Fortunately I had my GPS."

"Did you get a look at them?"

"They had ski masks on." No doubt the same guys I encountered in Houghton. "This is the only place I know where I am completely safe. I needed to figure out what to do next."

"Maybe I'm just paranoid, Sally, but I think I may have been followed here."

She moves into my arms, and I feel her shudder. "Did you see them?"

"No. I only saw movements in the woods. It could have been animals I suppose, but—"

"I'm scared, Wil. I'm not sure what we're up against." She grips me tighter.

I'm not sure either. "Apparently Norstaad thought there would be some kind of terrorist attack on the Great Lakes. Maybe that doesn't make sense, but somebody else obviously thought it did. They killed him before he could tell you about it."

Sally sighs. "And now they're trying to kill us."

Yes, but Sally is alive. That's the main thing at this moment. She is alive. "I think we're safe here," I say. "I don't think anyone could have followed me after I cut in from the ridges. Where are you camped?"

"Not far. I'll get my stuff and bring it over. I'm glad to see you have a tent. I didn't have time to grab mine. And you have a stove."

"Yes, but hardly any food, so—"

"I've got some freeze-dried meals that were in the stuff I grabbed." She laughs. "A piece of advice, Wil. When you're planning a backpacking trip, you really should take more than thirty seconds to prepare." I kiss her. Just one kiss. A quick one. A promise of things to come.

We put her sleeping bag next to mine in the tent, then open a pouch of freeze-dried beef burgundy and pour in some boiling water. We sit cross-legged on a small tarp around the stove, which puts out almost no light but provides a little warmth on this chilly night.

As our meal is ending, Sally says, "Why did you come back, Wil?"

There's just enough light flickering across her face to see her eyes. "I guess I was worried about you. I shouldn't have left before."

"I'm very glad you're here." She then leans over and kisses me delicately on the mouth.

"Sally, there are things I need to tell you." I pause, almost stumbling with my words. "Things about me."

"Are you married?"

"Oh no, it's nothing like—"

"Then later, Wil. I don't need to know anything else. Not now. For now, you being here is the only information I need."

I feel momentary relief, knowing I'm off the hook for a while longer. I didn't really want this confrontation now anyway. What I want instead is … well, I pull her into my arms and kiss her again. Her arms slip inside my fleece and encircle my waist. We break away, both of us breathing hard. Then I stand, extend a hand to her and lead her into the tent. It's just a two-man backpacking tent, low to the ground, so we have to kneel to get inside. Once inside, we tumble together onto the fluffy down bags. The kisses resume.

Suddenly she pushes me away.

"What?" I say, not wanting any interruption.

She's looking toward the opening in the tent. "I heard something."

"It's nothing," I say, then try to pull her back toward me.

She pushes me away again. "No, I'm sure I heard something." Her whisper carries urgency.

We both lie still. I hear it too, a soft crunching of footsteps drawing nearer. I feel like ice water has been poured down my spine. I jump from the tent and Sally is quickly beside me.

There is something, a person, coming toward us. I look around for my branch spear, but don't see it.

"Who are you?" calls out Sally while clutching my arm in a vice grip.

The person approaches. I can now make out shaggy hair backlit by streaks of moonlight. He's tall. Whoever it is says nothing, but continues toward us slowly. The situation feels menacing. I glance around us for indications of others circling in from behind.

There is now no more than thirty feet between us. I step in front of Sally, who peeks around my shoulder. "Stop where you are," I bark, with an attempt at an authoritative voice. The person keeps coming.

"Oh my God," Sally gasps and clutches my arm tighter.

I don't take my eyes off the intruder, who continues to approach us. "What?" I breathe to Sally.

"Oh God," she gasps again. "It's Sven."

Chapter 49

Sally's fear has caused her to hallucinate. I'm certain of that. The shadowy figure, still so enshrouded in shadows that I cannot yet tell if it's a man or a woman, stops just ten feet away and remains still. "Who are you?" I ask, trying to sound in control. The figure makes no sound, doesn't move. It doesn't seem poised to attack us, although this could be a diversion, while killers move in from the darkness. I keep turning my head, my eyes probing the night for others.

"Sven," says Sally.

No answer.

Now Sally steps in front of me. "Sven," she says again.

A soft, gravelly male voice says, "You need to fix it."

"Fix what, Sven?" Sally is speaking with an artificially calm voice, like you'd use to talk someone down off a window ledge.

The man is silent again.

"Would you like to sit down?" I ask. Silly thing to say, since there's nowhere to sit. But he doesn't make a sound.

"He's like that," Sally whispers to me, still clutching my arm. "You have to wait him out."

My God, maybe this really is Sven Norstaad, I think.

The moonlight is now full upon him, and I can make out a gaunt and ruddy face, disheveled hair. He wears a plaid shirt, like the one the man in the bushes had. He must be cold. He looks straight ahead, as if in a trance.

"We thought you were dead," Sally finally says.

This seems to get the man's attention. "Good," he says.

"Are you … are you … really Sven Norstaad?" I ask.

"I used to be," he says, then chuckles a low growl, like this is funny.

Sally says, "Are you hungry, Sven? We have some food."

"I take care of myself."

Sally takes a step toward Norstaad. "Sven, tell us what's going on."

More silence. Off in the distance I hear an owl, the only sound.

Then Sven looks at her and begins to speak. "They tried to kill me." Another low cackle. "But it didn't work." Then he looks toward me, and even in the dim light I feel his piercing eyes on me. "You," he says. "Wil Weathers."

My flesh crawls as he says my name. "Were you the man who grabbed my ankle in the bushes?"

I see the flashing of his teeth—a smile I think. "You saved me."

"I what?"

He seems more lucid now. "They chased me down before I could get to Ladke. Three of them. I had to get to her. She has to fix it." He goes silent for another moment, then says, "When you came, they had dragged me into the bushes. They had knives." He laughs again, deep and throaty, and says, "But I'm a wild animal."

"Three of them?"

"The unholy Trinity." He chuckles at this. "I killed one of them. One ran away when you showed up. The other was there, would have finished me off. But you came." The eyes I saw in the bushes.

"I thought you were dead," says Sally.

"I've been dead for a long time." Then he looks at Sally and says, "You must fix it, Ladke. HOMES kill."

"Kill the Great Lakes, Sven? Is that what you mean?"

"It depends on you, Ladke. You're the one who can fix it."

"I don't understand, Sven," Sally admits.

He looks back at me. "Did you see your picture?"

"What picture are you—" Suddenly the pieces come together. Norstaad is the one who broke into the church and took my phone and pack. He's the one who used my phone to call Sally, he's the one who returned my phone, he's the one who took the picture that's on my phone.

"You're the one who brought my phone back? Why?"

Again the deep laugh, which sounds more like a series of grunts.

So Norstaad broke into my apartment. That also explains why he bought new tires—to make the drive to Milwaukee. "Why?" I ask again.

"It worked, didn't it? You're here. You help her fix it. Now show her the picture."

I pull out my phone. The battery is nearly dead, but I'm able to bring up the strange picture of the green lake. "You took this?" I ask. I'm amazed that someone who's been off the grid for twenty years would be able to take a photograph with an iPhone.

"Show Ladke," he says.

I hold the phone so Sally can see it. She looks at the photo, then looks back to Sven. "Cyanobacteria," she says. "That's ugly, but what's the big deal?"

"They're going to kill the lakes. You must fix it, Ladke."

"Sven," Sally says, "You're not making sense now." She blows out a loud breath of frustration. "They're going to harm the Great Lakes with cyanobacteria?"

"HOMES kill," Norstaad says again.

"What's cyanobacteria?" I ask.

"Blue-green algae," Sally says to me, without taking her eyes off Norstaad. "That doesn't make any sense, Sven, and you should know that. Cyanobacteria have only a limited viability in the Great Lakes. Parts of Erie, yes, but the cold water and lack of nutrients always limit it to—"

"I know all that, Ladke. This is different. HOMES kill."

Sally turns to me and whispers, "He can be so ... so ... he makes me want to scream." Then she looks back to Norstaad and says, more emphatically than before, "Sven, you know that—"

"You must fix it. You and Ethan Ross. You are the ones. But he's gone. So take Weathers."

I recall the disturbing articles about blue-green algae that I saw outside Ethan Ross's office at Michigan Tech.

"Sven, you've got to tell me more," Sally says, but Norstaad has gone quiet again.

I take another tack. "How did you find this lake?"

Norstaad turns his eyes toward me again, but it seems like he's looking right past me. I spin and look behind me, but nothing's there. I repeat, "How did you find the contaminated lake?"

Now he looks me in the eye, like he's just become aware that I'm there. "How did you find the contaminated lake?" I ask again.

"I smelled it," he says.

"Where is this lake, Sven?" Sally asks.

No answer.

"Why haven't you told the authorities, Sven?"

"There are no authorities," Norstaad snaps.

Sally shrugs, obviously exasperated. "So who's doing this, Sven?"

Norstaad's eyes widen, like he's seen something terrifying. "The QUEEN always takes the PAWN."

"What do you know about QUEEN?" I ask him.

"The QUEEN always takes the PAWN."

I turn to Sally. "What do *you* know about QUEEN?" She's never mentioned this before.

She shakes her head. "I didn't know it really existed. There were posters around town, but everyone thought it was just some crazy quack, not anything real."

"How do you know it's QUEEN?" I ask Norstaad.

"They followed me. They left their name on my door. I had to leave."

"Who are they?" I ask.

"They are the darkness. They followed me. They are still following me." Another moment of lucidity seems to be occurring. "That's why I couldn't come to see you again." He's quiet for another moment, then says, "It depends on you, Ladke." Norstaad begins to edge away toward the shadows.

"Wait," I call out. "If you're alive, then who died in your truck?"

He stops and looks at me. "No one died in my truck." He gives me a sly smile. "He's the one I killed in the bushes. I put him in my truck, set it on fire. Maybe they'll think I died, stop following me." He cackles again. "Cost me my truck and my damn ring. Hated that truck anyway. But I miss the ring."

It all makes sense. "But of course," he adds, "I've been dead for years." Well, not all of it makes sense.

Sally interjects, "Sven, we can't do this by ourselves. We need your help."

"You will fix it," he says, looking first at Sally, then at me. "I'm dead." Then he turns and disappears into the darkness.

Chapter 50

Sally looks at me and lets out a big sigh of frustration. She slowly shakes her head, but says nothing.

"So that was Sven Norstaad," I say. "I'm glad he's alive, but he is scary."

"Like I've told you, he may be crazy, but he is a genius."

"Yeah, but he's hardly a guy who gets to the point. Must have been a heck of a teacher." Then I add, "So he's the one who broke into the church?"

"Checking you out, I guess. Nice that there's someone worrying about the guys I hang out with." She giggles, and it calms me to hear her laugh in the midst of what we're dealing with. It obviously hasn't hit her yet. I have a sense that I will need this memory of her laughter to sustain me in the days ahead.

We stand there quietly for a while, letting the enormity of what Sven has told us sink in. Then Sally says, "I'm getting cold." Without words we climb back into the tent and snuggle down, both fully clothed, into our bags.

I lie on my back next to her. Moonlight now streams down through the thin yellow nylon of the tent fabric, filling the inside with a warm glow. I shift over onto my side to face her, leaning up on an elbow. "Sally, tell me about what Norstaad said. Is it possible to kill the Great Lakes with algae?

That seems so ... far-fetched." I remember Ethan Ross's colleague, the fish guy, and his skepticism about an algae threat.

She is on her side facing me. She's so close I feel her warm, moist breath against my face, and I want to kiss her again, even in this deadly serious situation.

"I suspect it is possible," she says, "but I don't know how probable it is. There are several technical issues involved."

So here I am in the woods alone with a beautiful woman on a moonlit night, and we're having a technical discussion. Leave it to two nerdy scientists.

"Like what?" I ask.

"I think the main challenge would be to find a toxic algae that could survive a low-nutrient and cold-water environment like most of the Lakes present."

"And that's why the algae blooms in Lake Erie never spread farther."

Sally runs a hand slowly along my cheek. "You've been doing some research. I'm impressed."

"I just saw some articles outside Ethan Ross's office, when I went up to Houghton."

"Anyway, yes, it is possible to cause great harm to the Lakes. But I don't really know how possible. Apparently Sven thinks this QUEEN has found a way to do it. There are so many varieties of blue-green algae—actually, they're not algae, but bacteria—and frankly there's still a lot that's not known about them. New strains are being discovered all the time."

Her face is bathed in the soft golden glow, and I'm wondering why we're having this discussion. "How bad could it be? Wouldn't it just be a nuisance, like in Lake Erie?"

"Oh, no. When Sven says 'kill the Lakes,' I think he means it. You realize, of course, that the Great Lakes hold over 80 percent of the fresh water in North America and over 20 percent of the fresh water in the world, so destroying them would have global impact."

"But how could algae destroy the Lakes?"

"There's a whole list of ways: it could ruin drinking water, make the Lakes unsafe for recreation, damage aquatic life, destroy the fishing industry, and make the Lakes unusable to farmers. Not to mention the aesthetic impact. There are about sixty million people who live around them. I don't know much about economics, but the impact would be enormous. This would be a catastrophe."

"Is this stuff really poisonous?"

"There are certain species of cyanobacteria that are very toxic. I don't want to bore you with the details, but two types can be especially bad: certain species of *Microcystis*, which contain toxins that damage the liver, and some species of *Anabaena*, which attack the nervous system. I've seen reports about farm animals that have ingested just a small amount of *Microcystis* and died violently in an hour. Apparently it's fast and painful."

"Have people been killed?"

"I think most people are so grossed out by the smell and taste and general yuckiness of the algae that they don't want to get near the stuff. Ethan Ross would know more about that, but I do know there was a man down in Madison, who fell into an *Anabaena*-infested pond and died."

"So you studied algae up at Michigan Tech?"

"I studied environmental threats in general, but I did spend some time looking at blue-green algae."

Now we're quiet.

Then Sally says, "What do you think we should do, Wil?"

There's a first. Sally asking me what to do. The freshwater ecologist, the one who knows about cyanobacteria, the one who bounces around comfortably in the woods without getting lost or falling into bogs, the one who Norstaad says will fix it, whatever "it" is. She's asking me what to do? Well, it turns out that I've already been thinking about what we should do.

"I think we head out in the morning. Lander will be waiting for us. Then we go straight to the cops, tell them the whole story. It sounds like something very criminal is going on. Plus, we need to clear my name, so that every guy with a gun—and that's a lot of folks up here—isn't looking to take a shot at me."

Sally nods. "I agree. We go there first. Even if I'm not sure Sven has got his facts straight. But I'm worried that fast action is going to be required. The urgency in Sven's voice, the determination of these people to silence us. Wil, we need to find that lake, find out why Sven thinks there will be an attack on the Great Lakes, as crazy as that sounds. And if there is something like that brewing, we've got to stop it."

That's not what I'm thinking at all. We should inform the police and let them take care of it, while we get ourselves to a safe place. Maybe Sally will come with me to Milwaukee until all this blows over. Sure, Sally is a qualified technical resource and she'll be needed to consult with the authorities, but I say let's do that at a safe distance. Skype's just as good as being there. Bottom line, Sally is safe. I want to keep it that way. But I know that Sally won't buy into this.

So I say, "Fifteen thousand lakes in Wisconsin? And most of them, I suspect, looking pretty much like the one in my picture. Time to call in the pros to handle this, I'd say."

"Sven says we're the ones who'll fix it. But I ..." Her voice trails off and she turns away from me. I think she's crying. I lay an arm across her. Even through her thick down bag, I can feel her heaving sobs.

Then she turns back toward me, lifts her arms from her bag and puts them around my neck and looks into my face. There's enough filtered moonlight in the tent to see her tears. She sniffles, then wipes both eyes with the backs of her hands. She's done crying. "I don't mean to be a crybaby," she says, "but I get very emotional when I think about anybody harming the environment."

I stiffen as I imagine Joe Gerlach talking with her. *Sally did you know about Wil? What he did back in California? How he was arrested and convicted for starting a fire in the national forest that burned ten thousand acres of trees? A real monster, if you ask me.* I've got to tell her, tell her before Joe does. Even though this will mean the end. I just can't do it now.

Chapter 51

The White Pine County Sheriff's Department is located a block south of Main Street, just behind the Ace Hardware, in a nondescript one-story stucco building painted an institutional gray. After Lander dropped us off in front of Mrs. Grabowski's garage, we got my car and came straight here without even going inside to see Hazel.

Inside the sheriff's office, a receptionist behind a wide window beams when she sees us. "Hey, Sally, how goes it?"

"Fine, Ruth. We need to see the Sheriff, if he's in."

"I'm afraid Sheriff Tom is over at a conference in Green Bay for the next couple days. Darby's here though." *Well, we're off to a great start here*, I think.

"Sure," says Sally. She flashes me an it-will-be-okay look. "That'll be fine."

Darby sits at one of the three desks in the office area behind the receptionist's window. Just as I could have predicted, he's got his feet up on the desk. When he sees us, he jumps up. "Sally," he blurts out. He comes around the desk and stands close to her. "You're okay." He then shoots me a confused look. "And I see you've brought him in." He reaches for the handcuffs on his belt.

"Hold it Darby," Sally says, "Wil's with me." She lays a hand gently on my arm. Darby frowns, and you can tell he liked it better when I was a dangerous drifter. He shrugs and asks us to sit down. Sally and I tell him the whole story.

Darby probably should be taking notes, but he isn't. He listens to us with a dropped jaw, as if struggling to absorb it all. "You say there were three guys who attacked this Norstaad guy? And then two guys jumped Weathers up in Houghton, and you think the same two tried to attack you, Sally?" He doesn't look at me. "Did you get a good look at them? Do you know who they were?"

"Like I said, Darby, they had ski masks on. They weren't polite enough to leave their business cards."

"You're not giving me a whole lot to work with here. What we really need is—"

"What we really need is for you to take this seriously!" Sally has risen halfway out of her chair.

Darby seems to finally sense her impatience. "Okay, okay, settle down, and—"

"We are settled down, Darby. We need some action."

"Sure, there'll be action. Just trying to get the facts sorted out. I'll notify the Houghton department, and we'll compare notes on this. Weathers, you said there was a guy in Houghton who saw the attackers?" Darby finally pulls out his small notepad and, after rummaging around in the top drawer of his desk, comes up with a pencil.

"A guy named Lucas Tanner," I say. "Don't know where he lives, but he works at the Downtowner Lounge. Should be easy to find him."

"Okay, got it. We'll be—"

"But that's not the main thing, Darby," interrupts Sally. "Like I told you, Sven Norstaad didn't—"

"Yeah, he didn't really die, he faked his death. So we'll need to talk to him too. And just where might we find Mr. Norstaad?" He raises his pencil likes he's waiting for our answer.

"We don't know, but—"

"You don't know. Dammit, Sally, can't you see that you're—"

"Darby, just be quiet and listen for a minute." Sally leans forward and glowers at Darby. Everyone is now quiet. Then Sally continues. "The main point is that someone is going to use toxic blue-green algae to contaminate, maybe destroy, the Great Lakes."

"Yeah, I heard you say that," says Darby. He puts down his notepad and leans forward. "And just where do we find these villains?"

"We don't know," Sally says, "but they're apparently preparing the algae in a lake around here somewhere."

I show Darby the photo from my phone. He lets out a big sigh. "I've got to say, I'm having a little problem with all this. You come in here and tell me that somebody is going to destroy the world with algae?" Now he stands and paces in a little circle behind his desk. "Look, Sally, I respect you and all that, you know that. But sometimes your save-the-planet crap just goes too far. FYI, this is a sheriff's department. We have real problems to deal with here—people and property to protect. We can't be off chasing through the woods looking for some guy growing pond scum." Now he stops behind his desk, leans forward with both palms on the desk, and looks hard at Sally and then at me. "And even if we cared about this pond scum, which I'm not sure anybody does, we only have the word of some guy, who's supposed to be dead, who you met wandering around in the woods at night." Now he throws his hands into the air.

Sally stands, and so I do. "So the sheriff's office refuses to help?"

"No, Sally, the sheriff's office is going to help. We're going to look into those attacks. We'll get to the bottom of this. That's our job. And, by the way, I suggest you lie low for a while, until this all settles down. And Weathers, for what it's worth …" He looks down for a moment and sighs. "… I'm glad you helped Sally, but I'm still not clear on what you're doing hanging around here. I'll make sure the APB gets stopped, but life would probably be better if you just decided to head back down to the big city."

Outside, Sally turns to me and growls. "Grrr … I could just wring his neck." I'd be happy to give her a hand. Then she says, "We should go to the DNR. They're going to need to know about this. But until we can tell them where the lake is, that's probably not going to be any more effective than what we just went through." Now her angry eyes soften. "Wil, it looks like it's up to you and me."

Just like Norstaad said, it's going to be up to us to fix it. But it seems a lot more likely that it will fix us first.

Chapter 52

We sit around Sally's kitchen table with mugs of coffee in front of us—a deceptively peaceful scene. We've left my car behind the church, just in case the gray SUV is cruising the neighborhood, which it probably will be. I've moved my stuff back into the dormer room on Sally's top floor. My laptop is up and connected into Sally's wireless. We've locked the doors.

I'm happy to strategize with Sally about our next steps, but with the goal of accumulating enough evidence that we have something credible to turn over to the authorities. It would be foolish for us to try to take down a violent criminal gang by ourselves, which is what I fear she may be gearing up for.

"Other than Norstaad's fears, why do we think the blue-green algae is a real threat?" I ask. "Sure, there are some hoodlums chasing us, but maybe it's more like pot farmers shooting at intruders. A crime, yes, but not really a threat to the world." Truth is, I don't know much more about blue-green algae than Darby.

"Well, for the most part there is no threat from blue-green algae. You can find it almost everywhere," says Sally. "Darby's right in a way. Most of it is just harmless ugly pond scum. A nuisance, but hardly dangerous. In fact, there are some blue-greens, like spirulina, that are good for you. People use it as a nutritional supplement. High in protein. There are farmers who actually grow spirulina and press it into tablets. But I don't recommend we have it for supper. It's really smelly and tastes disgusting." She makes a face.

"How do we know that what Norstaad saw wasn't just somebody growing spirulina?"

"Well, I have to believe that Sven could tell the difference. But in any case, if someone was just growing nutritional supplements, I don't see why they'd try to kill Sven because he saw it, and then try to kill us."

I sigh. Sally has on that Isle Royale National Park T-shirt she wore the day she picked me up in Florence. Not sure I noticed then how tight-fitting it is around her curvy figure.

"Now we have to find that lake," she says.

I shrug. "There are thousands of lakes around here. And what do we have to go on? A photograph that could be one of a thousand—" I stop suddenly, as Sally's and my eyes lock. "Are you thinking what I'm thinking?"

Sally jumps up and rubs her palms together in excitement. "Geotagging. Your phone geotags all your photos, doesn't it?"

I pull out my phone and bring up the photo. Then my heart sinks as I remember that the GPS was turned off during the time the phone was stolen. I don't want to tell Sally the embarrassing story about me falling for Del Behrens's silly lecture on identity theft, so I just lay the phone on the table and shake my head slowly. "My phone's location services were turned off. I'm afraid there was no geotagging."

We sag, then Sally laughs. "That would have been too easy anyway."

"Yeah, but now we're at the end of the line."

She nods slowly, then we're both quiet for a while. We're both pacing her kitchen now, too antsy to sit. Then Sally sits again, and stares at the floor. She's either in deep thought or she's dejected about our apparent dead end.

We need a respite, so I say, "Tell me about Isle Royale National Park. I've never been there."

Sally looks up at me and smiles, obviously aware of what I'm trying to do. "It's a beautiful place, a wilderness island in the middle of Lake Superior. And I'm not surprised you've never been there—most people haven't. It's the least visited national park in the country."

"What's so special about it?" Not that I'm so interested in a tour-book summary of scenic destinations right now—I'm just trying to lighten things up a bit.

"It's a pristine wilderness, isolated from mainland development. It even has a population of wolves and moose."

I nod with appreciation and try to keep the conversation going for a while. "Wolves and moose? Is there enough food on an island for them to survive?"

Sally now stands and walks slowly to the refrigerator, but doesn't open it. She leans her forehead against the refrigerator door and taps her fist softly against the metal surface. She's clearly not very interested in this conversation right now. But she humors me nonetheless. She turns toward me, but she looks at the floor. She says, with her mind elsewhere, "Well, the wolves and moose are starving over there, actually. But I guess there's enough for them to survive."

She gives me an idea. Not an idea, really, but a question that I think might help us. I walk toward her, until our faces are just inches apart. "Okay, let's say you were trying to grow blue-green algae. What does it take for it to survive?"

Her eyes now meet mine, and I can see the wheels turning. "You need to provide nutrients."

"What kind of nutrients?"

"Mainly phosphorus. The reason the blooms in Lake Erie initially thrived was because of the fertilizer runoffs into the lake."

"But you said last night that they are probably trying to develop a strain of algae that would thrive in a low-nutrient environment, like Lake Superior."

She nods, pondering this for a moment. "That's correct, but I suspect you'd probably want to start the algae off in a nutrient-rich environment, before beginning to reduce the nutrient level."

Then I see something click inside Sally. She licks her lips, then steps back away from me. She says, "Maybe we're not at the end of the line, after all." She smiles and crosses her arms like she's about to present the winning argument in a courtroom case. "I was just thinking about the Bible study last week. Do you remember Ed talking about his delivery?"

"Yes. Sacks of fertilizer, as I recall."

"He said it was chemical fertilizer. Fifty bags. Farmers buy that stuff in bulk, not in bags. Who would be purchasing bags of fertilizer, and who would be needing that much?"

She's on to something. I say, "You're thinking someone was using the fertilizer to grow algae?"

"I'm guessing it was ammonium phosphate. It's often used because it's high in nitrogen, but it's also very high in phosphorus. Phosphorus, the breakfast of champions for blue-green algae." Sally now paces around the room in quick nervous steps.

"And didn't Ed say he dropped off his deliveries out in the boonies somewhere?" I ask.

"That's right, and that would make sense. The bad guys purchase the fertilizer, but have Ed deliver it to some remote spot so they won't be seen. Then they pick it up—they'd get it in bags so they could easily do that—and take it to the lake. Probably ordered it over the phone, so—"

"So they may have used a credit card. Bingo!"

Sally stops her pacing, puts her hands on her hips and faces me. "Perhaps. But also if we can find out where Ed dropped the fertilizer, we may find a road that leads to the general vicinity of the lake. So with that info and the approximate size of the lake from your photo, we may have this problem nailed."

I nod my approval. "I think it's time to go find Ed."

Chapter 53

Darby said there had been a wolf sighting near Ed's place, and I must admit that Ed lives in the kind of country where a wolf might hang out. A mile north of town, off a county road, a painted sign proclaims "Ed's place" at the entrance to a long gravel drive leading back into a large lot backed by thick woods. At the rear of the lot sits a double-wide, which I'm guessing is Ed and Tracy's home. A small building sits nearer to the front, and this seems to be where Ed runs his business. And his business seems to be about a lot of things. Sharing the real estate around the building are several large bins of scrap metal, a long rack of propane tanks, various kinds of lumber piled in more or less random patterns, several snowmobiles in various stages of teardown, and a big John Deere tractor. There are no cars, and it's pretty clear that no one's here. Ed's no doubt out making one of his deliveries. "Let's go see Tracy," says Sally. "She'll know where Ed is."

The former Northwoods State Bank is a grim, gray, all-business-looking building, but inside, where Irene's Hair and Nails now occupies the first floor, life is anything but grim or gray. At a glass counter, a stylishly-dressed young woman converses with one of the customers. She looks about as New York as I suspect anyone in White Pine ever does. Behind her, extending to the rear wall, four of the six stainless-and-vinyl salon chairs are occupied. Track lighting illuminates wallpaper designed to look like the peeling paint on an Italian villa. The place has the clean fragrance of an aromatic shampoo. There is a lively chatter in the air, the kind of energy that reminds me of my Starbucks mornings.

Tracy's at the last chair near the back, sweeping up hair from around her area. When she sees Sally, she drops her broom, runs up to her and explodes in sobs. "Oh, God, Sally, he's gone."

"What, Tracy?"

"Ed's left me." She collapses into Sally's arm. After a few more sobs, she says, "Took off yesterday and never came back. We had a fight the night before, and I said some things. I wish I hadn't ..." She can't finish the thought before more sobs come.

Sally continues to hold Tracy. Sally, the dependable caregiver. Seems like everyone needs her.

Tracy starts to regain her composure. She steps back, runs a hand through her hair, and looks around at the other customers, as if to say everything's okay now. She turns back to Sally. "He took his truck, left in the morning, but never came back."

"Do you know where he went?" Sally says, one hand on Tracy's shoulder.

"I've got my suspicions. He had a girlfriend in Duluth before we met. I bet he's gone to see her. Oh, God," she shrieks. The sobs threaten to return.

"He said he was leaving you?"

"That's what's so awful, Sally. He didn't say nothing. He covered it well. Cold-blooded really. Makes it hurt even worse. Said he was goin' out to make deliveries." Her words come gushing out. "I was totally unsuspecting. He always calls me from his cell, no matter where he is, during the day. But he didn't yesterday. And when I tried to call him, there was no answer. God, Sally, I'm so sorry I yelled at him."

Sally and I exchange glances.

Sally turns back to Tracy. "Maybe he didn't leave you, Tracy. Maybe he broke down somewhere, maybe—"

"He would've called. And if there'd been an accident, somebody would have found him by now. That big red flatbed ain't easy to miss. No, he left."

I interrupt. "Do you know what kind of deliveries he was making yesterday?"

Tracy looks at me for the first time. Her cheeks are streaked with black mascara. Her eyes are bloodshot. "No, not really. I don't pay much attention to that stuff."

"He mentioned at Bible study last week that he sometimes delivers bags of fertilizer. Could it have been—"

"Maybe, maybe not," she interrupts. "Like I said, I don't pay attention to stuff like that."

"I know this is hard," I say, "but if we knew where his deliveries were, then we might know where to look for—"

"He didn't go on his deliveries! He left me. Didn't you hear me? He left me!" Her voice is now almost at the screaming level.

Sally asks, "Have you contacted the police?"

"What's the point? He's left me. He's just—"

"Now, Tracy, we don't know for a fact that he's left you. I think you should tell the police he's missing."

Tracy looks at us goggle-eyed. "I guess so. I've just been so upset about this, I didn't know what to do."

After Sally has given Tracy more words of reassurance and at least two more hugs, she and Tracy call the police. We leave only after Sally has extracted a promise from Tracy that she will keep us informed if she hears from Ed. Out in front of the old bank building, Sally says to me, "Do you think Ed's disappearance might be tied up with this mess?" The golden-hours light of the late afternoon gives her face a warm radiance.

She's clearly thinking what I'm thinking. "It's possible," I say, "that Ed is off in Duluth frolicking with the old girlfriend. But it's also possible that Ed was delivering chemicals that are being used to grow blue-green algae, and he got just a little too close to the action for his own good." In any case, we will now have to proceed not knowing where Ed's drop-off point was.

Chapter 54

Back at Sally's house, we pace around her kitchen, nervously munching on bread and cheese she has set out for lunch.

Sally stops and shakes her head, while blowing out a frustrated breath. "I can't believe Sven would warn us about this mess, then not give us any hint about how to find the lake."

I have an idea. "Sally, you were telling me that spirulina is really smelly, right?"

Sally nods.

"Are all blue-green algae smelly?"

"I suspect most of them are. Why?"

"Do you remember that Norstaad said he smelled that contaminated lake?"

"Sure."

"Maybe that was his convoluted way of telling us where the lake is. What way does the prevailing wind blow around here?"

"Hmm … usually from the southwest."

"Look, Norstaad seems crazy to me, but he was smart enough to break into my apartment in Milwaukee, and he found us in the woods. And he figured out how to use an iPhone, even though he's been off the grid for two decades. I have to believe he wouldn't tell us to fix it without giving us some kind of information. So I'm thinking that lake may be southwest from Norstaad's cabin."

"Nice try, Wil, but how do you know he was at his cabin when he smelled it?"

"I actually have a good answer for that. Sure, Norstaad had a car, which means he could have been anywhere. But I suspect he seldom used it. The tire salesman in Iron River said his old tires hadn't been made for years. That tells me he seldom drove. Sure, maybe up to Houghton once in a while, but I'm guessing that's about it. Plus which, he said he hated his truck. Now, he did drive to Milwaukee. My theory is, that's probably why he bought the new tires. And we know that Norstaad is capable of walking great distances. I mean, he made it to the sentinels, didn't he? Still, I'd say the most likely place he smelled the contaminated lake is from his cabin. And if that's true, the lake is probably more or less southwest from his cabin."

Sally stands across the table from me, hands on her hips, looking at me like I'm some kind of superhero. "I must say, Wil, you are pretty clever at figuring out stuff. I can see why you teach physics." She pauses, then says, "Come to think of it, did you take more time off from your work to come back up here?"

I look into Sally's earnest face, and I must come clean. If I'd told her up front about my job, it would have been no big deal. But now it feels like a big lie has been uncovered. "Sally, I didn't tell you last week, but I got laid off at the end of last semester. A funding shortfall. So I'm ..." I stop there, as I see a hurt look come over her. I feel like crap. I look down.

"I don't understand, Wil. You led me to believe that you were teaching. Why didn't you tell me?" Her eyes wash over me like searchlights, scouring my face for some understanding.

I can't look her in the eye. I seem to have not learned an important lesson in life. It's one thing to have a misfortune or a screw-up. That's bad enough. But in my life, at least, the shame caused by those screw-ups has often caused more harm than the screw-ups themselves. "I don't have a good excuse. I guess I thought I'd never see you again. I ... I ... I was ashamed."

"You should have told me, Wil. You shouldn't feel ashamed." She stands and paces around the kitchen, stopping at the window to gaze out onto the front yard. She is silent for a while. Then she returns and takes her seat across from me.

"Look at me, Wil," she says. "You came back to find me. You didn't have to, but you did. That tells me more about you than any fear you might have had about me knowing you lost your job. It's okay." She extends her hand and rests it on mine. "Now about that lake."

This woman is amazing. But then she hasn't heard the bombshell yet. The really big news that the man whose hand she is caressing has probably harmed the environment more than QUEEN ever will, a man some have called a monster.

I fight my way back to the present moment. "Yes, about that lake," I say. "The other piece of data we have is the photograph."

"Okay, so what else can we learn from that picture?"

"Well, the photo gives us some idea of how big the lake is and maybe what its shape is." I send the photo to my laptop. Sally comes around next to me, resting her hand gently on my shoulder, as I bring the photo up.

The photo, now magnified on the laptop screen, is out of focus. Still, it's incredible that Norstaad, who'd probably never seen a cell phone before, could have figured out how to take a picture with my iPhone. We stare at the screen in silence for several minutes, looking for clues. It's a relatively small lake. Perhaps a half-mile across. The shoreline is lined with maples and oaks in various stages of turning color. The lake surface is a brilliant iridescent green, almost yellowish. The far side of the lake looks to be a slightly lighter hue, but that could just be the sunlight. It looks unnatural, creepy. "Can you tell what kind of algae it is?" I ask.

"Afraid not. Cyanobacteria can take on different colors, depending on the local conditions. You need some lab equipment to make a positive ID."

"So the authorities will have to get a sample and take it to a lab?"

"Not really. I'd rather look at this stuff at high magnification, like with an SEM." Gotta say, I find it a little sexy to be with a girl who knows what a scanning electron microscope is. Then she says, "But I have an optical field microscope, right over there under my desk. It will do just fine." She sees my amazement, then laughs, "Don't you always carry a microscope with you on hiking trips, Wil?" Even more sexy.

She's obviously thinking that we'll hunt for the lake ourselves instead of handing our ideas off to the authorities and heading for safety in Milwaukee. "So once the lake is found, you can tell if the algae is the bad kind?"

"Perhaps. There are many types of algae, and I'm guessing the best I can do is narrow it down to a few different possibilities. Like I said, it's probably some form of *Microcystis* or *Anabaena.*

"After you ID the algae, how do you get rid of it?"

"That's a problem for the DNR. But it isn't easy. People use a number of techniques to kill algae, but none of them works perfectly. And frankly, some of the remedies can be almost as hazardous as the algae, as far as toxicity."

We turn our attention back to the photograph. I examine the far shoreline carefully to try to determine the shape of the lake, but can't really tell much.

"Let's pull up Google Earth," I say, "and find the location of Norstaad's cabin. Draw a line to the southwest from there and look for lakes that are about the size of the one in the picture." With a few clicks we bring up a satellite image of northern Wisconsin and zoom in to the region west of White Pine, roughly where Mackinaw Lake is located. The satellite view shows a huge expanse of green conifer forests, interlaced with patches of golden yellow. Apparently the satellite photos were taken in the fall, which could be a break for us, as there was some fall color in Norstaad's picture. Dozens of tiny blue lakes dot the view. "I'm not sure which one is Mackinaw, sorry to say."

"Here, let me look." Sally nudges in closer and moves her hand over the mouse, brushing mine slowly as she does. "It'll be hard to spot. Out of those fifteen thousand lakes we like to brag about, I'm guessing half of them are right in our part of the state." She pulls out her GPS and taps a couple of buttons. "I put in the coordinates when I was there. Here it is," she says. Then she enters the coordinates into Google Earth, and the view shifts, then zooms in to a small round lake. *This is pretty cool,* I think.

The detail is amazing, yet the tree cover is so heavy I cannot make out Norstaad's cabin or the trail leading into the cabin. "Sven's house would be right about here," she says, pointing to one side of the lake. Then she zooms out on the image so that we're viewing a region that is probably a few miles square. "Okay, let's try your theory, Wil." We pan down toward the southwest, where the terrain is peppered with lakes.

We look for a lake that's about a half-mile across and is probably more-or-less round in shape and has deciduous trees around the shore. Too bad these satellite photos were probably shot before the lake was contaminated. Recent photos would have made the lake easy to spot.

After several minutes, we conclude that three lakes fit our requirements. None of them has a name, and none of them appears to be connected to a road, although we know that narrow roads aren't visible due to the tree cover. Sally right-clicks the mouse on each of the three lakes, which brings up its longitude and latitude. Then she enters these coordinates into her GPS. "So, we've got three lakes to explore. Let's start at Sven's cabin and try to hike to these lakes. That's probably what he did."

I turn toward her. "Sally, we're getting in over our heads on this. I say we turn this information over to the police or the DNR and let them track down the lakes."

"No." She shakes her head violently. "You know as well as I do that they won't take action based on our flimsy evidence. We've got to do this ourselves."

"But Sally, I can't let you—"

Sally places a hand across my mouth. Not harshly, but gently. "First of all, Wil, who gave you the authority to *let* me do anything?" She sighs, as I cringe. Poor choice of words on my part. But then she adds, "I know you're thinking about me, Wil, and I'm touched by that. But this is too important to ignore. I say we just scout things out, keep our eyes open, make sure we're not followed. Then we take our proof to the authorities."

I'm not going to change her mind about this. And I'm not going to let her go it alone. "Okay," I say. "Let's leave first thing in the morning."

"I think we have a plan, Wil." She raises a palm toward me for a high-five. "Not bad," she says, "for a couple of unemployed scientists."

"Yes," I say, "but let's go see Lander on the way out of town and give him the coordinates of those lakes. Just in case...." I don't finish the sentence. I don't need to. Just in case we run into the people who are trying to kill us.

Chapter 55

Darkness has fallen over White Pine, and here I am, staying at Sally's house again. After all we've already been through, you'd think it would be more comfortable. There's clearly a romantic connection between us, and it's hard to keep my mind from pondering the possibilities for the evening. I suspect it's the same for Sally. I'm not sure what might have happened last night in the tent if Norstaad hadn't shown up when he did. Things were certainly headed in a direction that my mind has returned to several times during this day.

But tonight's different. We're facing something terrifying and dangerous, with implications and consequences that are so great, it's hard to get my mind around them.

I'll sleep in my dormer room tonight, and that's okay; as drawn to this woman as I am, I am also in awe of her character. And it makes me want to rise to a new level. To be a better person than I have been. To take more risks. To be more bold. To be more honest. Honest. I guess that's the main reason I'll sleep in the dormer room. I can't allow this relationship to progress any further until I tell her. And of course that will be the end. I'll tell her when all this is over. But there's no way I can tell her tonight.

Chapter 56

Fortunately, a corner booth is open at Danny's, and I steer us in that direction, feeling on edge about another encounter with Joe Gerlach. Sally and I both order the German potato pancakes, something that will stick to our ribs for the big day ahead of us. Sally wears a white, long-sleeve shirt under that pink Patagonia vest she wore last week when she took me to the sentinels, and heavy long hiking pants, perfect for serious bushwhacking.

The usual high-energy good vibes are in full force at Danny's, but they don't seem to be rubbing off on us. There is a cloud over our morning, especially for Sally, and I'm worried about her. I sense her somber determination, even as she tries to be light and cheery.

I lay a hand on hers and say, "Let's hope we find out that this threat isn't real."

Sally grimaces, then sighs. "I guess there's no way to know for sure. I'm certain this is no hoax; nor is it a case of Sven not knowing what he's talking about. I am a hundred percent confident in his judgment, even though I don't understand it most of the time. So, yes. I think it's real, and it scares me half to death."

"You said that most blue-green algae can't survive the colder waters and the lack of nutrients they would have to endure in the bigger parts of the lakes, but that maybe some algae could survive with reduced nutrients. Say more."

"Not much is known about this, but there are some troubling signs. I've been following an NOAA study—that's the National Oceanic and Atmospheric Administration—that's trying to understand why *Microcystis* seems to continue to thrive in places like Lake Erie even after the nutrient levels have been reduced. There seem to be indications that some algae have a genetic makeup that allows it to naturally adapt to reduced nutrient levels."

I take a sip of coffee. "That's pretty scary."

"We're going to find out soon enough." Then her worried demeanor softens. "What I do know is that I'm glad you're here."

I give her a silent nod that says "me too."

Just then, Lander appears at our table. "Good morning, you guys," he beams. "You wanted to see me? Danny's got me covered for fifteen minutes. What's up?" He slides into the booth next to me. He's wearing a white apron over his black T-shirt. I again notice the tattoo of a leaping trout on his right arm. There's a caption under the trout that I can't make out.

"First of all, we want you to have these coordinates." Sally hands Lander a slip of paper that contains the GPS information plus a printout from Google Earth showing the three lakes. "These are the lakes we're going to check out today. We're hoping one of them is the contaminated lake."

Lander leans forward, then whispers with urgency, "Look, you guys, I'm not feeling good about this. You both almost got yourselves killed already this week. Seems to me you could be walking right into a trap here."

"We plan to be careful and stealthy," I say, then pause to take another sip of coffee to show my nonchalance. "We don't plan to do anything other than find the location of the contaminated lake and examine a water sample to verify Norstaad's claims." I lean back and cross my arms in a confident way. "Then we'll hand everything over to the authorities." I glance at Sally to be sure she's still buying into this. "You know as well as I do, Lander, that they won't do anything until we give them some hard evidence."

"You're starting in from Norstaad's place?"

"Yes, probably going cross-country from there," I say. "The lakes range from three to six miles away, so we should be home tonight."

Then Sally adds, "There's one more thing, Lander. We ran into Tracy yesterday. She's really upset. Could use some cheering up. I wonder if you might pop into Irene's and check up on her." It seems that Sally never stops thinking about others.

After we give Lander a good-bye hug, we head out to my Fiesta, parked right out front. I stop halfway to the curb. Leaning up against the front fender is Lucas Tanner.

Chapter 57

"Lucas, what are you doing here?" I ask.

"I hope it's okay," he says. "Officer Darby called me yesterday about the attack on you, and I gave him a description of the two men, best I could. Gotta say, glad to see you're doing okay, Wil, but you didn't need to run off like you did." He then looks at Sally and nods. After just a moment of hesitation, she nods back.

"I never got to ask you about the men. Did one of them have a shaved head and rimless glasses?" I ask.

"I didn't see them real well. But yes, maybe one of them did have a shaved head."

"What can we do for you, Lucas?" Sally asks.

"Officer Darby told me that Professor Norstaad is still alive and that he believes there is some kind of algae attack being planned. Once I got into White Pine, it wasn't hard to find you."

"Darby talks too much," Sally whispers to me.

"And so," Lucas continues, "if you're going out to hunt for a contaminated lake, I'm all in on that. Student of Ethan Ross, member of PAWN. How could I not be all over that? I do know something about cyanobacteria, so maybe I could be useful."

Sally says, "I'm not sure we need another—"

"I understand, but I thought it was worth a try." Lucas begins to back away. "Okay, so I'll see you—"

"I don't see what harm it could do," I say, looking at Sally and wondering why she might have reservations about this. Surely Lucas's expertise could only be an asset. "As a matter of fact, we were leaving right now to head out there."

Lucas stops. "I've got my stuff. Just have to get it out of the car. Do you have a microscope, Sally? I've got one in the car, and that could be useful in—"

"I've got one."

Lucas hurries back to an old Tercel and soon returns with a large pack. "Thanks for letting me tag along. I've been away from this stuff so long, it will feel really good to get back into the field."

Sally sighs as Lucas climbs into the back of the Fiesta, and the three of us head out. I don't know why she would be reluctant about Lucas going with us. I say there's strength in numbers, and Lucas's biology knowledge could come in handy to supplement Sally's. But Sally is quiet for now, looking straight ahead as we head west out US 2.

Chapter 58

Norstaad's cabin holds no pleasant memories for me. And I'm sure it doesn't for Sally either. We've left the Fiesta down at the clearing and walked up the rutted trail to the cabin, all the while remaining on the lookout for the gray SUV. The day is cool and sunny and calm. There's no wind that might send the smell of algae in our direction.

When we arrive at the cabin, Sally runs around to the rear to check on her car. I follow. She grabs the key and takes a few more items from her base camp, then locks the car. Sally is all business. No cheery laughter this morning. She checks her GPS, looks off into what appears to be impenetrable forest, and says, "It's that way."

"How do you know where the lake is?" Lucas asks.

I start to speak, but Sally cuts in. "It's complicated. We're not even really sure this is it. It's a shot in the dark." She then shoulders her pack, gives me a here-goes look, and strides toward the woods. Lucas and I follow behind.

If it weren't for Sally's GPS, I'd say we were lost. We struggle through dense understory for at least a mile, then come out into a huge stretch of maples and oaks. The going is easier here as we walk atop a brilliant carpet of red and gold leaves. I walk alongside Sally now, with Lucas bringing up the rear. "You seem uncomfortable having Lucas along," I say, keeping my voice low.

"It's just that we can't have anything compromise what we're trying to do."

"You have some reservations about Lucas?"

"I don't know, he's kind of weird. I never really got to know him very well. He always kept to himself. He was just part-time, although I heard he's brilliant."

"He's had some hard times in his family, I think."

"Yes, that probably explains a lot. He's about as animated today as I've ever seen him. And then there was the accident...." She trails off.

"Yeah, that was awful. I understand he was up on those logs with Jeff Yardley."

"It all happened after I left. What Minji's had to go through is terrible. You know she was Jeff's girlfriend."

"Yes. I'm sorry. Is that what caused PAWN to disband?"

"Oh yes. Things came apart quickly after that. PAWN died with Jeff."

"And Jeff's father …"

"Dennis. Used to be my friend. But I think he somehow holds me responsible for what happened to Jeff. Since the accident, he's really different. Losing a son must be the worst."

There's a sadness in Sally's voice now, and I decide I need to change the subject. "So what should we do when we find the lake?"

"I'll need to look at some samples, try to determine what we're dealing with, then see if there's any evidence that someone's intentionally growing this stuff. Then skedaddle without being seen and get our tails back to the DNR. And pray." She stops and looks at me. "Wil, this is really scary business." Her voice drops to a whisper. "And yes, I'd feel better if Lucas wasn't along. I'm sure he's fine, but I don't know him well enough to feel comfortable with him."

Then she goes up on tiptoes and kisses me softly on the lips. Lucas stops behind us, while the kissing continues, but Sally doesn't seem to care that he or anyone else might be watching. When she pulls away, her smile has returned. I touch my fingers to her cheek, and let them stay there for a few moments. I say nothing.

The going has become difficult again, as we enter a forest of second-growth white pines with a dense understory. After another two sweaty hours of making our way through this dark, trailless wilderness, we suddenly see light ahead. We are approaching a lake.

Ten yards from the edge of the trees we stop. "Let's be careful," Lucas whispers, sounding afraid for the first time. "We don't know who may be out there." We all nod, then move silently toward the shore. We stay close to the trees to avoid being seen.

There is no sign of human activity. As we step out onto a narrow rocky beach, Sally checks her GPS and pronounces, "This is the correct spot, but obviously the wrong lake." The water is a pristine blue; not a sign of algae anywhere.

"Where do we go next?" Lucas asks.

Sally's studying her map and cross-checking it with the GPS. "The next lake is another two miles. You guys need to take a break or should we keep going?"

"Keep going," Lucas and I say, almost in unison.

Sally nods and heads off around the shoreline.

Lucas walks beside me now. "I know Sally would rather I wasn't here," he says, "and I don't blame her."

I say nothing, and Lucas continues. "I'm sure she holds me responsible for Jeff's death, at least partially. Hell, I do too. If only I could have grabbed him."

"It was an accident, Lucas."

"Yeah," he says, unsatisfied. "It's just that I have to live with that every day."

"It must be hard." Then I try to shift the subject. "Tell me about your research with Ethan Ross. Don't think I heard you talk about that."

"Sure. I loved it. I wasn't a full-time student or anything. I had to work to make ends meet, and I didn't have a family to help me with tuition. Anyway, I heard one of Professor Ross's seminars on freshwater invasives, and he had me. I went and talked with him, and after he checked me out, he was willing to let me do some work in his lab."

"Working on invasives?"

"Blue-green algae, actually. He was quite into that."

"Yeah, I know. Sounds interesting."

"It was. While it lasted. Until I had to quit."

"So what do you think about the idea that someone could destroy the Great Lakes with blue-green algae?"

"I don't know. Far-fetched, I'd say. But if someone was determined and knew a thing or two about biology, then ..." He doesn't finish. We see light coming through the trees, indicating a break in the woods ahead.

"I think we're almost there," I say.

In moments we see another shoreline through the trees. We make the same stealthy approach as we did at the first lake. Seeing no indication of human presence, we step out onto the beach.

We are silent and breathless. Although the lake appeared fairly round in Norstaad's photo, we must have come out onto a small bay. From our vantage point, I'm guessing we can see only a third of the lake. I estimate the lake to be a half mile across. There is no sign of human activity. Yet there is no doubt that his is the lake from Norstaad's photo. All that we can see is covered in an iridescent scummy green. At the water's edge, the odor is intense. It's a musty, almost choking, smell that tests your gag reflex.

"What do you think?" I ask Sally.

"Dear God, it's even worse than I thought," she says.

Chapter 59

"Do you think it's the bad kind?" I ask.

"We're about to find out," she says. Sally drops her pack and pulls out a rugged aluminum case, from which she unpacks a microscope. She connects a battery pack and clips a light to the microscope stage. She places several plastic implements next to the microscope, then puts on latex gloves. While Lucas and I keep our eyes on the shoreline for any motion, Sally kneels at the water's edge. She leans out and scoops up some of the slime onto a spatula, then puts a dab onto a glass slide.

Our eyes now turn to Sally, as she studies the sample, shifting the slide left and right, then readjusts the focus. Finally, she stands and says, "It's pretty clearly *Microcystis* of some kind, but it's different from anything I've seen before. Lucas, why don't you take a look and see what you think."

While Lucas looks through the microscope, I photograph the lake from several angles with my iPhone. Finally, Lucas stands. Shaking his head, he says, "I agree. Some type of *Microcystis*. Are you going to collect a sample to take back, Sally?"

"Yes," she says. "Let's do that now." Lucas assists her in putting some samples in plastic jars. When Sally's finished, she says, "Now let's explore the lake a little more. I don't see any sign of human activity around here. If someone's farming this stuff, like Sven believes, there should be a facility here."

We make our way only a short distance around the lake before we see it.

Across the lake, no more than a couple of football fields away, sits a metal prefab building. Near the building, a long wooden pier extends into the lake. Radiating from the end of the pier are several wooden partitions that look as if they are separating different parts of the lake.

"A cocktail," Sally says.

"A cocktail?" I ask. As I look closer I can see that the slimes in the different sections of the lake are of slightly different hues.

"I suspect they may be growing different types of cyanobacteria in those different sections of the lake, for their different toxins. Blending them to maximize toxicity. I bet there's *Anabaena* out there too." Sally turns toward me. Her face is flushed with what looks like a mixture of despair and rage. She continues. "It produces toxins that attack the nervous system, and its effects can be ten-thousand times greater than the effects of cocaine."

Lucas jumps in here. "Yeah, this looks bad."

I look from face to face. "You guys are really scaring me now."

Lucas continues. "Not to make things worse, but there's evidence that ingesting an ounce of affected water would lead to a quick and painful death. Hemorrhaging, extreme pain, breathing failure, then the end. It's called the very-fast-death factor. I suspect we're dealing with that too." He puts his hands to the sides of his head, like he's overwhelmed. Then he adds, "Sally, do you think they might also be growing various cyanobacteria for different lake depths?"

"Yeah, maybe," she says, "like one variety that thrives in shallow water and another that thrives in deep water."

I'm still not satisfied. "But say they dump this crap in the Lakes. The lakes are vast. How would it ever spread?"

"Oh, several ways, actually," says Lucas. "First, the reproductive cysts of the cyanobacteria can become airborne, and with the prevailing winds from west to east across Lake Superior, which is where I suspect they'd plant it, they could easily spread."

Sally adds, "There's also the natural water currents in the lakes, which would move the algae toward the other lakes. And another factor—and it's a big one—is the shipping industry."

"Shipping industry?" I ask.

"Ballast water," she says. "When ships unload or take on cargo at a Great Lakes port, they usually pump in or discharge ballast water. That water provides a way for undesirable things to be spread all across the lakes, and—"

"Like zebra mussels," Lucas says. "We know exactly when they arrived at one spot on the Great Lakes back in the late eighties, in one freighter from Russia, but through ballast water exchanges from all the shipping within the lakes, the zebra mussels contaminated all the lakes in less than ten years."

"I saw a study that said that the invasion of zebra mussels and other invasive mollusks have cost our country over five billion dollars so far," says Sally.

"Now," adds Lucas, looking out upon the lake, "imagine something a thousand times worse."

I shake my head in disbelief. So Norstaad was right.

Lucas isn't finished yet. "There's one other way the cyanobacteria might spread. Some of them exhibit a property called gliding motility. Okay, technical words, but what they mean is that certain cyanobacteria can move under their own power. Not fast—maybe only a few centimeters per hour—and nobody knows for sure how they do that ... is that right, Sally?"

Sally nods slowly. "Yeah. Most of the studies I've seen are for motions on a solid surface, but there's reason to think they might move on a water-air interface also. When you study their motions in the lab, they seem to be pretty random, but it could be a mechanism for spreading. A few centimeters an hour can add up to a few kilometers over a year. Slow, but relentless."

So the blue-green algae can move under their own power. This sounds like some kind of sci-fi lunacy, but I'm hearing it from two scientists. "So there's no option," I say. "This operation has got to be stopped." *HOMES kill,* I think. *I couldn't have said it better.* "I say let's collect our samples and get out of here."

Lucas takes a step toward the buildings, then shades his eyes with his hand. "Have either of you got binoculars? I for one would like a closer look. We need as much information about this operation as we can get."

We don't have binoculars. "Let's keep our distance," I say. "These people won't just welcome us in for a cup of tea. At least not the kind of tea I want to drink." I begin to back away.

"We can move in a little more, but let's stay close to the trees," says Sally.

We edge toward the algae-production facility. Now I can see a web of horizontal racks, covered in green, near the building. Next to the racks are an open garage door in the side of the building and high stacks of plastic barrels, no doubt intended for transport. Three men are busy at work, tending their slimy green harvest.

"It looks like they're drying the algae," I say. "Doesn't that kill it?"

"Hardly," says Sally. "The drying causes the algae to produce cells that will protect it from adverse conditions. They're called akinetes. It's like the hard shell of a seed. Just what you need to survive transport in the back of a truck and a cold Lake Superior winter. I'm guessing they're compressing the dried algae into cakes inside that building, then preparing to ship them out in those barrels. Must have some generator power inside that building."

So far, my ignorance has protected me from the overwhelming reality of what we seem to be dealing with. But now I'm beginning to sense the distress that Sally and Lucas must be feeling. My eyes sweep across the area on the other side of the building. I see several vehicles. One is a gray Suburban. There are also several trucks, some partially loaded with the barrels. Apparently they are preparing to make their deadly shipment. One of the trucks is a red flatbed. A chill shoots through me. Ed.

I take several more pictures and some video. "Okay," I say, "let's get out of here." I look at Lucas and see he's staring at Sally, his mouth open in shock. I quickly turn to Sally and my heart nearly stops. Standing directly behind her is the man with the shaved head. Before any of us can react, he pulls a black cloth bag over her head and seizes her arms. My instinct is to lunge toward her, but before I can do anything, blackness comes down over my face and my arms are pulled roughly behind my back and confined. I cannot breathe.

Chapter 60

It's dark. I'm on the ground. There is cool dirt beneath me, that much I can tell. I feel the cloth constricting around my face. It's a heavy opaque material. I cannot see anything. Have I been unconscious?

My hands are secured behind my back. It feels like they may be wrapped in duct tape. There is complete silence. I scream, but I can tell the heavy cloth around my face is muffling the sound. It allows barely enough air for me to breathe. I try to move my body, but my ankles are also bound.

I saw the man with the shaved head take Sally, and I'm guessing the same thing has happened to me. Is she near me? I call her name, but I suspect that little sound makes it through the shroud around my head. And if she answered, would I hear her? I am able to roll, side over side, which I do. After no more than three rolls, I come up against a wall. It yields a bit as I bang into it. Thin metal. I roll in the other direction, and after no more than a half-dozen rolls I hit another thin metal wall. I conclude I'm in an enclosure no more than ten feet wide. Probably a tool shed.

So far, I've not allowed my mind to go wild with this. But now it does. *Where's Sally? Is she alive? Why couldn't I have saved her? Why haven't they killed me yet?* Panic threatens to overwhelm me, and I know I must not yield to that old enemy. I try to calm myself. I have no chance unless I can remain calm. *The polhode rolls on the herpolhode* ... That will do no good here. I scream again, but I only feel the hot blast of my breath reflected back on my face. I picture Deacon Ellen, standing before the four grumpy men, her hand on my shoulder, saying "It's okay, Wil. It's okay." This seems to help. I say those words softly over and over to myself, as if Deacon Ellen were right here to comfort me.

Why haven't they killed me yet? I've got to think this through. I must try to understand this. If I can, then I might have an idea of what to expect next, and if I have an idea of what to expect next, then I might be able to craft a plan. *Why haven't they killed me yet?*

I begin by reviewing what has just happened. While Lucas, Sally, and I were talking, we were attacked. My best guess is that Sally and Lucas are both imprisoned like me. So what are they going to do next? My mind is racing, but my thought processes are chaotic, driven by terror. I picture Deacon Ellen again, and I begin to calm once more.

I am certain they plan to kill us. After all, they attempted to kill Sven Norstaad, and the attack on me in Houghton seemed bent on doing me in—although those attackers did try to put a shroud over my head, like the one I'm trapped in right now. So maybe they only tried to kill me after I put up a good fight.

Oh, God. I want to weep. This isn't going anywhere. There is nothing I can do but wait until someone comes for me, and what happens then I'm guessing will make me wish they had killed me quickly.

I picture Sally. Sally, that beautiful girl, that brave girl. How is she doing right now? I try to project a thought to her—silliness, I know. But if there is anything to this psychic stuff that I have always ridiculed, then maybe she can hear me. *Sally*, I want to say, *don't be afraid. I'm okay and I'm with you. Sally, I want to be next to you right now. Even in this awful place, I want to be next to you. I want to hold you and make you feel safe. I want you to know that I love you.*

I let out another shriek and roll over again, thrashing like a dying fish on the deck.

Are you there God? It's Wil. I have no right to speak to you. I'm not even certain you exist. In fact, I tend to think you don't. But if you do exist, then maybe you're hearing me. Yes, me, just one of the seven billion humans, and not a very noteworthy one at that, on this tiny inconsequential speck of dust in the universe. But if you're there, God, I really need your help. I'm about to die, and I've let down every person I've ever known. But, God, if you're listening, please protect Sally. Do something, God. Please. This is desperate. Save Sally. Save Sally. Save … My prayer ends in sobs.

Then I hear something. There's something in the shed with me. I go rigid, lie perfectly still. *What is it?* Maybe I imagined—but no, there it is again. Maybe just mice. But no, it's something large. I think a person is in the shed with me. Are they coming for me already?

Then I feel a touch on my forearm, which is bent behind me, and I feel a tearing, a cutting. I tense up, but it's not flesh that's being cut. It's the tape that secures my hands. "Who are you?" I cry out into my heavy shroud, but I hear no response. Then it's quiet again.

I lie perfectly still, waiting for another sound. My hands are free. I rip the remaining tape from them and quickly pull the bag from my head. I'm still in complete darkness. There is no sign of anyone near me or in the dark quarters where I am confined.

I rip the tape from my ankles, and now I'm completely free. I stand on shaky legs, and feel around me.

I see a thin vertical sliver of light. It's from a door, slightly ajar, just a few feet away.

Perhaps this is a trap; I'm not certain. I'm not certain about anything right now. Beside the narrow opening I peer out. I see the lakeshore and the metal building not far away. Just beyond the building, several men work with rakes at the drying area. Next to the building are the vehicles. Maybe I could make it to one of them and escape. Unlikely. No one would leave a key in the ignition. Bad idea. I'm not sure what to do. Perhaps I could just stay here and wait until someone comes for me and jump him. But what about Sally? Every moment that passes, her chance for survival goes down.

Who cut me free? I'm sure it wasn't Lucas or Sally. They would have said something to me, and in any case, I'm certain they're still confined.

I push the door slowly open and step out into the light, which momentarily blinds me. Then I quickly dart behind the shed, out of sight from the building and the drying area where the men are working. I crouch behind the shed. Where are Sally and Lucas? They must be somewhere nearby. Is it possible to find them and free them? That's something that usually works in the movies, but I'm pretty sure anything I try now would be a long shot.

But I can't just remain here. I've got to do something. Then I feel something cold and metallic at the back of my neck. I've never felt anything like it before, but, even so, I know what it is: the barrel of a gun. I go rigid and instinctively raise my hands. The barrel pushes against me, and I step forward, out into the open space between the shed and the lake. Then a hard kick sends me to the ground. I come to my knees, but stay there as I look up into the face of Lucas Tanner.

Chapter 61

"Where's Sally?" I ask, as I rise to my feet, keeping my hands up.

Lucas says nothing.

"What's going on, Lucas?" I say.

Lucas's face is without expression. The sadness I had earlier seen in his eyes has been replaced by a lifeless, cold glaze. "I'm reshaping the world, Wil. And it's a good thing."

"Where's Sally?" I ask again.

"That's none of your business, Wil. But let's just say she's been undergoing a little interrogation. She knows a lot, Wil. Maybe too much. I've been trying to find out just how much. She knew how to find this place, and I must know how."

"I can tell you that, Lucas, so why don't you—"

"It doesn't matter anymore. We've moved beyond that point."

"Is she alive?"

"That's none of your business, Wil."

"Why haven't you killed me yet?"

"I'm not a killer, Wil." Lucas gives me an easy smile, but his eyes remain cold. "I'm a soldier. A good soldier doesn't kill just to kill. A good soldier kills when it is necessary, when it will serve the cause." He gazes out onto the lake. "A greater good, you might say."

A shaft of terror stabs me. I see where this is heading. He hasn't killed me and probably not Sally either, because he plans to kill us with the algae. Our poisoned corpses will help his cause, striking terror when they are found, a nice little appetizer before the full-blown devastation of the Lakes. The QUEEN always takes the PAWN.

"I'm sure you're enjoying your moment of glory, Lucas, but—"

"I'm not enjoying anything, Wil. I'm only doing what I need to do. My ability to enjoy anything ended when the extremists like Sally Ladke killed my father."

"How can you say that Sally had anything to do with your father's death? You said he died of a heart attack."

"My father had a mine. Out near Superior. He'd been a miner all his life, and his father before that. They'd gotten into taconite, Wil. You're a smart guy. You've probably heard of that. A nice source of iron ore. But they said my father was evil, that he was destroying the environment. But this country needs—"

"I'm sure your father wasn't evil, Lucas, and I'm sure he wouldn't want you to become evil."

"I'm just being faithful to him. My father was doing good for people, good for the economy. The extremists shut him down. Fifty people were out of work. My dad stayed up nights worrying about that. Then the heart attack came."

"So this is your response? Destroying millions of lives?"

"It's my way to fight back. I saw the opportunity at MTU, the chance to develop the tools I could use to ..." He looks out at the lake again, like a proud father pointing to his child. "To do this."

"If Professor Ross had any idea what you were—"

"Ross is another ivory-tower idealist. He never had a clue." A smile comes over Lucas' face.

"So you developed the cocktail, Lucas. That's a real contribution to—"

"Oh, it wasn't that hard, really. I recall you saying you're a physicist, Wil. So let me just say that what I've done isn't rocket science."

"But you're harming a lot of innocent people."

"Like Norstaad? Ladke? PAWN? You call them innocent? Look what people like that are doing to people who've worked this region for generations. They want to stick their noses in where they don't belong. They're always looking for a new cause, a new threat to work on. So I'll give them one. Sorry you've got to suffer, Wil, but it is for a greater good."

"So you infiltrated PAWN."

"It was so easy, Wil, that I'd have a hard time calling it infiltration."

"And you killed Jeff Yardley, maybe gave him a little push from the log pile?"

"Wil, you are a great guy, the kind of guy who could be my friend, but I think that's not going to be possible. Jeff Yardley was the kind of person who's ruining this country. Full of simplistic ideas. Thought he was doing good things, but ultimately believed he was superior to ordinary people— people who don't have a banker father, people like me. Let's just say I did the right thing." He's looking toward the lake, obviously getting impatient with me.

But I continue. "And then I'm betting you hit up Jeff's dad for funding for QUEEN. Exploited his grief, turned it into hatred for PAWN, which you convinced him was responsible for his son's death."

"Wil, you're a bright guy. Yeah, you and I could've been friends. You're not like the Sally Ladkes of the world, who want to preserve their sacred little forests and their endangered species while real people get hurt."

"I'm sorry about your father, Lucas. I'm sorry he suffered. But Lucas, what you're doing is wrong. You can't fix a hurt by hurting someone else, someone who—"

"Shut up, Wil. You've made some bad choices, and you're going to have to pay. Too bad, but that's the way it is. And I don't need to hear any of your sentimental moralizing. This country is headed in the wrong direction, a direction that is destroying what many people have worked for. What I'm doing will get their attention. Yes, people will be hurt, and that may seem like a tragedy to you. But it's simple economics. Terrible things have been done, and a price must be paid."

Lucas makes a sweeping gesture out to the lake. "Someday—and it won't be long—imagine the waterfronts at Chicago and Toronto looking and smelling like this." He pauses, as if to savor the idea. "Imagine the water unsafe to drink. Imagine the fishing industry gone. Imagine the beaches ruined. Imagine people afraid to go anywhere near these lakes. Yep, ingest a teaspoon of that beautiful froth and you die a painful death in thirty minutes." He steps closer to me, still a good ten feet away, and adds, "Imagine the whole world knowing that radicals like your friends brought it all upon themselves. Oh, don't look so sad, Wil, sometimes things have to get worse before they get better."

My mind is racing for a way out of this, but the panicky jumble that is my thought process right now comes up with nothing. So I keep talking. "Lucas, you're way off base. Sally hasn't—"

"Sorry to interrupt, Wil. I'm sure you think your words have a lot of merit, and I admire your earnest attitude, but the ball has already been set into motion. This will be painful for you, no doubt, but you probably ought to check this out."

I follow Lucas's eyes toward the lake. The man with the shaved head roughly pushes Sally out along the rickety pier extending into the middle of the lake. She has a black bag over her head, and her hands are bound by tape.

Lucas says, without even a trace of emotion in his voice, "Yep, she loves nature so much. Now she's going to get a mouthful of it."

Chapter 62

I am a physicist, grounded in reality. I know the difference between real life and fiction. In the movies, the bad guy always keeps the good guy around long enough to explain all the intricacies and motivations of his crime—the how-he-done-it and why—thus giving the hero enough time to figure out a way to prevail over the villain.

This is not the movies. I'm standing before a very real person in the middle of the woods in Wisconsin, where only very real things ever happen. This very real person is holding a pistol aimed at my chest. I know that if I make any quick move, he will shoot me before I have a chance to do anything at all to him. In the movies, Vin Diesel would do a quick roll or some other amazing gymnastics maneuver and disarm the villain. Such will not be the case here. And maybe I'm only thinking about this because I cannot face reality, the reality that Sally is about to be killed while I stand by helplessly and watch.

The man with the shaved head pushes Sally ahead of him. With each push she stumbles, and at one point it seems she is about to topple into the algae-ridden lake.

A physicist would have a plan, would have the details worked out. But details and plans be damned, I whirl so quickly that Lucas is caught off guard. His gun fires but he apparently misses me—at least I don't feel anything yet. He fires again, and now there's an intense burning in my shoulder. But I am already halfway down the shore toward the pier. I hear the gun fire again, and I feel like I've been kicked. There is another intense burning. I'm still on my feet. I know I'm hit, but I must keep going.

I stumble onto the pier. It wobbles, probably not designed to support three people in motion. The man with the shaved head turns toward me, holding Sally in front of him. But I cannot pause. If Sally goes into the lake, she will die. I cannot allow this to happen.

In moments, as the man tries to wrestle Sally over the edge of the pier, I am upon them. I leap through the air the last few feet, diving to grab hold of Sally before she goes in. But in the same instant, he pushes her behind him, and I fall short.

He faces me, and I see the silvery glint of a large knife blade. As Sally crouches behind him, he comes down on me hard, and I shift quickly, but not quickly enough. His knife slashes into my forearm. I probably have mere seconds before my wounds debilitate me. I lunge up into the man, my full body weight plowing into him. He falls backward over Sally. The man struggles to regain his balance, but it's too late. Flailing as he goes, the man with the shaved head disappears into the vivid-green lake.

"Sally," I cry out, as I kneel and clutch her to me. As I start to peel the bag from her head, the man in the lake surfaces and thrashes and screams for help. He tries to make his way back up onto the pier.

I know Lucas and others will be upon us in moments, and I have no plan to avoid their attack. I work frantically now to free Sally's hands. We are trapped at the end of an unstable wooden pier in the middle of a pool of certain and rapid death.

Lucas stands at the entrance to the pier, his gun pointed toward us. Two other men, who've obviously heard the gunshots, have run up to join him. I turn to face them, still in a kneeling position, while Sally is behind me, struggling to unbind her ankles.

"You are a fool, Wil," Lucas says. His voice projects an artificial calmness, but he's shaking—with rage, I suspect, not nerves. I expect him to start firing.

Over my shoulder I see that the man with the shaved head has now clambered back onto the pier and is slowly making his way toward us. He's coated in a green slime that makes him look like an alien. We are boxed in, with no place to go but into the lake.

"Wil, I'm so sorry I got you into this," Sally breathes from behind me. "I want you to know how proud I am of you." I feel a sense of calm wash over me at her words.

On our knees, Sally and I edge toward Lucas, as the green man closes in on us. "Lucas," I shout, "you'll never get away with this." A B-movie cliché, but it's all I can come up with.

"I already have, Wil. See those trucks? They're being loaded right now. By tonight it will begin. And then it cannot be stopped. After this is over, after millions have paid the price, do you think my life matters? What will matter is my faithfulness to my father. A few will remember me as a hero."

We are now within ten yards of Lucas. Within gunshot range. Behind us, the man with the shaved head can almost reach Sally. I hear her praying behind me. I turn toward her. She's in my arms, holding tight, looking up at me. I want the last thing I see to be her eyes.

Chapter 63

Just a few steps away from us, the man with the shaved head staggers, then stops. He glares with unfocused eyes, then clutches his stomach, moans and collapses on the dock just inches away. He lies still.

I expect gunshots, but instead I hear loud grunts and a crash from behind me. I turn back toward the shore to see Lucas and the two men on the ground in a pile, stacked one upon the other. Beside them stands a huge man. As I struggle to comprehend this, Starla and Lander run out from the trees and stand beside him. Starla calmly retrieves the gun that has fallen from Lucas's grasp.

Still shaking, Sally and I stand. We say nothing. There are no words that can adequately respond to what we've just gone through. There are no words needed. We make our way slowly to the shore, where the outstretched arms of friends await us.

Starla is the first one to speak. "Wil, I want you to meet Sam. These three dudes—she gestures to Lucas and the two men on the ground, "they've already met him."

Sam, a mountain of a man, gives me a friendly nod, then Starla continues. "And this, I presume, is Sally." She enfolds Sally in a sisterly embrace and holds her close. Then she looks at me again. "Dear God, Wil, you're hurt."

I look down at my arm and only now, feel the sharp pain. The shoulder and sleeve of my shirt are drenched in blood. Lander is quickly beside me and helps me remove the shirt. "Crap," he says, "this time we're going to have to get you a doctor."

I look down at the wounds—two round holes in my left shoulder, bleeding profusely, and a slash across my arm, just below the elbow. The pain is now escalating. It's gone from a four to a ten in the last minute. The adrenalin must be wearing off. I feel the now-familiar wooziness that precedes fainting, just as I did in Houghton. But this time is different. I will not allow myself to pass out. "How did you all find us?" I ask, still holding it together.

Sally stands at my side, a steadying arm around my waist, helping Lander to wrap my shirt around my shoulder to stem the bleeding.

Starla says, "Your friend Lander here, he's one resourceful gentleman." She waves Lucas's pistol around as she speaks—which makes me nervous—ready to launch into a story, and it's clear she's trying to distract me from the wound. It helps. "We got lucky," she says. "Couldn't reach you, Wil, and I was gettin' worried. Friday's my day off, so I say to Sam, how 'bout a drive in the country?" She pauses and looks over at Sam with a romantic smile. He's keeping his eyes on the three men on the ground, but he shoots her a quick grin. "When we hit town, we stopped at some café, and the guy there—Danny, I think—sent us off to find Lander. So here we are."

"It all started with Tracy," Lander says, not looking up from his bandaging work. "When I went to see her this morning, she said you had asked her where Ed was making deliveries, and she remembered that he had a calendar in his office. We went out to Ed's place and found out that he was in fact delivering fertilizer again, and the calendar listed the intersection for the drop-off. When I realized that the road headed down into the general direction of the lakes you guys were exploring, I knew it was time to get mobilized. But I gotta say, finding this place wasn't easy. The last mile is just a wide spot through the trees."

"Speaking of Ed," I say, "I think they may have him somewhere around here. We need to find him."

Starla keeps Lucas's pistol aimed at Lucas and his two partners, still on the ground. I don't know if she knows how to use that thing, but I wouldn't want to press my luck with her. She looks like she means business. Sam hurries off to the other buildings to find Ed.

"And what's with the green guy out on the pier?" Lander asks.

"He fell into the algae. I'm not sure he's alive."

"Darby should be here any minute," says Lander. "He wasn't very interested at first, but Starla here—I swear—is one persuasive woman." He chuckles. "Darby's probably still trying to find his way through the trees back there. He and Bart will take care of these creeps."

I have one more question. "Who cut me loose?"

Starla answers. "Wasn't us. We just got here."

Then Darby's cruiser arrives from the woods, bounding over the uneven terrain, with lights flashing, like in a scene from *The Dukes of Hazzard*. But I'm not tracking any of this very well. I'm drifting into a fog, the effects of my wounds now beginning to numb my senses. I am only focused on Sally close beside me. This is all I care about.

As we are led to Lander's Eurovan, I cast one last glance toward the lake. At the edge of the trees, I see a solitary figure. Tall and thin, he wears a plaid shirt. He's pretty far away, but for a moment it seems that we lock eyes. Then he disappears into the woods.

Chapter 64

As the nurse pushes the portable x-ray machine from the cubicle, where I lie on a hospital exam table, she says, "The doctor should have the results in just a few minutes." They've already cleaned and bandaged the wounds and started an IV. Antibiotics, I'm told.

"The knife wound, fortunately, wasn't serious," the nurse says. "The gunshot wounds are another matter. But since the bullets went clean through, that makes our job a lot easier. We'll want to see if there has been any damage to the bones and muscle, though."

I'm in the ER at the White Pine County Medical Center, and I'm overwhelmed by all the attention. Sally, Starla, Sam, Lander, Deacon Ellen, and Darby are all gathered around the bed. Ellen had everyone, including the nurse, join hands around me, while she said some prayers. That was pretty cool.

Darby, swaggering as usual, has his best taking-charge-of-the-crime-scene persona going, but even he has mellowed.

"Damn, Weathers, that was impressive, what you did out there. Thanks to our good work, we're gonna nail those creeps good."

Never mind that twenty-four hours ago, he was denying that any such creeps even existed. Now you'd think we were good drinking buddies who spent our Friday nights swapping lies down at one of the local watering holes.

I don't know what all the fuss is about. I don't feel that bad, and I'm hoping they'll let me out of here soon. Of course, the painkiller they shot me up with probably helps my rosy outlook.

Lander steps closer. He's wearing the same black tee shirt he had on at breakfast. For the first time I read the fine print underneath the trout tattoo: "Fisher of Men." He fiddles with the red spikes on his head and seems awkward being here, which I understand. Hospitals aren't my favorite places in the world either. So I try to divert attention away from medical topics.

"What did Tracy say when you called her?"

This brings a grin from Lander. "You should've heard her squeal when she heard Ed was okay. I'm not sure whether she was happier that he was alive or that he wasn't partying over in Duluth. He's just down the hall from here. Tracy's there with him. They're looking him over, but it seems he's fine. I can't imagine being tied up like he was for all those hours."

"So I'm guessing they commandeered his truck to make their nasty deliveries up to Lake Superior?"

Darby has to interject here. "Yep, but we've got state troopers all over that now. They've already located their boats up on Keweenaw Bay, all ready to deliver that crap out into the lake."

I return to Lander. "In case I haven't said it before, Lander, I want to thank you for being such a good friend to me." I choke up a bit as I say this, and I chalk up my schmaltz to the drugs.

"Hey," he says, then looks down while swallowing hard.

Starla and Sam stand back from the bed, big smiles on their faces. Starla's eyes meet mine and I almost lose it. Yep, must be the drugs.

A serious-looking doctor enters the room, carrying a clipboard and a stack of films. He studies his notes for a while before speaking, then says, "Mr. Weathers, we've looked over the x-rays and they look good. Gunshot wounds are very serious things." At this, Darby sidles back up to the bedside, as if his presence is necessary when things like gunshot wounds are being discussed. The doc continues. "The bullets made clean entries and clean exits. Blood loss was minimal, probably due to the prompt response of your friends here. In some cases like this, we'd probably want to get a CT scan, but that would mean sending you over to Escanaba. I don't think we need to do that here. You're a very fortunate man, Mr. Weathers. We could probably boot you out of here this afternoon, but we're going to keep you overnight, just to be on the safe side."

When the doctor leaves, Sally comes up beside me and takes the hand of my good arm. Everyone else slips out of the cubicle, wisely sensing that we need time together.

"Wil," she says, then melts into sobs. She quickly pulls herself together, then laughs, while sniffling and wiping away tears. "I'm just so grateful that you're okay."

"Sally," I say, then stop. I just want to look at her. Her eyes. Those brown eyes, full of emotion, bathing me. Her soft baby-like skin with just a touch of rosiness in her cheeks and those full lips. I must not be too sick, because I really want to kiss those lips right now. Only after a while, I say to her, "You're amazing, Sally. We did it. We fixed it."

She opens her mouth to speak, but then just smiles. I want to kiss her even more. "Yes, I guess we did," she says.

Sure, I'm riding on a wave of painkillers, but I know that what I'm feeling right now is not due to any drug. What I'm feeling right now is a peace that I can't recall ever experiencing. No solution to any physics problem ever felt like this. No response to any other person has ever felt like this. Whatever it is feels really good.

Chapter 65

It's the usual madhouse at Danny's on this Saturday morning. Sally and I have found a corner booth. I've just been released from the hospital, where I got lots of attention overnight, being the only patient in the small medical center that must have no more than a half-dozen beds. Sally spent the night in the room with me. She took the recliner across the room from my bed, but at one point she slipped into the bed next to me, on my good side, away from the wounds. She covered my face with soft kisses and let her fingers stroll across my chest. We talked about small things, the rigors of the day making anything more just too much. There was no talk about the lake, about Lucas, the algae, Norstaad or what's going to happen between us.

No sooner has Marge dropped off menus and filled our coffee cups than both Danny and Lander slide into the booth. "How's the wing?" Lander asks.

"Almost good as new," I say. Well, not quite. I've still got a pretty impressive bandage on it, and the doc said I might be needing painkillers for a few days.

Danny is glowing. "Just wanted to come over and welcome our resident heroes. Lander's already filled me in on the whole thing. We're awfully proud of you guys, and I was wondering if there's anything I can do for you." Last night,

Danny sent a couple of his guys out to pick up our cars, dropping Sally's Outback off at her house and leaving the Fiesta at the hospital.

"You've already done plenty, Danny," Sally says. "And we appreciate it."

Lander leans forward and addresses Sally. "Do you think they could have pulled it off? I mean, would their attack have really worked?"

Sally takes a sip of her coffee, then shakes her head slowly as if burdened with a grave thought. "I don't know. It's possible that the algae would not have taken hold in the Lakes the way QUEEN was hoping. You could come up with a lot of reasons why it wouldn't work. But Lucas knew what he was doing, and it is possible that it could have worked. And if it had, well … well, it didn't."

"What will happen to that stinky lake?"

"At least the algae is contained there. But the DNR is going to have a major cleanup problem. Probably soak the whole thing with copper sulphate, I suspect. I'm hoping they'll study the lake before the remediation, though. It's important to learn just what Lucas did and how it can be prevented in the future."

The tech talk is apparently too much for Danny. "We probably should get back to work, Lander," he says, standing. As they head back to the kitchen, Danny says over his shoulder, "Breakfast's on me, guys."

No sooner have Danny and Lander left than I see Dennis Yardley standing by the entrance, looking our way. As my eyes meet his, he nods and heads toward us.

As Yardley stands at our table, I notice Sally stiffen. "Would you like to join us?" I ask.

"No thanks," he says, "this will just take a moment."

I wait. Yardley's eyes are cast down as he says, "I've made some pretty bad mistakes." Sally now looks up at him, but remains quiet. Yardley continues, and his voice is slow and deliberate. "When we lost Jeff, that was just about the end of our world." He clears his throat. "I guess I channeled my anger toward that group he was in." He now looks directly at Sally. I'm no longer seeing the confident banker, but rather a broken man. "Sally, it was easy for me to blame you, even though I knew you weren't even there. If Jeff hadn't gotten involved with ..." He trails off, and for a moment I think he might cry.

"It's okay, Mr. Yardley," Sally says. "Jeff was a wonderful man, and I know how proud you were of him."

Yardley clears his throat again. "Anyway, I did some terrible things. When Lucas Tanner approached me and seemed to be grieving himself, I thought I'd finally found someone who understood. He told me that, even though he'd been a member of your group, he was now intent on stopping its radical excesses." He puts a hand down on the table as if he needs to steady himself.

"Please sit down, Mr. Yardley," Sally says. She shifts in her seat so that he can slide in. Which he now does.

"I gave Tanner some money. Quite a lot of money. I believed he was going to organize counter protests or something like that. That he needed money for publicity. I had no idea what was really ..." His voice trails off for a moment. "I'm headed over to the sheriff's office now to tell them. Whatever happens to me, it's okay. But Sally, I wanted to tell you face to face that I am very sorry."

Sally's eyes are getting misty. "Mr. Yardley," she says, "thank you for speaking to me. That means a lot. Jeff was a very courageous person, and I see that you are too."

Yardley nods as he swallows back a sob. He shoots Sally a quick look with eyes filled with pain, nods at me, then stands and leaves.

For a few moments, Sally and I sit in silence.

Then Sally says, "So Wil, what are you going to do now?"

I pick up my glass of ice water and begin to take a sip, but put it back down. "Well, I've still got job applications to send out. I guess I should be heading back home."

"Oh."

"Look, Sally, I've got to—"

My words are interrupted by another visitor to our table. It's Joe Gerlach. My heart sinks.

"May I join you two for a minute?" he asks.

I nod, and Joe slips into the booth next to Sally, across from me. He motions for some coffee, so apparently he's going to be here for awhile. I brace myself.

He looks first at Sally then at me. "You two have been busy, I hear."

We both nod.

"Look, Wil, you and I have got some unfinished business, so I'm glad I caught up with you this morning. It won't hurt Sally to hear this, either."

I nod as I look down. Here it comes. I'm wishing I had told Sally about the fire. This will only make it worse.

"Wil, as I mentioned to you the other day at the church, I spoke with a secretary in the physics department at UWM last week, and she said you were not employed there."

I nod, but remain silent. At least I've told Sally this part.

"The next day I got a call from a Dr. Michaels, I believe."

I nod, but keep looking down. "Yes, Grace Michaels, she's the department chair."

"Well, I'm glad she called. She said she had learned of my call and wanted to speak with me, just in case I was thinking of offering you a job. Wil, she told me that you are an excellent teacher. She said that you have a passion for inspiring students with a love for physics." I now look up, my jaw dropping, as he continues. "She said you were let go because of a funding shortfall, but that she could give you the highest recommendation."

I let out a huge sigh. He continues. "About that other thing, Wil." He now shoots a quick glance over at Sally. "About that other thing, Dr. Michaels brought that up. I didn't mention it. She said I should know about it."

"Look, Joe," I interrupt, "I didn't mean to run out of the church like that the other night. It's just that—"

"Let me finish, Wil. Then Dr. Michaels told me what a person of integrity you are, and how unfortunate it was that had happened to you. So, Wil ..."

I look at Sally, whose eyes are glued on Joe. My mouth feels dry, and I reach for my glass of ice water.

"Wil, I'm offering you a job to teach science at our high school. Now let me go on before you say no. I realize that this isn't the university. It doesn't have the glamour of the University of Wisconsin. But this would allow you to teach kids about science and fire them up, just like you got me fired up the other day here in Danny's. You could make a real difference."

"Gee, Joe, I don't know. I mean, I've never thought about, uh ..." I realize I'm stammering, so I just shut up.

Joe goes on. "Take a few days and think it over, Wil. We could make this happen very quickly. I've already got the green light from the school board, and because all the background checks have already been done at UWM, I imagine you could start almost immediately. Wil, I'd be honored and our kids would be well served if you decided to come." Then he stands and says, "Well, I've already interfered too much with your breakfast time. Sorry about that. But, Wil, please do think about it, and let me know. Okay?"

Sally is beaming as Joe leaves. "Wow. Just wow. What do you think, Wil?"

"Well, I … look, Sally. About that other thing that Joe mentioned, I—"

"Maybe I talk too much, Wil. Maybe I jump right in too much, instead of waiting. But I've got to tell you this." She lays a hand on mine. "With me, Wil, you would never have a girl who sews frilly curtains for your windows. I'd probably be planning our next expedition." This makes me smile. "But, Wil, I want you to know that I would always be there for you."

I swallow hard and cannot look at her.

"Sally, please let me explain this to you." She slumps in her seat, mouth opened slightly, obviously disappointed over my apparent rebuff of her romantic invitation. "You are a beautiful woman, and I would be—"

There's fire in her eyes now. "If this is the easy let-down, just don't say anything. I deserve better than—"

"No, wait, please. Just listen." She's quiet. "God, Sally, this is so hard for me, especially because of who you are. And who I am when I'm with you."

Then, as she watches me in silence, I tell her everything, forcing myself to look into her eyes as I do. My carelessness in putting out the campfire. The ten thousand acres of prime national forest land that burned. The lives that were threatened. The arrest. The conviction. The depression. The long recovery. My shame. I explain how I'd wanted to tell her, but couldn't.

When I'm finished, Sally is silent and breathing hard through her mouth. She shakes her head violently, as if trying to awake from a horrible nightmare. Her eyes are large with ... what? Disappointment? Betrayal? Hatred? Sadness? All of the above? Whatever it is, I am not surprised. I try to see myself through her eyes, and all I come up with is the image on the TV of the deranged-looking man being led to the jail. "Is this the face of a monster?" I've had enough.

With all the visitors to our table, Marge hasn't even taken our breakfast order yet. I drop a five on the table to cover the coffees, then get up and leave.

Chapter 66

Sunday morning at Starbucks is a familiar scene. I've got a seat right by the window, which affords me a view of the activity along Brady Street. I sip my house coffee, while I watch an old man with a walker making his way along the boulevard. Across the street, cars vie for parking at a Walgreens. I haven't even cracked open my laptop yet. There are just too many things scrambling around in my head.

Someone has left the front section of the *Milwaukee Journal-Sentinel* on the table next to me, and I thumb idly through it. I find the article on page eleven. It's a short article, sandwiched between blurbs about a meth bust in Mequon and some misbehavior by a state legislator.

> *Houghton resident, Lucas Tanner, and three others were arrested by the White Pine County Sheriff's Department for growing blue-green algae in a remote northern Wisconsin lake. One man, apparently a co-conspirator, was found dead at the scene. The men allegedly intended to pollute the Great Lakes. They are being held awaiting arraignment.*

That's all there is. Most readers, more interested in reading about how the Brewers are doing or in catching up on the latest political in-fighting, will miss it completely. I let out a big sigh and look out the window again.

There's a lot to think about this morning. I haven't opened up the laptop because I'm still pondering the text on my iPhone. I read it again. It's from Grace Michaels. Short and sweet. Hurried, even. "Wil, just heard there might be some funding for a temporary position in the spring. No promises beyond that. Interested? Give me a call."

So my desperate days of searching the *Chronicle of Higher Education* may be over for a while. Sure, it's only temporary, but it's a start, a stepping stone. I have one more unemployment check at the end of October, and that won't quite stretch until January. But with the promise of my old job back, sort of, I'm less hesitant about asking my parents to float me a short-term loan.

And this could get me out of the Bali Hai. So how come I'm not overjoyed by this news?

Joe Gerlach said I could start soon. What would that be like? I could go at my own pace. Linger on the exciting parts. Really get into it. For sure, high school isn't the university. Joe admitted that much himself. But how is it different? Students are students. And students need a teacher. And that's what I am, a teacher. But living in White Pine—a deal-breaker?

The old man with the walker now stops, turns and looks behind him, like he's waiting for someone. No one is there. Then he resumes his slow journey along the sidewalk.

White Pine. I made more friends there in two weeks than I have here in seven years. Living close to the woods, hikes after work. The potlucks at the Tuesday night Bible study? It's odd that would seem appealing now. Maybe it's because of Ellen, who allows me to ask hard—or stupid—questions, who honors that I'm still struggling with a lot of this stuff.

But I can't let my mind remain on any of these things for long. Because of Sally. I let out a troubled sigh. I can't let this pull me down. I've only known this woman for two weeks. But I'm fooling myself if I think I'll walk away from this unscathed. I look out the window again at the gray street, then down at my hands. They're trembling.

Back at the Bali Hai, I pause to look at the plastic flamingos. They don't make me laugh this morning. I feel a twinge in my arm. I'll have to pop a couple Advils when I get up to the apartment. Here I am, a physics teacher, walking around with two gunshot wounds and two knife wounds. I shake my head. I actually charged past an armed gunman. And got shot. I wonder if that experience is what it's like in combat. I shudder as I think about charging an armed man right now. But then, at that moment, I didn't think twice. I reacted. Pure instinct. Sally. That's what caused my reaction. Has there ever been another time when I did something like that? Odd that the most terror-filled moment of my life, the most out-of-control moment of my life—and there have been very few of those—was also the moment when I felt most fully alive.

At my door, I have my head down, so I don't even notice Starla there in the hallway until she speaks. "Good morning, Wil," she says. "Was wonderin' when you'd show up." I see Minji standing next to her.

I haven't told her about my separation from Sally. In fact, this is the first time I've seen her since I left White Pine yesterday morning. "I was just down at Starbucks. Doing some work." I look at Minji and ask, "So why are you here?"

She has a little smile that makes me uneasy. "To see you, of course," she says. "Sally called me after you left. We always talk about important stuff. She told me what happened. The whole thing. Pretty bizarre tale, Wil. And Starla here, along with Sam, was amazing, I hear."

I'm not up for a visit right now. "And?"

Starla says, "Well, sounds like you kind of burst out of there fast, don't you think, Wil?"

I reach for the handle on my door. Am I going to have to go through my fire story with these two? I can't deal with that right now. "I would say the situation was pretty clear."

Minji says, "Really? Maybe you were jumping to conclusions, Wil."

That smarts. Jumping to conclusions, a specialty of mine. "I don't think so."

"Did you stick around long enough to hear Sally's response?"

I guess Sally has told them about my past. Great. I turn towards them now, bristling. "Oh, I didn't need to wait for words. I saw that look on her face, and I understood. It's just how I would have reacted. Some things cannot be forgiven, and Sally's a person with principles."

Minji smiles again. "That she is," she says. "The most principled person I know. But it seems, Wil, like you may not understand what her principles are."

I'm getting a lecture, and I'm in no mood for that right now. I take a deep breath to calm myself before I reply. "Meaning?"

"Sally's a strong person, but I suspect you already know that, and she won't let anyone push her around. A doormat, she is not." Her eyes are now pounding into me like a jackhammer. "But when it comes to forgiveness, she's amazing. I don't know where she gets it."

I suppose I do. Deacon Ellen's words about the four grumpy men come back to me, and I sag.

Starla now speaks. "So, Wil, I guess it's now a matter of what you want." These two are ganging up on me. She then says, "What do you want, Wil?"

What do I want? That's not the question I've been asking. More like, what do I deserve? *What do I want?*

There is quiet now. Then Minji says, "I'm heading back up north in a few minutes. If you're interested, I suggest you grab a few things and hop in the car with me."

Chapter 67

Darkness has fallen as we arrive back in White Pine. Minji stops at Sally's house, but her car is gone. "She's probably at the church," I say. "She usually cleans up over there on Sunday nights."

A minute later we climb up the steps to the parish hall. Like on that first Sunday night, a light is on inside, the only light on this dark street. I can see movement inside through the wavy glass. As we knock, I see a figure move toward the door. My heart is in my throat.

But then the door swings open, and the friendly red face of Hans Gerlach greets us. "Oh, hello, Wil," he says. "Bet you were hoping to find Sally here."

"As a matter of fact, I was."

Hans gives me a wry smile. "Sorry to disappoint you. I've got the clean-up duty tonight. You'll find Sally over at Hazel's."

Several cars are parked in front of Hazel's house, which worries me. Maybe she has died. But Hazel sits in her recliner, a quilt pulled around her, doing fine. "Oh Wil," she cries, as Minji and I enter the room. "Now my day is complete."

The room is packed. Sally is there, and I feel a need for air as our eyes meet. Others are there too. Tracy, Deacon Ellen, and several women I don't know. "I hope I'm not interrupting anything," I say.

Sally comes up to me and rests her hand on my shoulder. She looks hard at me, like she's trying to look inside me. She says nothing, but her eyes say plenty.

"Not at all, Wil," Hazel says. "We're just doing some planning. I've got to tell you about this. They were getting ready to move me into a residential facility over in Iron River, and I was going crazy. I just couldn't have handled that, being away from my home and all my friends. But now I don't have to go. These wonderful women, all of them angels, are going to stay with me here, one every day." She's beaming.

"That's wonderful, Hazel," I say.

"It was all Deacon Ellen's idea," she says. "She organized the whole thing."

Tracy chimes in. "Ellen is amazing. Is there anything she can't do?"

Ellen says, "There are a lot of things I can't do, Tracy. After all, I am a deacon and not a priest."

Tracy says, "You mean like the Eucharist and baptisms?"

I look at Tracy and say, "And maybe weddings?" All eyes are suddenly glued on me.

Tracy shrugs and nods toward Ellen. "I don't know. You should ask her."

I'm ready for this. So ready. *What do you want, Wil?* I look deep into Sally's eyes, as I address the whole group and say, "Actually, I was hoping Sally and I might ask her together."

The look on Sally's face? I can't begin to describe it. Let's just say that I've come up north once more. This time for good.

Technical References

This story is fiction. Yet, the statements about cyanobacteria are based on fact. Relevant technical references follow.

101: *One posting near the bottom of the CNN page ...*
Melissa Gray and Joe Sutton, "Algae Bloom Kills Record Number of Manatees." CNN.com, March 12, 2013: http://www.cnn.com/2013/03/11/us/florida-manatee-deaths/.

175: *... a satellite view of Lake Erie ...*
"Toxic Algae Bloom in Lake Erie," NASA Earth Observatory, October 5, 2011.
http://earthobservatory.nasa.gov/IOTD/view.php?id=76127.

175: *"Harmful Algal Blooms are Growing Once Again around ..."*
D'Arcy Egan, "Harmful Algal Blooms are Growing Once Again around Western Lake Erie, Threatening Fishing, Boating, [Cleveland] *Plain Dealer*, August 24, 2013: http://www.cleveland.com/outdoors/index.ssf/2013/08/harmful_algal_blooms_are_growi.html.

176: *... can cause death in mammals in ...*
P. R. Gorham and W. W. Carmichael, "Hazards of Freshwater Blue-Green Algae (Cyanobacteria)," in *Algae and Human Affairs*, ed. C. A. Lembi and J. R. Waaland (Cambridge and New York: Cambridge University Press, 1988): 408.

252: *I think the main challenge would be to find ...*
"Establishing the Sources of Toxic Cyanobacteria Blooms in the Great Lakes," National Centers for Coastal Ocean Science, accessed March 18, 2014:
http://www.coastalscience.noaa.gov/projects/detail?key=47.

252: *... and new strains are being found all the time ...*
P. R. Gorham and W. W. Carmichael, "Hazards of Freshwater Blue-Green Algae (Cyanobacteria)," in *Algae and Human*

Affairs, ed. C. A. Lembi and J. R. Waaland (Cambridge and New York: Cambridge University Press, 1988): 418.

253: **There are so many varieties of blue-green algae— they are actually not algae, but bacteria ...**
"Introduction to the Cyanobacteria: Architects of Earth's Atmosphere," University of California Museum of Paleontology, accessed May 3, 2014:
 http://www.ucmp.berkeley.edu/bacteria/cyanointro.html.

253: **...over eighty percent of the fresh water in North America and over twenty-percent of the fresh water in the world.**
"Great Lakes: Geography and Hydrology," U. S Environmental Protection Agency, accessed April 11, 2014:
http://www.epa.gov/glnpo/basicinfo.html.

253: **... two types can be especially bad ...**
Robert Edward Lee, *Phycology*, (Cambridge and New York: Cambridge University Press, 2008): 33-80. Much of the discussion of the toxic forms of blue-green algae evolved from helpful discussions with Prof. Robert Bell, University of Wisconsin–Stevens Point.

260: **There are some blue-greens, like spirulina ...**
Steven D. Ehrlich, "Spirulina," University of Maryland Medical Center, accessed July 15, 2014:
umm.edu/health/medical/altmed/supplement/spirulina.

278: **... that allows it to naturally adapt to reduced nutrient levels.**
"Establishing the Sources of Toxic Cyanobacteria Blooms in the Great Lakes," National Centers for Coastal Ocean Science, accessed March 18, 2014:
 http://www.coastalscience.noaa.gov/projects/detail?key=47.

288: **A cocktail?**
Concept suggest by Professor Robert Bell, University of Wisconsin-Stevens Point, private communication.

288: ... *toxins that can attack the nervous system* ...
P. R. Gorham and W. W. Carmichael, "Hazards of Freshwater Blue-Green Algae (Cyanobacteria)," in *Algae and Human Affairs*, ed. C. A. Lembi and J. R. Waaland (Cambridge and New York: Cambridge University Press, 1988): 418.

288: ... *very fast death factor* ...
Fernando M. Rubio, "Development on Antiboldies for the Detection of the Toxin Anatoxin by Immunoassay," U. S. Environmental Protection Agency Report EPD06014, August 31, 2006:
http://cfpub.epa.gov/ncer_abstracts/index.cfm/fuseaction/di splay.abstractDetail/abstract/7932

289: ... *through ballast water exchanges from all the shipping within the lakes* ...
Felicity Barringer, "New Rules Seek to Prevent Invasive Stowaways," *New York Times*, April 7, 2012:
http://www.nytimes.com/2012/04/08/science/earth/invasiv e-species-target-of-new-ballast-water-rule.html?_r=0.

289: ... *zebra mussels and other invasive mollusks have cost* ...
Dane Konop, "Zebra Mussels Changing Great Lakes Ecosystem," Press Release 96-11, March 1996, National Atmospheric and Oceanic Administration, accessed June 15, 2014: www.publicaffairs.noaa.gov/pr96/noaa96-11.html.

290: **There's one other way the cyanobacteria might spread** ...
E. Hoiczyk, "Gliding Motility in Cyanobacteria: Observations and Possible Explanations" *Archives of Microbiology* 174, no. 1-2 (August 2000): 11-17, doi 10.1007/s002030000187.

291: **akinetes**
Robert Edward Lee, *Phycology*, (Cambridge and New York: Cambridge University Press, 2008): 45*ff*.

Acknowledgements

It is a pleasure to acknowledge the many people who have made the writing of this book possible. I am grateful to Professor Robert Bell, Department of Biology, University of Wisconsin—Stevens Point, for excellent discussions and insights about potential hazards of toxic cyanobacteria. I am also grateful for technical discussions about environmental threats with Professor Earl Spangenberg, College of Natural Resources, University of Wisconsin—Stevens Point and Professor Wes Halverson, College of Natural Resources, University of Wisconsin—Stevens Point.

I wish to acknowledge Dr. Jack Rhodes for useful discussions about bus travel in northern Wisconsin. I learned much about conservation history in Wisconsin through the resources of the Wisconsin Conservation Hall of Fame, Stevens Point, Wisconsin.

I deeply appreciate the excellent work of Nicole R. Klungle, who did an outstanding job of editing this manuscript and providing many insights into the story. I thank Bill Fitzhugh, who provided useful critiquing on parts of the manuscript, as well as Chris DeSmet, University of Wisconsin—Madison, who critiqued parts of an early draft. The excellent programs and mentors at the Jackson Hole Writers Conference, Jackson, Wyoming, and the Writers Institute, Madison, Wisconsin, were influential in helping me develop the manuscript. I am grateful for expert guidance from Jane Friedman, at the 2014 Writer's Institute.

I benefited from discussions with Sister Mary McDonald Corcoran, prioress of the Benedictine Transfiguration

Monastery in Windsor, NY, about transformation in human lives.

The names of the characters Sally Ladke and Danny Piper were selected in memory of Sally Phillips and Danny Piper, two friends from my high school class, who died as this book was being written.

It is a pleasure to acknowledge those wonderful servants, the deacons of the Episcopal Church, who inspired my character Deacon Ellen.

Much of this story was motivated by love and appreciation for the beautiful wilderness and gracious people of the state of Wisconsin.

I am deeply indebted to my wife Mary Trainor, my sister Patty Trainor, and my kids—Erica, Karl and Lucas—for their helpful insights, support and love.

About the Author

Jim Trainor is the author of *Grasp: Making Sense of Science and Spirituality* and three novels.

He is a professional physicist (Ph.D., University of California), and served at some of the world's leading research centers, authoring over sixty articles in physics. He is also an ordained Episcopal priest and is active as a speaker on topics in science and spirituality.

Jim lives on a lake in central Wisconsin with his wife Mary. They have three grown children. When not at his desk writing, he's hiking in the wilderness or paddling his kayak across a lake.

More information on Jim and his books at
www.JimTrainorAuthor.com

Also by Jim Trainor

ISBN 978-1490936789

Karen hopes that Maui will rekindle the firs in her marriage. But the flames that engulf her are of betrayal and murder, from which there may be no rescue.

The Sand People blends laughter and tears in grappling with issues that plague our lives: broken relationships, addiction, shame and death -- and pointing toward the victory of hope over failure.

ISBN: 978-0615709215

Honorable Mention
Foreword Reviews 2012 Book of the Year

Josh Waverly had lived a quiet, low-risk life, until a beautiful woman jumped into his car, pursued by a sadistic killer who wants them both dead.

ISBN 978-1456354084

We have big questions about the meaning of life.

Why are we here? Have discoveries of modern science made God obsolete? Is there a conflict between science and spirituality? How do we know what is true?